# Highland
# Salvation

### Highland Pride,
### Book 4

# Highland Salvation

## Highland Pride, Book 4

*Lori Ann Bailey*

Entangled Publishing, LLC
2614 South Timberline Road
Suite 105, PMB 159
Fort Collins, CO 80525
rights@entangledpublishing.com

Amara is an imprint of Entangled Publishing, LLC.

Edited by Robin Haseltine
Cover design by EDH Graphics
Cover photography from Period Images, 123rf, and Deposit Photos

Manufactured in the United States of America

First Edition April 2019

*For two men who possess hearts of gold and the internal strength of the bravest Highland warriors, my father, David, and my father-in-law, Arnie.*

# Chapter One

*How do ye tell a lass the man she is betrothed to is dead?*

Finlay Cameron, the bastard son of the English Earl of Middlesbrough and the Cameron laird's aunt, had practiced the words over and over on the endless journey north from the successful, but bloody, melee in Edinburgh to the Macnab lands. A battle that had been fought in a futile attempt by the Covenanters to eliminate any Royalist lairds still loyal to King Charles.

But now, as the sun set both on the day and his time, he felt as if he had not adequately rehearsed the words he knew would change Blair Macnab's world.

It would most likely be easier if he didn't have a tender spot for the beauty. Not because of her looks, but because he'd seen there was more to her when he'd accompanied the Cameron laird to visit the man's sister and her friend Blair. He'd always harbored hope that the bonny lass would look his way.

After entering the castle's gates and stabling the horses, feet heavy as if he'd walked the journey instead of riding comfortably astride his mount, he rubbed his hands together and trudged toward the Macnab keep with Blair's brother John. Dread spiked its way into his lungs like the thick mist that floated on the morning moors, making it hard to take a full breath.

Hell, he'd never been good with words.

What would he do if she cried?

"Are ye certain ye wish for me to tell her?" He'd done his part and delivered the news to John Macnab, but the man had taken a few moments then looked him over as if he were the answer to some prayer.

"Aye. 'Twill be best if the news comes from one who saw it happen." Blair's brother's lips quirked to the side, and he wasn't certain if the man wanted to avoid witnessing the pain it would bring to the lass or if he was worse than Finlay with women. "I had left before the fighting started. She may no' believe me," John insisted, but he had a strange gleam in his eye, more like he was plotting versus mourning the man who had been slated to become his brother by marriage.

"All right then, but ye should be there in case she needs someone to cling to."

The thought of Blair trembling in his arms over another man would be almost as bad as watching helplessly as that same man mistreated her only two weeks earlier. If it had been within his rights, he might have killed the man himself for the way he'd abused the lass.

Shaking his head, his steps carried him under the ornately carved crest above the entrance to the Macnab stronghold. Despite the motto etched into the stone, *Let Fear Be Far From All*, he had the urge to turn and charge for the familiar embrace of the battlefield. Swords he knew how to face, but his tongue went numb when he tried to talk to a bonny lass, and it had been no different the times he had been around Blair.

"Did she love him?" His lips moved before he could stop the question that had been plaguing him for the last few nights. His parents had loved each other, but it hadn't been enough to change the circumstances of his birth or the life he'd been forced to live.

Bloody hell, he was certain she'd had relations with Henry Montrose. She'd spent a couple nights in the arse's room.

His steps faltered, and he froze. His blood drained from his head so quickly he thought he might tip over.

*Nae.*

The thought that churned in his head now solidified like the weight of a great oak felled by a mighty wind, leaving the landscape changed forever.

*She can't be with child.*

Images of his mother, hardier than the petite Blair Macnab who looked as if the slightest breeze would work against her, toiling to keep them fed and refusing help from his father flashed in the back of his mind. A boy tossed back and forth between parents who were like thunder and rain when they came together, but oil in water when it truly mattered. No child should have to live with the stigma of being a bastard.

"Who really kens with a woman's heart?" He detected a hint of bitterness in the reply as if John was speaking of someone other than his sister.

He turned his gaze to meet John's. Blair's brother wore the expression of a man doomed to the gallows, but his thin lips also hinted at currents hidden beneath the surface. "But truly, I think Henry may have only been the best choice in a line of no options."

Turning appraising eyes in his direction, John peered at him a moment, sighed, and apparently deciding he could be trusted, blurted, "I was hoping to make a match for her with a Royalist clan. She had options, but none as well-spoken and comely as Henry. The others were also twice her age."

"I'd assumed The Macnab had made the arrangements."

So, she'd probably had little say in the matter.

Finlay had known Henry Graham for years and had always been aware the Earl of Montrose's cousin was an egotistical bastard, putting himself above others. The man had no heart, risking the future of a vulnerable lass only to take his pleasure with her before seeing to it they were properly wed first.

Why had Blair Macnab chosen him? Were her other options that much worse? Aye, the arse was easy on the eyes, but as far as he knew, it was his only redeeming quality.

"Nae. I had to talk my father into it. His health is failing, and I'm afraid it affects his judgment."

"What will ye do now about her?"

A grin spread across pale skin as eyes the same sapphire blue of John's sister's glanced upon him with a glint that raised the hair on his arms. "Ye will marry her."

Pulse pounding in his neck, he pushed away the odd thrill that shot through him, along with the dread that tightened his muscles. "Nae, ye cannae mean that. She willnae want me."

It was time he took a wife, and he'd considered looking, but he had visions of a wife who would care for him, one who would remain by his side no matter the odds, and one who wouldn't be tempted to leave him when he was torn between two homes that both required his loyalty.

And, he'd seen the way Blair had looked at the Graham arse and the way she'd not given Finlay a second glance; the lass had no interest in him.

Still, the thought of coming home to a bonny lass like Blair heated his blood and made him ache for the gentle touch of a woman, something he'd only let himself indulge in a handful of times.

"Trust me. 'Twill be a solid match. She would be in good hands with yer ties to the Camerons and the king. I cannae trust Father no' to marry her to a Campbell Covenanter. I bet he'll be planning it as soon as he hears the news of Henry's demise."

"There has to be someone else."

He hated the way his heart thumped, the shortness of breath. But, most of all, he despised the part of him that was denying he wanted Blair Macnab.

The lass would likely want nothing to do with him. Henry had known how to woo a woman with words and a charm his half brothers taunted him that he could never possess.

"Nae. It must be ye. I've kenned ye long enough to trust ye with her, and there is nae time to find someone else before my father marries her to a Campbell who I will have to stand against if it comes to war."

"Are ye certain?"

"Aye, she will be amenable."

But that's not what he wanted in a wife.

Could he grow to care for her? Would it be enough that she had the intelligence to help him with his complicated life? Could he settle for a wife who didn't want him?

Shaking his head, John held up a hand, "Dinnae decide now. Stay the night and think about it. I'll talk to Blair."

Finlay thought to protest, retrieve his horse, and leave for England. He kept his objections to himself, because he was exhausted and needed to rest. But if he was honest with himself, he wanted to see the bonny lass one more time.

• • •

"Nae, Father. Ye cannae mean to sign that document."

Blair Macnab's father had always been able to drive her

mad with anger, but this was the first time his actions had inspired disgust. Fisting her hands on her hips, she glared at The Macnab as he sat at his desk, ignored her protestations, and studied the papers in front of him as if they were a shield against her words, ones which held no sway with him.

"Aye, I do." He peered over the top with his imperious gaze that implied nothing she ever did would break through his tough facade, and she'd never live up to his expectations. But that no longer mattered to her; he was not the hero she had once believed him to be.

How could he sell his soul to his highest bidder or to the man who offered safety at the expense of denying the very principles that had held their clan together for centuries? But then, their people's desires wouldn't matter to him, because the best option he'd given her was to be betrothed to a man who had forced her to do things she would never be able to confess. She shivered and pushed away the thoughts of her impending marriage and the poor choice she'd made.

"Then ye will be sending Macnab men to England to fight for a cause they dinnae believe in."

Balling her fists so tightly that nails dug into her palms, her voice barely rose above her normal calm demeanor, but 'twas a strain to keep the tenor down to a somewhat respectable level when she had the urge to scream in defiance. It was the one emotion she'd never let her father see, always doing her best to be a loyal daughter and devoting her entire self to being the best at all she set her sights on, proving a woman was valuable as something other than a vessel to an heir.

"Ye dinnae ken what has to be done to keep a clan safe."

She understood more than her father believed. Signing the papers she'd discovered on his desk meant he'd be sending Macnab men to England to help the English Parliament defeat King Charles. It was suicide, on top of a betrayal of their country.

"And 'tis why ye agreed to let Henry Graham ask me to be his wife." Fingernails dug into her palms. Had her father known the man she'd been fooled into accepting had the temperament of Satan when he was challenged? She was furious with herself for being fooled by Henry's charm. She prayed her father had been unaware of the man's true nature, because it would destroy him completely in her eyes, if he'd known of the man's proclivities.

"Aye, he is a good match. If 'twill keep the Grahams from raiding our lands 'tis worth it." Setting down the papers, he swept his hand across the parchment reverently then turned his full attention to her. His face darkened to a shade of red that made her think of the blood of the men he was willing to sacrifice.

It was too late for her, but perhaps she could persuade her father to save their clan. "Ye cannae play both sides, Father. 'Tis dangerous." Shaking her head, she sighed. He'd not give her words the credence he would give those of a minstrel spinning some farfetched tale about chivalry and true love.

"I'm doing what I need, and I will discuss it with ye nae further." Flattening his palm on the table, a loud *thwack* echoed through the room.

She flinched, but it jolted her anger to an escalation point. "When I'm ensconced in the Graham household and yer Covenanting friends come in the night to slit our throats, 'twill nae matter to ye."

"My signing that agreement may be the only thing that keeps ye safe." Standing, he towered over her and glared down with the full weight of his wrath and the disapproval he'd always held for her.

This time, she didn't cower. "How could ye no' stand up for yer clan's beliefs and support yer countrymen?"

Lips pinched and jaw ticking, he pointed toward the door.

She stomped for the exit, determined to hold back the

fury that bubbled over before she said something she would regret.

Her father had used her yet again, based on her supposed attractiveness, not only devaluing her skills but selling her to the bidder with the most political clout, not caring that his actions would put her life in danger.

After pulling open the door, she marched through, only to freeze at the sight of two hulking forms stalking toward her from the main hall. Instinct screamed at her to flee. But, this reaction was new to her, brought on by her recent traumatic events, and she wondered if she'd ever be able to look at a man again without questioning his nature. Most likely not, once she was wed to the man who had instilled this panic in her.

She would not let Henry's actions rule her, especially not in the home she'd spent years managing. No other man had ever made her feel threatened.

She stood tall, even as she shut her lids to bolster her courage.

"Blair," broke into her thoughts as a familiar voice reached her ears. She opened her eyes.

Her brother, John, halted just shy of her. She'd not seen him since she'd left Edinburgh almost two weeks ago. As she threw her arms around him, hope and comfort replaced the despair that had taken root. He returned the embrace then drew back.

"Och, I'm so glad ye have made it home."

"I'm happy to be back."

Blinking, she took in the man beside John, and the panic from before melted. It was Finlay, a clan member and guard to Kirstie. She'd seen him on many occasions when he'd been here with the Cameron laird to visit her friend, who had been living with her the last few years. Swallowing, she met his gaze, tamping down her confusion. "Is Kirstie with ye?"

"Finlay has news for ye," her brother cut in. Curious, she tilted her chin toward him.

Dread settled into her chest. John hated delivering bad news. And it would be just like him to bring in another to do the deed. "Och, no, where's Kirstie?"

"Henry Graham is dead." Finlay seemed to put himself between her and her brother, as if shielding her from the news he stated so calmly.

Time stopped, and her heart pounded as the men in front of her stilled, blurred, and faded into the background.

Stunned for the first time in her life, she didn't know what to say. Her mouth fell open as if she should reply, but nothing came out. Only two weeks earlier, she might have broken down in tears, but she'd gotten to know her betrothed too well on her recent trip to Edinburgh. It only felt like yesterday that Henry was looming over her, forcing her to do things she'd not wanted.

She gasped.

Ramifications spun through her head. Bile rose in her throat, and her hand flew up to cover her mouth. She lowered her hand and gripped her skirts, leaning into the wall for support. "How?"

Finlay studied her, and he looked as if he wanted to take her in a reassuring embrace but didn't want to intrude on her personal space. She wished he would; she needed to be grounded as the world was swept from under her feet.

What would her father do now? At least with Henry she'd been able to choose, even if he had been an awful decision. She fought back the tears that threatened to spill as she imagined being required to wed a man who would force her to follow the Covenants and denounce the things she held dear.

"A group of Covenanters attacked us in Edinburgh the day after the meeting." Finlay broke into her thoughts as he imparted the rest of the story.

Maybe there was hope for a better match.

*Och*. She was being insensitive. Henry had lost his life— she should show some concern for the man who would have been her husband, despite the indifference he'd shown for her well-being. The man had treated her like a whore.

But, he was dead.

Her stomach knotted, and her limbs numbed. What would happen when she was ordered to marry and her new husband discovered she was no longer a maiden?

Nae, now was not the time to think about herself.

Lifting her gaze to the Cameron man, she said, "Was he in pain? What happened?"

Finlay answered, "I was near him when it happened." His hand took hers as those hazel eyes met hers. She was surprised she didn't flinch and wasn't repulsed by the gesture. His touch was reassuring, kind, and she found herself being pulled toward him without really moving.

"'Twas swift, and I am certain he didnae feel much." Licking his lips, he swallowed then broke from her stare, tilting his head down only to once again give her a reassuring glance. Was he hiding something?

Trembling now, she wondered if it was from pain at the loss or fear of what was to come. She'd worked so hard to find a husband that both she, John, and her father could agree on. Her friend Kirstie had been certain there was real danger waiting for the Royalists in Edinburgh. She'd never once considered Henry might be in peril or that *he* had been the threat she should have feared.

Knees wobbling, she struggled to calm her breathing and think logically. "I need to sit." She regretted the words immediately because Finlay released her hand, and it fell limp to her side.

"Come," John said as he moved, raising his hand to

knock on their father's study. Shaking her head, she backed from the door.

"Nae. He doesnae wish to see me just now." Her eyes pleaded to beg off.

Facing her father so soon, and with this news, would cause her to step across a line and let him know how she really felt about him and his plan to side with the Earl of Argyll and men of his ilk.

Her brother's fist stopped before striking the door, his eyes taking in her concern, then they lit with some mischief she'd not seen since he'd come up with the plan to wed her to a Royalist.

Her brother loved their father but didn't share his beliefs. He'd already been making plans to join forces with James Graham, the Marquess of Montrose, the man willing to lead the Royalists in opposition to those wishing to force the Presbyterian religion on others. John would be furious when he learned of their father's latest plan, but she couldn't speak of what their father was doing in front of a Cameron, who were known for their loyalty to the king.

"Why do ye no' take Finlay to get a drink. 'Tis been a hard ride here, and ye may need one yerself right now. I'll tell Father."

"Aye. Och, I'm so sorry, after yer journey, ye must be famished. I only just arrived home this morning, so I can imagine ye didnae stop much." She'd been so focused on her own problems she'd slipped in her usual role of taking care of the keep and those within it. Heaven knows, her mother never took any interest in it. Now, those duties might be the only thing to keep her thoughts from going down the mole hole into the twists and turns of doubts that spiraled in her gut like sailor's knots.

Glancing back to the hulking Highlander, she vowed to show him Macnab hospitality while he was here. She could least keep alliances with the Camerons and Macnabs on steady ground.

"John, I'll have something prepared and waiting for ye as well."

"This way, Mr. Cameron." Cringing inside, she recoiled at the words, they sounded so formal and distant. A wedge she had purposely put between them in the past.

"Finlay." His deep voice washed over her, a melodic tune that sounded too intimate.

In his eyes, she saw nothing but warmth. She suddenly wanted to call him by that name, wanted a familiarity with this man who had guarded her friend so closely during their recent trip, but her tongue wouldn't work. Instead, she nodded then held her hand out to indicate the way to the great hall.

Maybe she could talk John into sending her to stay with Kirstie until the whole matter of her new match had been settled.

"Och, how is Kirstie? Alan?" She had no idea where her friend was or if Kirstie's beloved had made it through the same conflict that had taken Henry.

"Alan is safe, but when I left, no one could find Kirstie."

Chills spread through her arms, up into her shoulder blades, and then down her back as her hands started to tremble. Fear for her brazen friend settled in to latch onto her heart and squeeze like the jaws of a dog on an old rag soaked in cooking oil. "What of the Cameron laird and Malcolm?"

"They are unscathed."

"Kirstie." Her voice hitched. What had happened to her friend?

"I'll send word when I hear." Finlay was a man of few words, but somehow, he managed to convey concern and strength.

Reassured he meant what he said, and knowing there was nothing she could currently do, she nodded as they reached the large room, festooned with hanging tapestries and weapons that thankfully lay unused on the walls. It was a place of revelry and the space where her clansmen celebrated and gathered on special occasions, but the chamber felt like a cold, endless cavern instead of the warm hall of her youth.

"Sit," she indicated after leading him to a long table reserved for close family and honored guests. "I'll be just a moment."

Her nape felt oddly warm, as if his gaze had fixated on her back as she moved to the kitchen door to arrange some refreshments to be brought. Finishing her instructions, she pivoted and strolled back to the tables.

Finlay briefly recounted the conflict that had taken place in Edinburgh, sparing her most of the bloody details. As they talked, a server came in with ale and two plates of meats and cheeses.

Her fingers trembled as she raised the cup of ale to her lips as the uncertainty about her future returned. She fought the fear her father might now wed her to a Campbell. She hoped her brother would again be able to sway him into choosing a family that would share her beliefs and perhaps even to a man who would appreciate her.

"Ye arenae staying long?" she asked him.

The last thing she wanted to do was entertain while she imagined her father and brother down the hall arguing her fate. But she smiled politely, focusing on the Cameron man's full red lips instead of the unnerving gaze that seemed to see too much.

"Nae, I have business to attend to."

She nodded as he took a bite of the cheese. "Ye must be tired."

"Aye."

"I'll have a room prepared for ye."

He smiled. "I'll only be tonight."

Her brother stormed in, red faced from obviously dealing with their father, and sat where the servant had left a plate for him.

"What did he say?"

"He was quite angry to have to deal with it and that the alliance might be lost. I think he will be searching for a new match for ye straight away. He mentioned Henry's brother, but I reminded Father that he wasnae kenned to be kind to women."

She shuddered.

She couldn't deal with this in front of their guest. "I'll see to a room for Finlay." His name flowed easily from her tongue, and she found her gaze drifting to him.

He nodded, and she left the men to talk in private.

# Chapter Two

Thinking to break her fast early, Blair meandered through the corridors of her youth, making her way absently toward the great hall, the news of Henry's death beating at her with all its ramifications.

There was too much to do to be lying in bed wondering at the twist of fate that had once again left her helpless to the whims of men. Although there was still hope—her brother was open to listening, and he valued her opinions.

She'd spent the night tossing and turning, trying to feel awful about Henry's death, but all she'd been able to muster was relief, until thankfully, she'd been able to squash that unfortunate response down with guilt. What did that say about her? Surely, she should seek God's forgiveness and counsel. No matter what the man had done to her, she owed him her sorrow.

Was it enough to be haunted by the man who had promised to care for her but treated her like a serving goblet, using her then tossing her back with the dregs of his meal until the next time he needed to quench his thirst? Did she owe the brute her grief as well as the adoration she had so naively given him?

She uncrumpled the still dry handkerchief she'd brought from her room. Guilt stabbed at her as she looked at the scene depicted on the cloth—King Charles's coronation. How had she shed no tears?

Her opposite hand trailed across the cool stone walls as she turned her thoughts to the most pressing problem. Her father could now force her into something worse. Her only hope was that John might yet intervene and save her from having to turn her back on her clan for a husband she didn't want.

After reaching the large empty hall, she strolled into the room, making her way to her usual spot at the table and plopping down, only to stare unfocused at the grain patterns on the wooden table. A plate landed smoothly in front of her.

She tilted up to see one of the younger serving boys. "There is a man waitin' to see ye. Should I show him in?"

"Aye." She straightened, thankful for the distraction, as the boy scooted out to retrieve the visitor.

The guest was most likely a merchant she'd been negotiating with over the quality of their candles. The ratio of tallow was too high, and she wanted him to increase the beeswax, which would eliminate some of the unpleasant odor on the candles.

The pompous cousin of her betrothed—well, former betrothed—slinked into the hall, and dread assailed her. Perhaps he'd come to deliver word of Henry's demise, but the smirk on his face looked out of place. It was as if he was having trouble finding the right emotions to express over his loss, just like her.

If she'd known Bruce was the visitor, she'd have instructed the kitchen lad to send him away. Now, stared down by another of the Graham family, who incited a sickening anxiety in her belly, she wished she'd stayed abed, perhaps even feigned illness.

Standing, she forced a smile. "Hello, Bruce."

"Blair." The sound of her name on his lips gave her the impression she wouldn't like his news, but she already knew the truth. He must be wracked with heartache. Anytime she'd seen Bruce in the past, he'd always been at Henry's side. The man now looked lost without his kin, like he'd been so engrossed in despair that he'd not groomed himself in days.

"I'm so sorry ye've come all this way. I have already heard the news. I'm saddened for our loss." *Och*, she wished she truly felt those words. She tried to remember something positive about Henry, but his looks were the only thing that came to mind.

Bruce took the seat next to her, settling in as if she'd welcomed him to dine with her. She eased down to her spot. The man was possibly beside himself with grief. She supposed he must be when he picked up her kerchief.

She was about to expand on her condolences, but he cut her off. "Ye will marry me."

Shards of ice pierced into her chest. Another Graham man ordering her about.

No, she would not marry this arse.

"Nae. I havenae even had time to mourn Henry." That would have to do. *Och*, she couldn't let her father know another Graham was seeking her out.

"Precisely. Henry bedded ye, and now ye may be carrying one of our clan. 'Tis the right thing to do."

Sinking farther into her seat, she struggled for a response. He must have taken her silence as proof.

"We shall wed in two days."

"Nae." She was certain all color had drained from her face as she ceased to breathe.

The man loomed over her like dark shadows of the

phantom that had plagued her childhood nightmares.

"I amnae with child."

"Can ye prove it?" he shot back as the flesh on his face tightened.

There was no way to prove such a thing, but she was certain, with the way her stomach had cramped this morning, her courses would be here any day.

"Nae, ye must go on my word. I wouldnae lie about something so serious." Wringing her hands in her lap, she prayed he'd stand, turn, and leave, that she could rewind the clock and never agree to have anything to do with the Graham family, despite their loyalty to King Charles.

"Ye are a Macnab. Yer clan cannae be trusted."

Her father's reputation of playing both sides was well earned, but John and she were loyal to the king and couldn't be swayed. Resenting the slight to her character and her clan, she turned her nose up at the toad whose gaze drifted down to her midsection.

"'Tis the truth. Time will tell." She wouldn't grow large and round with the passage of time, but that wouldn't stop Bruce from spreading gossip and ruining her possibilities.

"Ye have two days to decide."

Blair wanted to scream. The desire to lash out consumed her as she stared down at her untouched plate of mutton and bread instead of meeting the cold eyes of her dead betrothed's cousin, a man apparently as ruthless as Henry.

She shook her head with a certainty she didn't feel, as if she were the one who could make the call. "I need time to grieve."

"What better way than to be welcomed into Henry's clan."

"Nae." She clenched her fists under the table and met his stare straight on.

"If ye dinnae marry me in two days' time, I will tell

Henry's family." Bruce's lips twisted up on one side like the treacherous bend at the nearby river where she'd seen many children slip in. Something in her stomach lurched.

"Ye ken ye will be forced to wed Norval, and he isnae as kind and generous as yer former lover."

She cringed as her father's suggestion from last night loomed. He had mentioned she should wed Henry's brother.

She'd seen Norval accost a kitchen lass and force her into a closet once. Henry had even spoken of his aversion to his brother's temperament in public. She couldn't imagine what the man was capable of when no one was looking.

"And what do ye gain from marrying me?" Fisting her hands, she forced her gaze to his. His catlike grin turned to that of a lad about to get his hands on the coveted prize at a caber toss.

"The right to claim yer clan's allegiance for the Royalist cause and gain the favor of the Marquess of Montrose."

"Ye are mistaken if ye think my father has chosen a side. My marriage willnae sway him."

"I will still gain my cousin's favor and get to bed ye every night. I cannae lose." He shrugged.

She wanted to shiver but steeled herself to deny him satisfaction and pinned him with a disgusted stare.

Eyes turning cold, his voice thickened. "Or ye can take yer chances with Norval." This time, she couldn't hide the shudder that rolled over her. "'Tis what I thought."

If Bruce told Henry's family they had been together, the lot of them would appear before her father and demand the arrangement, especially if they believed she carried the eldest and favorite son's child in her belly. Her father would turn her over without another word, probably happy to be rid of her.

She could tell John, but what could he do? He might attack Bruce, but that would put him in jeopardy and possibly harm the Macnab clan's relationship with Montrose, the leader of the Royalist forces. A wave of dizziness unsteadied her.

"I'm staying at the Duck's Head Tavern. If ye dinnae come to me by tomorrow night, I'll be on my way to the bonnet laird. I'm sure the man would love to ken his precious son's seed was spilled inside such a bonny and well-connected lass."

Gaze returning to her full plate, nausea swept over her as the implications rushed through her. If she told her father, he'd push her into Norval's arms or even worse, force her to wed a Campbell.

The air shifted beside her. When she glanced back up, she glimpsed Bruce's back as he skirted out through the kitchen doors along with removing any opportunity to plead for some other outcome.

Deep male voices startled her. Bruce must have heard the men coming. Looking up, she was met by warm hazel eyes.

Finlay Cameron had been the man who had protected and been kind to Kirstie and her. His gaze made her want to believe there were good men in the world, but the only one to see any value in her was John.

While jumping to her feet to greet them, her stomach churned with despair, and her hand flew to her mouth. Hoping to find a quiet place to contemplate her options, she ran from the room without even saying good morn.

• • •

Finlay's gaze followed Blair from the room—he'd never seen the vibrant lass so pale. She'd always overlooked him, but to ignore him in her own home was a new insult to his pride. Perhaps the grief had overcome her manners. Shaking it off, he continued to follow John into the hall, happy to be filling his belly. He needed to be on his way, but now he had John's proposal to consider. The one that had him tossing and turning during the night. Should he wed Blair? And, would she want him?

Coming north to share the sad news with Blair's family before vicious rumors reached her might have been a mistake. What's worse was the rumors were true—Blair's betrothed had pushed another man into the thick of battle to save his own skin. He'd wanted her to think Henry had died an honorable death and spare her the details. He'd given her most of the truth of the battle. He hoped no one who had seen the incident would feel the need to come forward.

She had a right to believe the best about the man she'd given herself to, even though the man had been a despicable craven. He'd only left out the specifics of Henry's cowardice. It had been to protect her. He had to acknowledge the truth. From the moment he'd met Blair Macnab and the calm confidence she possessed, he'd been in awe of her.

Instead of being here, he should have rushed to England to tell his brothers and father the Puritan propagandist papers were for once telling the truth instead of the lies and over-exaggerations they were prone to print.

Prince Rupert, the leader of the Royalist forces in England, was skilled, but his tactics were not always civilized, and the English Parliament had seized onto the crimes he had committed. They had perpetuated a false narrative, leading the public to believe King Charles approved of his nephew's atrocities, further enraging the Protestants determined to oust him based on his love for his Catholic queen. Finlay knew better. King Charles didn't care for his nephew's ways and would probably send Prince Rupert away if he weren't so desperate for help.

If the English Parliament succeeded in this scheme, it could lead to the downfall of the king, and at the hand of the Scots, no less.

After John and he took a seat at a long bench on the raised platform toward the interior of the large hall, he studied the tapestries of the Macnab symbols and ancestors that overlooked the spot and indicated the place of honor. It was similar to the hall at Kentillie, but something about the scene left him cold like his estate in England, instead of feeling fulfilled like he did when he was on Cameron lands.

Movement caught his eye as a servant appeared in the empty room. While the Macnab heir gave some instructions to the lad, he remembered the conversation he'd overheard outside his door this morning.

A gaggle of maids had been discussing a lass who had missed her cycle and appeared to be with child. The group seemed quite scandalized. Could they have been talking about Blair?

John broke into his thoughts as the lad scurried off. "Have ye considered my offer? My father may wed Blair to a Campbell if I dinnae present him with a better option."

"Would he risk the wrath of Montrose over such a thing?" His chest tightened. Blair's union with a clan loyal to the Covenanters would cement the Macnabs' loyalty firmly on the side pushing Parliamentary rule onto the people of Scotland.

For his king and country, it was important she marry into a clan with Royalist ties.

"I dinnae ken. 'Tis why ye must take Blair as yer wife." John's stare met him straight on.

"Ye are no' yet the laird and cannae make that decision." Placing his elbows on the table, he clasped his hands and leaned into them, analyzing what a union between them would mean. John pinned him with staunch blue eyes that conveyed the veracity of his intent.

"I'll convince him." The man pinched his lips together, then gave him a bright smile that reminded him of the first time he'd seen Blair smile. It had been when she'd convinced the servants at the Macnab keep they could entertain several of the Cameron clan, after his kin had shown up unannounced just before the late day meal. And she'd been able to pull it off as if the extravagant meal had taken weeks to plan. It had been the first time she'd caught his attention, and he'd been amazed at her efforts and the results.

"Ye are certain ye can?"

If her brother had the same uncanny ability to make things happen and win people over that Blair possessed, Finlay would soon be wed to one of the most beautiful lasses in all of Scotland. It would ensure the Macnab clan stayed faithful to the king.

"Aye. He plans to sign the Solemn League and Covenant. He will want to shore up alliances with Royalists as well, and what better match than to a family favored by the king." He caught on that John was referring to his English relatives and not the Cameron clan. Not many people knew of his connection to the king, and he'd not been one to parade about the Highlands acknowledging the family that only grudgingly accepted him.

"Ye canne let him sign the proclamation." Every muscle in his body tightened.

"I cannae control what he does as long as he is laird. Blair and I have both tried to talk him out of it. Now ye see how important it is that she be wed to someone faithful to our clan's beliefs."

"I dinnae have my laird's permission."

"Ye can take her to Kentillie and get his blessing."

But he wasn't planning on going to the Cameron keep. He was bound for England to give his family and King Charles an update on the loyalties in Scotland. By coming here, he'd already added time to the journey, a delay he couldn't afford.

"That doesnae change the fact she doesnae desire to be

wed to me." Reality set back in. He'd been visiting for years with the Camerons, and she'd not once looked at him with a hint of interest.

"'Tis nae true. She is just upset about the loss of Henry. She will grow to care for ye." John's eyes twinkled as if he'd solved the mysteries of life.

"Even so, I wish to have a wife who wants me." His past wouldn't let him commit to a wife who would not be a partner.

"Trust me. She wouldnae be averse to ye as a husband."

Hope blossomed in his chest. Could he have what he'd always dreamed of? A family that stayed together no matter where they lived, and a woman who could navigate her way through the tedious tasks of life on an English estate?

A lad from the kitchen peeked into the room, glanced around, and asked John, "Where's Mistress Blair?"

Pointing, the Macnab heir absently said, "That way." The lad nodded and ran after her.

A lass bounded out of the kitchen balancing two plates in her hands and smiled, then strolled over and set the trenchers down in front of Blair's brother and him. His stomach growled at the sight of cold mutton, bread, and cheese. The lass turned and made her way back to the kitchen, but his gaze landed on the plate left unattended next to him. It must have been Blair's. Her pallor had been slightly green when she'd run from the room, and now that he thought about it, she'd been holding her mouth. She might truly be with child.

If Blair married right away, no one would ever know her secret, but if she started to show, she might end up forced to support herself and the babe on her own. Shoulders drooping, he remembered his mother and the blisters and calluses on her hands from struggling to make his home in Scotland a happy one.

He couldn't let that happen to Blair.

"When will yer father make the arrangements?"

If The Macnab followed his typical pattern of positioning his clan on a fulcrum between the Royalists and Covenanters, it would be too long. Maybe John could push him into a quick decision. After picking up a piece of cheese, he tossed it into his mouth.

No wonder she ate it all—the milky, creamy texture was smooth with just a hint of smoke and sharpness.

"If 'tis no' ye, I'm sure 'twill take months to come to an agreement. He never does anything without deliberating every outcome and manipulating the situation until he has whatever he wants."

Dread snaked into Finlay's spine. Swallowing the cheese, his thoughts raced as he tried to figure out a way to save the lass from the life his mother had lived without forcing her into an unwanted marriage. But Blair didn't have the luxury of time.

He told himself not to worry. It would be different with her—she would find a husband, and no one would hold the babe against her. She was the daughter of a laird of a powerful clan, and she and the babe would be cared for, but the thoughts had a false ring in them. He knew her options would be limited if her state were discovered before arrangements had been made.

The lad stumbled back into the room, Blair breezing in behind him, shoulders back, head held high, like a goddess ready for battle. All signs of illness erased from her face. They were replaced by the smooth glowing skin and poise of the lass he'd seen all those years ago, the one who knew her way around the castle and could inspire confidence and delegate tasks to accomplish the greatest of feats.

Blue eyes the color of a cloudless summer day turned to him, and she smiled. Then nodded in some secret way as if apologizing for her behavior of only moments ago. The gesture enveloped him like a caress, despite the distance between them.

She strode on through the room to be met by a nervous-looking Highlander in the doorway. The slender young man presented her with a box, and a surge of jealousy jolted through him at the smile she granted the interloper, but there was something different to it. Her lips were curved up, but they were stern and set. A resilience and strength of purpose radiated from her, indicating the lad was no lover bringing her gifts to entice her heart.

Shoulders relaxing, he cursed, letting it bother him that she might be interested in another.

"Will this be better than the last batch?" Blair's words carried through the hall. All the authority of the lady of the keep were infused in them, dripping with confidence and poise.

"Aye, 'twill, me lady." Voice low, the man's head remained dipped, gaze just peeking at her through his lashes, showing her the reverence she deserved.

"Ye are certain these willnae have the same odor."

Raising the lid, he swung it up, but it caught on hinges mid-flight. "Aye." His face lit with a tentative smile.

"If this batch isnae better, dinnae bother coming back. I've reached out to another candle maker. I dinnae mind the tallow ones for outside, but they willnae do in the keep."

"Yes, me lady. I promise 'tis the quality ye seek and at a fair price."

Her delicate hand reached inside and pulled out a long bleached white candle. Raising it to her nose, she inhaled as the candle maker rubbed his nape.

She commanded respect from all those she dealt with. Finlay found himself intrigued, wondering where her skills had come from and why he'd always seen her taking care of these tasks and not her mother. Despite her small stature and gentle lilting voice, she was a fierce negotiator and ran this castle like she was the one in charge. And better still, she understood numbers, a skill that to this day eluded him, because they pranced around in his head causing it to ache.

He needed a wife who could run a large estate, and those were hard to find in Scotland. The English lasses wouldn't speak to him, not that he would consider a priggish Sassenach for a wife. Blair might not care for him, but she was what he needed. Still, she'd never really looked at him.

John cleared his throat, and his eyebrows were raised as if to say, *I know what ye are thinking.*

"All right," Finlay blurted as the beat of his heart increased, certain it was the prudent decision for his clan, country, and king. She was a Royalist, and it would be a good match for the Camerons and King Charles if their union could keep the Macnabs from joining the Covenanters. "But only if she says yes, and only after yer father and my laird have approved of the match."

"I'll get his approval." John's grin turned triumphant, the man's gaze turning back to Blair. "Ye will both be happy."

He still wasn't sure. "I have two conditions. Ye will join us on our way to Kentillie as a chaperone."

"I can do that. What else?" John relaxed, leaning back and popping a piece of cheese into his mouth.

"We have to leave today."

# Chapter Three

After dealing with the candle maker, Blair turned to see John's crooked smile spread into a satisfied smirk. He'd made some plans for her she probably wouldn't be pleased with. She inched her way toward the table, wondering why her brother's grin reminded her of the time he'd pushed her off the cliff into the freezing cold water.

Finlay, on the other hand, stared through her as if she were an apparition. His slack jaw tightened, and he glanced away as if embarrassed to be caught in the act. As she inched closer, his golden skin reddened, making him look like a boy of fifteen instead of a man several years her senior.

His gaze met hers and held her mesmerized. It was the first time he'd focused his regard on her long enough to pull her in. She was caught in a web of thick dark wisps of lashes which framed intriguing eyes so intense they screamed for attention. They were blue on the outer rim, then gray, and just around the black was a warm chocolate sun that spread out from the center.

Enthralled, she found herself wanting to study what some

may call hazel eyes, but there were hidden depths, and she'd been pulled in like a child seeing the stars for the first time. How had she never noticed him before?

And what had her meddling brother done now?

She blinked then reminded herself to breathe. After a sharp inhale, a wave of tension evaporated, and Bruce's ultimatum faded to the back of her mind. She would contemplate that unpleasant business when she had a moment alone. She walked toward the men and slid into the seat next to Finlay.

As they continued to stare at her, she asked, "What are ye two about?"

After raising her glass, she took a sip of the warm ale she'd left untouched earlier. Her appetite was ruined; she ignored the food. Curious, she gave her brother a sidelong glare meant to say "what have ye done."

"I have arranged for ye to wed Finlay."

Shrinking back at the surprise, she gulped and gasped for breath.

The brawny Highlander seemed to bristle at her reaction, the only indication he was part of the conversation. His stare met her straight on as he held his shoulders and head strong. He was a warrior, a Royalist, and a protector to her friend, Kirstie. He was a good man.

Fear of rejection hid deep in the depths of his hazel eyes, but also pride. She knew that feeling from her own failed attempts to gain her father's affections.

Could he be the answer to her prayers? Bruce's demands had left her paralyzed with fear, but something inside her recognized this man could be her salvation.

Did she deserve a husband like Finlay after what she'd done? It was too soon to rush into another hasty betrothal, but Bruce had left her little choice.

He must have taken her silence as a denial, because he

pushed back to stand, showing he was above her dismissal. "I believe it is time for me to take my leave." She'd never heard him sound so formal, so cold, almost English.

"Nae, dinnae leave." Her heart skittered and almost stopped as her hand clasped onto his arm. Finlay's gaze drifted to her hand, but she didn't remove it. Swirling, multicolored eyes climbed her arm to meet her stare, causing warmth to spread, a flush she wasn't familiar with. "Ye just caught me unaware. Give me a moment."

This might be her only opportunity for deliverance, her chance to have a good life with a decent man, a supporter of the king and her religion. But she was no longer the maiden she had been up until a week ago. She had to confess her secret, wouldn't let him be brought into a union he might resent when he discovered the truth on their wedding night.

Tearing her gaze from Finlay's, she pivoted to her brother. "May we have a few moments alone?"

"Aye, I'll be just outside." John nodded, stood, and strolled toward the door while her heart pounded so feverishly she could feel it in the back of her neck. Heat enveloped her. Her hands trembling, she removed the one on Finlay and clasped it with the other in her lap, hoping to steady them both.

Her gaze skimmed the room to be certain they were alone. But even so, she leaned in close so that if anyone entered, their conversation would remain private.

"Do ye really want me, or is John pushing ye into this?" Her pulse thickened, stalling the pounding in her chest as she awaited his reply. For some strange reason, it was important to her that this was Finlay's choice and not something her brother had pushed him into. She wanted to know that some part of him could care for her. She opened her mouth, but the confession eluded her voice, leaving her throat dry and empty.

She should be jumping at the chance to marry into the

Cameron clan. But his gaze warned there would be something different about this marriage. His eyes held secrets he might not wish to share, and she found herself wishing she'd asked Kirstie more about the man in front of her. She should have paid closer attention when Cameron visitors were in residence. But anytime the large group had visited, she'd focused on making sure the keep operated smoothly. She was so focused on duties, she'd barely gotten to know her friend's brothers, much less any other men with them.

She had no illusions any man she married would want her outside of her wifely duties, but she'd learned to make herself as indispensable and important as she could. Would he respect that and reach out to her for advice, or only on cold nights when he wanted a woman to bed?

She'd thought she had made the right choice with Henry, but her instincts had been so wrong. Could she trust the voice inside that told her Finlay could be a true partner?

Even so, did she have another agreeable option?

"Aye, I would be pleased to have ye as my wife."

She nodded.

"And," Finlay continued, "I am aware ye dinne ken me well, and I willnae claim to be something I'm no'. I will always be honest with ye, and I can tell ye, I respect ye. I believe marriage takes two people to make a family happy. I will do my best to be a partner, a friend, and someone ye can depend upon."

It was the most she'd ever heard him say, and every word of it rang true. Although she didn't love him, they might be able to make a relationship work. And…she believed that was genuine kindness in Finlay's hazel eyes, something Henry, his brother, and his cousin all lacked.

"Ye ken I was betrothed to Henry," she blurted.

He closed those beautiful eyes at the mention of her dead betrothed's name. She willed him to open them again, because he had to know the truth. Honor wouldn't let her go into this arrangement without him knowing what she had allowed. Nodding, his lids rose, and she met his intense focus straight on.

Swallowing, she fought back the sting in her eyes as the words spilled from her lips. "He took me to his bed."

Finlay glanced through thick dark lashes that hid his reaction. Suddenly, filling her lungs became hard and labored. Would he reject her now? A tear slid down her cheek, and she swiped at it, hoping he hadn't seen her moment of weakness and cursing herself for letting the monster who would have been her husband affect her so.

She glanced around the room to be certain they were still alone. Satisfied no one else would overhear, she returned her attention to Finlay. Voice shaking as she fought back the memories, she continued, "I willnae lie to ye. I want ye to ken that I willnae come into the bargain a maiden."

Silence greeted her, so she rushed to fill in the void.

"'Tis all right if ye have changed yer mind. I willnae hold it against ye, and I willnae let John either."

"Nae," his hoarse reply cut her off. Heart sinking at her best hope for a bearable future, she nodded and made to rise.

This time, his hand shot out, clasping onto her wrist. The warm touch was gentle but firm, a soothing caress which promised understanding and compassion, nothing like the way she had felt in Henry's arms when he'd pulled her to his room. "I mean, aye. I will still have ye."

A breath of air reached her lungs.

"I ken ye also believed ye would spend yer life with the man. I will never hold that or anything that comes from yer association with Henry against ye. Yer past willnae dictate how our future should be lived." His gaze penetrated into a part of her that wanted to believe his words. "I would be honored to have ye as my wife."

Relief flooded her senses. The pressure that had been building on her chest, threatening to suffocate her, eased as a tide of warmth rolled over her like a gentle breeze. She breathed a long, liberating breath. She wouldn't be beholden to a man of deceit or one with a brutal nature or to a Covenanter.

Hoping to let the sincerity in her heart show in the words, she focused on his eyes. "And I promise to be a dutiful wife, one ye can rely on, and someone ye will be proud to have at yer side."

He raised her hand, his regard not leaving her, as his lips brushed her bare skin. The touch was light, intimate, and promised he would cherish her. A peace washed through her, one she'd never experienced at another man's touch.

Finlay was the right choice.

Smiling, she eased back into her seat, Finlay's hand staying firm in hers as she lowered it to her lap. She felt the surge of happiness, thinking their clasped hands signified the seal of their agreement. Her eyes drifted down, and for the first time, she noticed how full his lips were, a light red, like slightly watered wine. She'd only ever kissed Henry, but somehow she knew things would be different with the man who was now to become her husband.

Satisfied, she called out, "John."

Her brother strolled back into the room, satisfaction plastered on his smug features. Had he been watching them?

"Do ye have a decision?"

"Aye, if father is agreeable, we will wed."

"I'll speak to him now."

Finlay rose. "I will come as well." He looked at her. "Excuse me. I think 'tis important I make the offer." A smile spread across his lips, then he added, "Only pack what ye need for a couple of days. I will send for the rest. I apologize for the swift departure, but I have urgent business to see to."

Nodding, she rose and followed the two men from the hall. Normally, she would protest the hasty departure, but there was a man in the village who would be back for her all too soon if she did not escape. It was best if she was well on her way to being wed before Bruce could collect on his demand. Once she was married, her biggest problem would be whether or not she could persuade her new husband that she was worthy of helping him run his house.

Later that afternoon, as the warm rays of the midday sun showered her skin with hope, she found herself riding next to her mother, who had insisted on coming along as a chaperone for the journey. Her mother, more likely than not, only wanted the chance to see Elspeth Cameron, the Cameron laird's mother. They had formed a friendship akin to Kirstie's and hers over the years.

Shortly after she'd left the hall this morning, John had hurried into her room to say her father approved, and they would be off within the hour. With the Macnab laird's failing health, he would not be able to make the trip with them. Her father was probably pleased to be rid of her so easily. She wished she'd been able to hear the conversation that had decided her fate.

Apprehension creeping in, she wished she'd asked Finlay why he was in such a hurry. She was prevented from seeking answers because John dominated his attentions, and the guards sent by her father kept her sequestered away from her betrothed. It was as if her father was trying to ensure her honor during the journey.

She was pleased to be going to the Cameron lands; not only would she be with Royalists, but she prayed Kirstie would be there. Surely she was safe and back at Kentillie by now. It was another reason she didn't argue with leaving for Finlay's home straight away.

Peace finally returned at the thought of the prospects

ahead. Until they passed by the Duck's Head Tavern, and a disheveled man stepped out through the front door of the nearby stables, glaring at her as if he intended to charge up and stop their procession.

*Bruce.*

# Chapter Four

The sun had dipped low in the sky, and despite the hour, Finlay appreciated that it still illuminated the clear Highland sky with a subtle light that would continue deep into the evening hours. The surrounding mountains were dotted with purple and blue hues that blew in the slightly chilled wind. The familiar sight made his heart sing. The pressures of the journey eased, just as it did every time he came home from England. Forgoing his own cottage near the edge of the village, he steered the group toward Kentillie, the Cameron seat and stronghold.

As they passed through the stone gates and walls and into the fortified courtyard of the castle, peace enveloped him. He'd been looking over his shoulder most of the trip because he'd felt like they were being followed. There was comfort in knowing he was now surrounded by men he trusted.

He turned to Blair. Her back was straight, a slight smile on her face as she glanced from side to side taking in the magnificence of the castle's stoic beauty. She was lovely. And he was happy to see she was pleased with the Cameron stronghold.

He'd wished for time to woo her before the wedding, but they had moved swiftly on the journey here, and the Macnab men had kept her well guarded and out of his reach. He wondered if her father didn't trust the Camerons.

From her alert, inquisitive scrutiny, Finlay could tell she had never been here. He found that odd, considering her friendship with Kirstie. Thinking back, the only time he'd seen Blair off Macnab lands had been their recent trip to Edinburgh. She had obviously been kept close to home most of her life.

How would she do on a journey to England, and then upon her arrival with all the gaggle of English servants and family demanding they follow silly protocols and English ways? A stab of guilt knifed into his side at the knowledge he would be throwing her in with the wolves and vipers on that journey.

With the Macnab warriors keeping them apart, he'd not had the time to tell her about the situation at his estate, and he wondered how much she knew of him and of his birth. Would she reject him once she learned?

He'd been just about to tell her of his double life, when she'd called John back to seek her father's approval. His moment was gone.

Anyway, he was marrying her to protect her and the babe. No matter what she thought of his difficult family situation, he hoped she would see that.

Now, it was too late. There would be no going back without hurting both his honor and hers. Besides, over the past few days, she'd looked miserable astride the horse she rode, sometimes looking green or as if she was in pain. She needed a father for her child, whether she knew it yet or not.

Unease washed over him as they made their way to the stables and started to dismount. He'd left directly from the battle in Edinburgh, and while he knew Lachlan and Malcolm had survived with no injuries, he was unsure of the fate of his friend Alan and the laird's sister, Blair's friend, Kirstie.

There was little activity around the castle, and he assumed most of the inhabitants were inside taking the evening meal. Stomach rumbling at the thought, he handed his steed off to a stable boy and strolled over to help Blair down from her horse.

Her dainty hands clasped tightly onto his shoulders as if clinging to him in an embrace. Although the touch was innocent, awareness shot through his chest and straight into his cock. He'd always found her attractive, but he never thought such a small gesture would affect him so. His need to be with her must be in anticipation of their wedding night. It wasn't the time to let his desire be known, so he pushed it aside.

"Kirstie should be here." Without removing her hands, Blair's sapphire stare locked on his, and he realized she was trembling, expecting her friend to be in the stables where she loved tending to the animals.

He wanted to wipe the worry from her eyes. "We'll ken shortly where she is."

Blair turned away, staring at the stables as the boys took the horses inside, looking for her friend to walk through the door and out into the open at any moment.

"Come."

Her hands fell from his shoulder, but he found himself reaching out for the one, entwining his fingers with hers. She didn't pull away. Either testament to the worry over her friend or acknowledgement he would soon be her husband.

He wanted to get to know her after days of seeing her but being kept apart. He guessed the Macnab men only backed away now because they'd made it here safely and John had captured their attention. Finlay seized the opportunity to guide her toward the castle and away from her guards. "Have ye ever been to Kentillie?"

As they stepped out into the open, she glanced around, appearing to take in everything. "Nae. My father didnae allow me to come."

"Then how did ye and Kirstie meet?"

"Och, we were wee things the first time she came to my home. Riding through our gate like a phantom chasing its prey. She made me think of far off places I'd never seen, and I was mesmerized by her right away."

"Sounds like her." The smile that breached his face came from down deep. He loved the Camerons and his clan, but it was the bit of nostalgia over Kirstie's exploits with the horses that warmed his heart.

"She continued to visit over the years, and we developed a strong friendship. She was like the sister I'd never had."

As their steps took them closer to the large gray fortress, he could feel the tension leaving her body as she spoke of her friend, admiration glowing in her gaze. He hoped one day she would hold him in such high esteem.

He released her hand and opened the large wooden doors to escort her into the great hall. Blair took in everything. And he wondered how was it that the most beautiful lass in Scotland was about to marry a bastard like himself.

Pushing away the doubts as they strolled into the cavernous room, he was pleased to see he'd been accurate—a large group of Camerons was gathered at the table. Kirstie and Alan were among them.

Alan waved at them. "Look who finally made it home."

Kirstie glanced up and saw the woman by Finlay's side. She let out an audible squeak then jumped up and ran for them.

"Ye are all right," Blair said, but it sounded more like a question as his laird's sister wrapped her arms around Blair, pulling her in. He was happy to see the joyous reunion and to know his friends were unharmed.

Alan appeared by his side, clapping him on the shoulder and drawing him in for a quick embrace. "Glad to see ye, friend."

"'Tis good to see ye as well and that ye found Kirstie. Was she unharmed?"

"Aye. I'll tell ye the story later, but for now, come sit and join us for the meal."

Nodding, Finlay caught a glimpse of movement behind him and realized the rest of their party had joined them.

"John, Sara, come join us. We are celebrating our marriage." Alan reached out, taking Kirstie's hand and pulling her back to his side as if he couldn't stand to be without her for a moment.

"'Tis happy tidings," Finlay said.

Blair burst into excited chatter as she took her friend's free hand and bounced with delight, showing that zest for life he appreciated in her.

He was pleased to see Lachlan, the leader of the Cameron clan, next to Maggie, who held their newborn son close to her chest. Scanning the rest of the table, he noticed the priest, who was thankfully in residence. He'd apparently already presided over Kirstie's and Alan's wedding. All Finlay had to do now was ensure he had his laird's permission and wed the lass.

They could be on their way tomorrow.

Moving toward the table, he approached his laird, nodded at Maggie, smiled at the little one, then glanced back to Lachlan. "May I have a few minutes to speak with ye in private?"

Lachlan stood and led the way out of the room, down a short hall, and into his study. As the door shut behind him, it clicked into place.

"I would like to wed Blair Macnab. I have already spoken

to the Macnab laird and have his blessing for the union. I seek yers as well." The words came out in a rush, partly because King Charles needed the information he possessed as soon as possible to defend himself. But also because now that he was here, he was afraid Lachlan might somehow have an objection.

"'Twould be a good match. I'm assuming since he is here, we have the approval of the Macnab heir as well." It was widely assumed that an alliance with John was of more importance than that of his rapidly deteriorating father.

"Aye. He suggested it."

"Ye have my blessing. I ken no better man to win the love of such a lovely lass."

He didn't know her heart, and she most assuredly didn't love him.

"Thank ye." Bowing his head, he smiled with relief then turned a straight face back to his laird. "Since the priest is here, can we wed now? I have delayed a trip to England for too long. I must get word to the king on the Solemn League and Covenant. Besides the ones we already discovered, Blair's father has decided to sign it. I have to warn him to expect resistance from the Highlanders who will be joining the war in England."

Lachlan nodded, a sad look crossing his eyes. "I agree. 'Tis better he kens sooner. When will ye leave?"

"If we can be wed tonight, we shall go first thing in the morning."

"Does Blair ken yer plans?"

"She kens we will be going to England, but I dinnae wish to tell her the rest until I ken for certain she will be loyal to our cause."

"I agree. With her father as an example, we can only hope that her brother has had more influence." Lachlan rubbed his chin.

"I have faith in her, just not her father."

Lachlan nodded then straightened his shoulders. "I have a request."

"Aye."

"Take Robbie with ye. He has some business to take care of. I'll send some guards as well."

Why would Lachlan send the boy with him? Robbie was practically walking into a war zone. The Cameron laird and Alan had taken a liking to the lad after rescuing him almost a year earlier and rarely let Robbie out of their sight.

He would have a wife to think of in the morning, too. Although he was confident in his abilities to keep her safe on the journey, having extra Cameron men with him would be welcome.

"Aye."

"Ye must protect the lad with yer life. I cannae tell ye more, but I'm trusting him with ye."

"Where should I take him?" He'd grown to like the lad himself, but Robbie was secretive, and there was something too familiar about him. Maybe Robbie reminded him of the lads he went to school with in England—not his attitude, but his education was similar to that of the English peerage he'd been forced to endure.

Maybe he was overthinking it. The boy was being raised by priests; maybe his education was to prepare him for a life in service to God. But why had he spied Lachlan training him late one evening in a secluded area near the base of Ben Nevis?

"He'll let ye ken when the need arises."

He had more questions about the lad than he had answers, but he had other concerns right now.

"Can they all be ready to leave in the morning?"

"I can arrange it. Robbie and some guards will be at yer house at daybreak."

"Guards are a good idea. They should travel light, so we

can make good time." Finlay liked the idea of having strong, capable Cameron men on the journey with them. He'd have them on alert as well, to be certain they weren't being trailed.

Lachlan nodded.

"All right then. Let's finish the evening meal and see to another wedding." His laird clapped him on the back then started for the door.

Finlay trailed behind him, wondering again what would prompt his laird to send a boy raised by priests to a country torn apart by civil war.

But that thought fled as they entered the great hall and he saw Blair's radiant face while she laughed at something Kirstie whispered. Her gaze met his, and she smiled at him, reminding him that he was about to become a married man and would be taking her to his cottage tonight.

• • •

Blair sat stunned as she heard the tale of how Alan had saved Kirstie and the harrowing events her friend had been through. A blessed peace washed over her as she reveled in her friend's happiness and met many new Camerons who welcomed her as if she were long-lost kin.

She was happy to see Brodie, the laird's cousin and frequent visitor to the Macnab lands, with a wife, Skye. The woman had a slightly rounded belly and wore the same glow on her face when she looked upon her husband that Kirstie did when she smiled at Alan.

Sara chatted away with Elspeth, seemingly as happy as the rest. It was a side of her mother that she only showed when her father was nowhere about. It soothed her when she saw her mother was more than the weak, doting wife Sara portrayed to her father.

It dawned on her that she'd been able to accomplish the

things she had because her mother encouraged her. She hadn't realized her mother's enthusiasm had been squashed by her father's belief that the place for a woman was at a man's feet or in the bedchamber. She questioned if her father even knew it was she who had been running the Macnab castle for years.

Movement from the corner of the hall caught her attention as Finlay strolled back into the room with the Cameron laird, who had a wide grin spreading across his face. As they moved closer to the table she guessed he had approved. Lachlan scooped up a trencher and a spoon, banging them against each other to gain the attention of all those gathered.

"Father Fergus. Would ye do us the honor of wedding this Cameron man to this lovely Macnab lass here?" The laird waved his hand toward her.

A blush crept onto her face as every eye in the room gazed at Finlay then pivoted to stare at her. Everything was happening so fast, she'd not even mentioned the arrangement to Kirstie, but no matter, her friend pulled her in for another tight embrace, whispering in her ear, "Ye have made the right choice. He will treat ye well."

Blair had already come to that conclusion. Finlay had been so kind on the journey here, looking out for her mother and her. She'd also seen how he'd cared for the men and horses that traveled with them. Despite his hulking appearance, he seemed to be a good man.

As she stood speechless, her friend drew back and gazed directly into her face with a pleased look. She flushed, then her friend chimed in, "'Twill mean ye will live here with us part of the year."

*Part of the year.* What did she mean? Would Finlay send her home sometimes? But she wasn't able to voice a question before Lachlan was taking her by the hand, drawing her forward, and placing her hand into Finlay's.

"I approve of this union between a Cameron and a

Macnab," he stated loudly as he turned.

From that moment, the world moved in a blur. Kirstie guided her from the room to be bathed. Before long, her friend had her in a clean gown and had placed ribbons in her hair. A short while later, Kirstie led her down the hall and into a chapel.

As they moved to the front, doubts crept in, until a vision of Bruce appearing haggard and crazed assailed her.

Finlay would care for her, and she would be among Royalists and friends. She'd also realized on the journey here she enjoyed listening to his deep, soothing voice.

This was what she had to do. For her own safety and for the good of her clan. If her father wouldn't make the right choices, at least John and she could salvage the clan name.

Blindly walking down the aisle, she stopped at the front of the chapel to face the man she was pledging herself to. The new shirt stretched across his broad shoulders was clean and a bit snug. He was a comely man. She inhaled and breathed in the scent wafting from him—fresh lavender.

*Och*, she would be in Finlay's bed tonight.

The unexpected warmth of Finlay's long fingers clasped onto her hands jolted her. She flinched. His touch hadn't bothered her, it was the shock of the touch she'd not anticipated.

Hurt flashed in his eyes, and she wished she could tell him, *nae, 'twas no' ye*, but words started spilling from Father Fergus's lips, and she was pulled away despite not hearing a thing. Her ears rang, and her knees became wobbly.

It was all happening so fast.

"Aye, I will." Finlay's husky voice was steady.

Swallowing, she scrutinized the man she was marrying. Her thoughts returned to the wedding night. He was large, much larger than Henry. Her hands started to tremble as uneasiness invaded over what the night might bring.

Finlay glanced down at them then back up at her, and his thumb brushed back and forth across her wrist. It had a calming effect, reminding her that this man was gentle, and he would never harm her.

"Blair," broke into her thoughts, but she wasn't sure who said it. Tearing her attention from Finlay, she noticed the priest was expecting her to say something. She just repeated what Finlay had said. "Aye, I will."

Would he be quick to anger? Would he respect her as a woman? Would he hate her when he discovered she was marrying him because she was being blackmailed?

But that wasn't the whole truth. She liked Finlay and would choose him before any other. Even as that dawned on her, she realized it was too late to ask questions now.

"Kiss her."

The sound registered, just as cheers rang out and hazel eyes dipped toward hers.

Finlay's full lips landed on hers like soft silk sliding against her flesh. Her eyes shut as a foreign sensation swept her into a world where only his touch existed. The soft pressure of Finlay's mouth was the only thing she felt until an arm coiled around her waist. It pulled her up onto her toes and into his hard body, deepening the embrace, making her insides quake.

The caress made her want to imagine a world where she was one with this man, a partnership in all things. It was like this were her first kiss, like everything before had been an illusion and this was what her body had known a man's touch should be.

This was magic.

Finlay's arm loosened, and she was sinking back to the floor, falling into a new world. One she felt had somehow righted itself, setting a course toward what she'd wanted from life.

# Chapter Five

The sun still illuminated the evening sky and trickled in through the chapel windows, which lent a magical glow to the holy space. Despite the hour and weariness from their journey, Finlay had a renewed sense of peace and a faith that God had given Blair to him, a precious gift he would guard with his life.

Until something faded in her eyes as they said the words that would bind them together. His heart lurched, thinking she might not be as moved by the moment as he. Still, he prayed it was just nerves, because he wanted her to come to care for him. He wanted the happy relationship his parents never had.

Blair's fingers trembled as they recited the vows. Someone told him he could kiss her, so he dipped his head and placed his lips on hers. She stilled, and the whole world stopped moving. Her lips were soft and subtle, and when he wound an arm around her waist to pull her farther into his embrace, she sighed like he'd done something right.

He'd kissed others, but this was the first time it sent

shivers right to his spine, immobilizing him, except for that part of him that wanted more. He deepened the caress. If this simple touch rocked him to his core, what would it be like when he claimed her body?

A cheer erupted from the gathered clansmen, pulling him from his thoughts. He loosened his grip, and Blair's slight form slid down his body to land on her feet. He'd not realized he'd picked her up.

His heart was thudding, breath coming fast as heat surged to the part of him that had come to life with a simple kiss, the part now throbbing with need. Her bright eyes rested on his, and she smiled. *Och*, thank God she smiled, but then he remembered where his thoughts had gone with such a simple touch and in front of a crowd.

Only a short while later, Finlay's new bride and he walked in silence toward the stables. The rest of Blair's family was settled in rooms at Kentillie, with the other Macnab men seen to elsewhere. He was eager to show Blair their home and sleep in a familiar bed. He glanced over at her, wishing to take her hand in his, but afraid she would flinch away as she had during their wedding. Still, he was willing to take things slow and let her get to know him first.

"'Tis a lovely night." Her soft voice carried to him on a wayward breeze.

"Aye, 'tis." He thought to say how lovely she was, but words had never been his strength. Instead, emboldened by her relaxed tone, he took her hand in his and was rewarded when she clasped on, inviting the connection.

"Kirstie said I may no' live here all the time."

He could hear the question in the statement. She sounded hurt.

"Will ye send me away part of the year?"

He stopped. Is that what she thought?

"Nae." He still had so much to explain, and he cursed

himself for his haste in their marriage and not fully explaining his life to her. If he didn't have to rush off to visit the king, he would have taken enough time to woo her properly; heaven knows she hadn't had that with Henry, either. She deserved so much more, and as soon as he had given King Charles the news, he promised himself he would court her properly and let her know that she was worthy of a man's respect.

"I dinnae ken, then."

Squeezing her hand, he confessed, "I live in England part of the year." His free arm clasped onto her and caressed Blair's smooth skin. How natural it felt to have her small hand in his, and how at ease he was becoming with her, because despite him neglecting to tell her, she had softened.

"Why? Is yer family in England?" The simple gesture of touching her seemed to calm her, the question coming out without the worry he'd heard in her previous words.

"My father is an earl. My mother refused to move to England with him, so I spent my years as a child, going back and forth between the two."

"Are they married? I thought a wife had to do as her husband instructed." There was no judgment, only curiosity.

"Nae. They never wed." Dropping his arm from hers, he continued to guide her toward the horses.

"Do ye have brothers and sisters? I thought ye were an only child."

"I have two brothers, but we only share a father."

He'd said enough, the conversation starting to turn his insides hollow when he should be celebrating. His English family was the last thing he wished to be thinking of now.

Coming to the edge of the stables, he signaled for one of the lads to retrieve their horses.

"'Tis why we leave for England tomorrow. I have important business to see to."

"How long will we be there?"

"Nae long this time. There is too much going on with the Covenanters and the rebellion against the king."

"Will yer family like me?"

"My father will love ye, but I never ken how my brothers are going to behave."

The lads arrived with their horses. He put his hands on her tiny waist and easily lifted her onto the seat of her mare.

After he climbed on his stallion, he noticed her coloring had changed pale, her hand flat on her belly as if it were giving her trouble again. If he'd had any doubts about her condition before the wedding, now he was sure she was with child. He'd done the right thing. This babe would have a father and a mother.

"Are ye feeling all right?"

"Nae. I think I may have eaten something that didnae like me."

*Och.* Did she still not know, or was she afraid to tell him? Some ladies weren't taught what happened when a man and woman were together until it was too late. Had she been one of those women who had been kept in the dark? Was it better when she did discover her condition if she knew it was Henry's babe she carried, or would it be better if she thought it was her husband's?

•  •  •

Blair thought she'd be feeling better by now. The whole journey she'd been plagued by cramps, and her courses had been so heavy she'd thought she would fall over from fatigue. She ticked off the food she'd consumed this evening to determine if it was something she ate.

The stew.

It had tasted lovely with a nice smooth texture, not like the brothy kind she was used to. *Och*, it must have had cream in it. The meal had already been prepared, and with the distraction of the wedding, she'd not thought to ask if any of the food had been made with cheese. She'd be lucky if she kept the contents of her stomach tonight, but luckily, she'd been nervous and had only taken a few small spoonfuls.

It was her wedding night. Finlay would want to take her to his bed. What would he think when she ran from the room seeking a safe place to relieve the pressure?

After arriving at a small cottage in a clearing not far from the castle, he helped her dismount and disappeared into a small stable while she studied the outside of the house, a quaint little place far from the bustling Macnab keep where she'd spent her youth.

The stones were gray, strong in appearance, but dull. While the home was surrounded by the beautiful backdrop of a mountain and the dark trees of the forest, it lacked the color and character she would have liked. Disappointment crept in, almost immediately followed by guilt.

All those skills she'd spent years strengthening in order to care for a castle and servants would not be needed in her new home. She couldn't help but feel a little saddened, like all her visions of what she'd hoped for in a future had been ripped from her head, swirled around and condensed into the small cottage in front of her.

Well, she would make the most of it.

Her stomach cramped, and she nearly bent over, nauseous with the pain. A hand landed on her back, and her instant reaction was to flinch. Finlay pulled his soothing hand away just as quickly as it appeared. She wanted to say, *Nae, it felt nice*, but another wave of pain washed over her, and her face heated. She did manage, "I'm sorry. I still dinnae feel well."

He looked understanding, almost as comforting as the fingers that had rested on the base of her spine. "Come." He tilted his head toward the house.

Pushing the door in, he gave her a warm smile before nodding for her to enter. It was darker inside, and she could only make out the outline of murky shapes. He stepped in behind her, a rush of air floating across her skin as he closed the door and bolted it behind them. A welcoming scent filled her nostrils, possibly apples and cinnamon mixed with whisky. Somehow it felt right. Freezing in place and breathing in the aroma, she waited on Finlay as he moved seamlessly into the room to light a candle.

The small, flickering light cast a comforting glow on the room that now reminded her of a warm hideaway she'd wanted as a child, a place where she could go and be herself. Sturdy wooden furniture was placed at odd angles around the room, a blanket strewn on the sofa, shoes and bags in a pile by the side of the door. But the first word that popped in her head to describe its appearance was sparse.

Her new husband was not the most organized of men. At least that would give her something to do, because they had not had time to discuss duties and what her role would be in the home. They had a lot to talk about, and suddenly, she looked forward to getting to know her husband. A small thrill rode through her like a butterfly chasing lavender.

Her stomach cramped again.

He had been studying her perusal as if looking for approval. She tried to give him her best smile.

"We must leave early. 'Twill need a full night's rest for the journey."

Mention of their wedding night brought a shiver to her shoulders, although she managed to keep it from being obvious. She didn't want her experience with Henry to taint her, but she was terrified of consummating their marriage.

Swallowing, she straightened her backbone, like she always did when something needed to be done, and determined she would follow through on the task at hand.

She would be a good wife.

Wanting to change and prepare for him, she thought on her attire—the same dusty gown she'd worn riding into Kentillie today. She'd brought little with her, and what she had, Finlay had sent to his home by Cameron men after they'd arrived at the castle. The trunk was in a corner. The energy to rifle through the small chest to find the new shift her mother had given her the morning they left felt daunting. He probably wouldn't mind if she just stayed in her current shift.

"Will ye show me to our room?" *Och*, somehow she sounded too eager. Would he think her a harlot after her confession about Henry?

"Aye." He guided her to a small room just off the main one.

She almost questioned, *this is it*, but somehow refrained, thinking it might hurt his pride if she diminished the size and meagerly decorated nature of their home. On second glance, although there were few items, each might tell a story about her husband.

Strolling over to a chair, she picked up a worn plaid, one that reminded her of the blanket she kept on her bed at home, almost threadbare. She drew it in and inhaled. Pure Finlay. Spice and security. Cinnamon and warmth, and now she was his. Hope surged as she thought of how he'd clung to this relic. Maybe he would find such an attachment to her. Yes, that's what she wanted to be to him—the blanket that kept him safe and comfortable the rest of his life.

When she turned back, it was to see in the light of the candle his eyes seemed focused, intent. But instead of being afraid, something in his dilated gaze made her feel treasured. She smiled then caught herself studying her new husband as his regard lingered. She only came up to his chest. He'd be difficult to kiss, but she'd wanted to kiss him again since the ceremony. His caress had been soft, tender, not like those punishing assaults by the weasel who had taken from her what she'd not been ready to give...what she should have been able to give to this man.

Heat rose to her cheeks, just as another cramp attacked. His eyes went from needy to worried, and she realized she'd not been able to hide her reaction to her body's protest. She'd have to inquire what was in the food at Kentillie before dining there in the future.

"Is there anything I can do to help?" Finlay moved closer.

"Nae. I think I just need rest."

"Ye get ready for bed. I have a couple things to see to and will be back to check on ye as soon as I am finished." He backed and placed the candle on the side table then walked from the room.

She undressed down to her shift and climbed under the covers. Her stomach finally returned to normal as she drifted off to sleep while waiting for her husband to return.

# Chapter Six

He should go in and bed his wife, that's what any other man would do. *Och*, but she looked so pale, and Finlay wanted her first experience with him to be pleasant. He'd come so close, too, about to kiss her when her face had turned green. Was it the baby?

Pacing the common room of his home, he vowed to give her a little space. He needed to tame the longing that had heated his blood the instant he'd seen her in his room. And when she'd smelled his favorite old blanket and nuzzled her head into the scent that could only be his, he felt a desire to claim her as his, cover her body with the scent of him, so she knew he would always keep her safe.

Instead of returning to the room, he made preparations for their journey then took the time to pen a letter to his mother, apologizing that he'd wed Blair without her presence, reassuring her that she would love his new bride, and promising to visit her as soon as they made it back from England.

The letters swirled and jumbled in his head, causing it

to pound as he struggled with the task of getting the lines in the right place. It should have only taken minutes, but he was certain a good hour had passed before he was done. He wasn't unlearned, but he'd always struggled with this type of task. Why was it so hard for him? What would Blair think if she ever found out?

Exhausted, he stood and stumbled back to his room and Blair.

Glancing down at her petite form, he smiled. He'd always thought her beautiful but never thought to find a woman like her as his own. On one of their last nights in Edinburgh, he'd watched Henry Graham drag Blair down the hall away from her room. Fists clenched, he'd struggled not to get involved, because doing so would go against her family's wishes and could threaten the Cameron clan's standing with both the Grahams and the Macnabs.

She was his now, and he would keep her safe. Taking in her peaceful slumber in the bed that until this night had been his alone, his groin ached for the release he was entitled to, the relief that only his wife would give him. He would take her gently and show her that he had already come to care for her. He wanted to do so now, but they had a long journey ahead, and she would need her strength.

She would be with him the rest of their lives. He could give her this one night to rest.

Leaning down, he blew out the candle, undressed, and climbed into their bed, wrapping his arms around her slight form and pulling her near.

• • •

Birds chirped and sun shone brightly through the window as light rushes of sound and movement brought Finlay out of the slumber he'd not been able to find until the wee hours of the morning. Although he could still smell lavender and summer rain, Blair was no longer by his side. She couldn't have been gone long, because the ache between his legs that had kept him awake deep into the night still raged on. A shuffle sounded in the other room.

Jumping up, he quickly dressed then walked out to find Blair rummaging through the trunk she'd brought with her.

Clearing his throat as to not startle her, which was something he seemed to be good at, she turned her head toward him and smiled. "Good morning. I didnae intend to wake ye."

"Nae, 'tis no' a problem. We need to be on our way. I usually dinnae sleep this long."

"Well, we havenae stopped long for days. Ye deserve some time to rest."

He moved into the space, inching closer to the bonny lass brightening his home, no, their home. His spirits lifted as he took her in his arms.

She melded to him, placing her arms around his hips and welcoming him, a reassuring sign she was pleased with their match. And he found himself wanting her to be happy. She didn't flinch as she had the night before. Maybe he'd taken the fears of a new bride and twisted them into something else.

He savored the feel of her, just wanting to know she was real and he hadn't dreamed it all. And she clung to him as if she, too, felt the same.

Easing back and reluctantly letting his arms drop, he said, "I'm sorry for whisking ye away so quickly."

"'Twill be all right. I've grown excited about the idea of visiting new places. My father never took me on his travels."

Sad, because that light in her eyes at the prospect of something new pleased him and made him want to show her the world.

"Once we are home again, I will take ye anywhere ye

wish to visit."

"I would like that." The smile she gave him differed from its usual radiance—it was wistful with a dreamy quality as if she wanted it but truly didn't expect it to happen. She'd taken well to Edinburgh, and he'd seen her excitement as he'd guarded her and Kirstie through the city. Blair genuinely enjoyed seeing new places. He vowed he would take her anywhere to keep her happy.

"What should I bring?" Blair cut into his thoughts as she glanced to her trunks then returned her gaze to his.

"We will travel light, just horses, so only a change of clothes."

She did this adorable thing where her smile quirked to the side and she tilted her head. Her reaction amused him.

"I was under the impression a trip to England took weeks. Surely, I will need more."

"I'll get ye whatever ye need when we get there, but for now, time is important."

Bewilderment swirled in her blue eyes. It almost looked as if he'd told her the sky was yellow. "I, I…" She looked down, her eyes skidding from side to side.

"'Twill be all right. I promise I'll take care of ye. Yer belongings will just get dusty on the journey anyway."

Gaping at him, she blinked, inhaled sharply, and nodded. It was as if she was telling herself she could do this, like facing down a feral cat standing between her and a drink when she'd gone a day without.

He reached out and offered a hand. She put her delicate fingers in his, and he drew her in. Misjudging her weight, she flew toward him, colliding with his midsection, and he had to swing his other arm around her when she floundered. The move pinned her to him.

Breathing in the cool scent of lavender, he dipped his head toward hers, burying his nose in her hair, seeking out the scent as his hands clung to her curves. Need clawed at him. Tempted to pick her up and cart her back to the bed to sate the ache that was making itself known again, he groaned inwardly. There wasn't time to thoroughly enjoy her body, and their first time, he wanted it to be special, no hurried affair that left her feeling used and uncared for. She was his wife, and he'd treat her with all the respect and reverence she was due.

Withdrawing, he let his hand slide down the slope of her back and fall away. He walked to a corner, picked up a bag, checked to make certain it was empty, then swiveling back around, he took two strides and held the satchel out for her.

"Just two gowns. We must make haste and cannae take a wagon."

She took the cloth sack and picked out her gowns.

"I've heard parts of England are lovely." The hint of excitement in her voice gave him hope.

"This will be a short visit, but at least ye will be able to get acquainted with the estate."

"Ye have an estate. Is it large?"

"'Tis half the size of my father's, but the land is what's impressive." Taking another bag, he walked into his room, filling the sack with coin, an extra plaid and shirt, and a second pair of boots.

Entering the main room, he halted at the sight of her arms wrapped around her satchel, hugging it as if she was afraid he was going to tell her she couldn't take it as well. Guilt stabbed at him, but he could delay no longer, and he wasn't going to leave his new bride alone.

Rushing into the kitchen, he grabbed the loaf of bread he'd brought from Kentillie last night.

"I'm sorry. 'Tis all I have this morn." Breaking it, he handed her half.

"'Tis fine. I have no' even thought of food yet this

morning."

"When we get back, I'll make certain the kitchen is well stocked for ye."

Smiling, she nodded.

"Do ye enjoy to cook?"

Her face went blank.

Hell, of course she didn't cook. She was accustomed to living in a castle and having servants, being able to wear whatever she wanted when she wanted, and wasn't rushed onto horses to take dangerous journeys into the heart of a civil war.

He'd make it all up to her when they got back.

"Nae. I dinnae ken how." Her shoulders straightened. "But I'll learn," she continued as if he'd challenged her. He'd not meant to make her feel inadequate.

"We can do it together. My mother taught me, and I'm no' so bad at it."

"I cannae wait to meet her."

"She's going to love ye, but she'll be sore about me taking ye off to meet Father before her. I'm leaving her a note to apologize for taking ye away so quickly." He strapped his claymore to his back before walking toward the door.

Moments later, they were leading the horses out of the stable, guiding them into a day with warm sunshine. As he helped Blair up on her horse, his steed snorted as if it were jealous of the attention he was giving his new wife or offended by the new horse's presence in its home.

Once she was seated, he turned toward Heddwyn, the name he'd given the beast because of its red coat and fiery temper. The horse snorted again.

*Och, get used to them, Heddwyn. They arnae going anywhere.*

The steed tried to show off by pulling back as he climbed on his horse, but he was able to mount and calm Heddwyn.

"Mayhap yer horse is still tired from the journey here."

"Nae, 'tis jealousy. Heddwyn is used to getting all my attention." He rubbed the steed's neck.

The sound of voices and hoofbeats resounded through the trees. Robbie cantered into the small clearing around his house, flanked by three of the most experienced Cameron warriors.

Two of the men in the group who were to accompany them on the journey puzzled him. One was Malcolm, his laird's younger brother; Lachlan normally kept him close to home. After the young man's performance in the battle in Edinburgh, however, the laird must have developed more faith in the lad's abilities.

Brodie was the other. He'd heard Brodie was good with a sword, but Finlay had never seen him lift anything heavier than a cup of ale. The laird's cousin seemed completely out of place, but he'd changed after Skye had returned and they'd married. Perhaps he had merits Finlay was unaware of.

Seamus and Tristan were the most accomplished and experienced warriors of the clan. Although he was glad to see them, he was accustomed to making the journey on his own. Now, he had a small group of men to lead along with a wife to protect.

"Good morn to ye both." Robbie tilted his head, and Finlay wondered if he was really in charge of his expedition, or if he'd lost that role to the lad of almost fifteen summers seated on the steed before him. The boy had a way of fading into the background but still commanding the attention of all those around.

"Good day." Blair's easy smile rested on the men as she took them in, and despite his negligence in letting her know they would have company on the journey, she appeared at ease with their sudden appearance.

"Good to see ye, Blair," Brodie said.

"Welcome to the Cameron clan," Malcolm said before she could answer, and he realized she'd not been startled by their presence, because Brodie and Malcolm had been to visit the Macnabs several times when Kirstie had stayed with Blair.

"Thank ye."

Finlay opened his mouth to introduce her to the rest, but Brodie beat him to it. "Blair, this is Robbie, Seamus, and Tristan. We will all be accompanying ye on the journey south."

"Pleased to meet ye all." The remaining men nodded their agreement but looked anxious to get going.

They rode out of the clearing and made their way down the well-worn path to the main road. The men took up position behind them, and Blair pulled her mare next to his.

Continuing on, Finlay studied his new wife out of the corner of his eye but kept a close watch on their surroundings. She seemed content to study the landscape, and many miles passed in companionable silence. As they followed the path and the cottage of a nearby farmer came into view, she asked, "Where does yer mother live?"

"Nae too far, just up the road a bit more, but ye cannae see it from the trail." He pointed in the general direction.

The brook that trailed the path came into view.

"Och, 'tis lovely."

"Aye, and there is a bonny waterfall no' too far away. When we return, I'll take ye to see it." The thought of his wife naked, bathing beneath the water, had him shifting in his seat.

"I'd like that." Her smile was genuine, and it reached into his chest, causing a flutter of something that seemed like contentment.

"There are many things ye will love about the Cameron lands."

"Do ye go to Kentillie often?"

"I usually go every day and practice with the men in the lists. When we get back, if ye'd like to go with me, ye can visit with Kirstie while I'm there."

"I'd love that. I'm so happy for Kirstie and Alan."

"Aye. 'Twas a long time coming."

Blair continued to pepper him with questions as they passed landmarks he'd long ago committed to memory. All of which had become mere scenery, but each caught her attention and reminded him of how lucky he was to have a home with the Cameron clan.

For a few years now, he'd made the trip to England alone and was accustomed to the silence. He found himself enjoying her soothing voice and waiting for the next question, yearning to know more about her by seeing what she was curious about. It seemed to be everything.

He hoped she would be as enthusiastic about the estate in England, and that the mistrustful, rude attitudes of the Sassenachs he called family wouldn't dampen her zest for life in the hostile landscape as it had his.

• • •

Stopping for the midday meal—well, really, it was almost late afternoon—Blair was relieved to climb down from the horse for a little while to rest her sore rear end. She wasn't accustomed to long travel, and between the trip to Kentillie and now this one, she was sure her bottom was bruised. But the last thing she wanted to do was complain to her new husband or the other Cameron men.

Her husband had not even tried to bed her on their wedding night. What if he wasn't attracted to her? Her chest ached at the horrid thought.

She'd lain awake for what felt like hours, terrified of what the act of intimacy would be like with him, finally falling asleep. She'd woken to Finlay cradling her in his strong arms after he'd crawled into bed. The embrace had been tender and reassuring.

When the soothing tone of his voice skidded across her ear as he whispered something about protecting her, she sank into the warmth of his body. It was the first time she'd ever felt treasured and appreciated by a man, and she feigned sleep so the moment wouldn't end. The last thing she wanted to do now was show him that she couldn't be a good and dutiful wife, so she would soldier on.

Her husband did not converse as freely as she did, but his actions showed he was attentive to her needs and cared for her well-being. The men behind them were as quiet and solemn as her new husband. If she'd been thinking, maybe she would have asked for a maid to accompany them, but she'd had no time to plan anything since the moment Finlay had walked into her well-organized world.

So far, although Finlay was caring, he seemed preoccupied. He pushed them on as if the devil himself were after them, even looking over his shoulder often and squinting to take in everything they'd left behind. She let it go and watched the scenery as they rode along, taking in the wildflowers and lavender blooming on the lush green mountains as they gradually faded into the distance. The weather had been beautiful, and she enjoyed the mild temperatures and sunshine on her face. But, the threat of coming storms surrounded them like a plaid that had been left in a cool loch, then draped over her shoulders.

After having the horses taken to the stables, they walked toward a medium-sized inn in a small village that lay at the end of a dense part of forest.

"Finlay Cameron. Welcome back. Is it that time again already?" A thin redheaded man with a full beard met them at the door before Finlay had the chance to knock or push it in.

Her husband nodded at the man who took a step back and looked at her.

"Ye have company with ye this trip." The innkeeper's eyes roamed over her and the rest of the group, and his face seemed to pinch in with confusion.

"Aye, my wife and some Cameron men. Can we have a table and whatever yer serving today? 'Twill be a short visit."

The man's eyes brightened, either pleased Finlay had taken a wife or that her husband had brought more business his way. "Och, let me see what we can do. The kitchen was closed a short time ago." The innkeeper's head bobbed as he gave the impression of counting them silently. His lips quirked to the side before he continued, "'Tis no' a problem. I'll check with the cook to see what can be done."

"I can help." Blair needed something to do after all that time sitting astride her horse, and she smiled at the innkeeper, who instead of insisting she not assist, looked relieved. She made her way through the door and into the quaint room that was darkening to match the gloom settling over the outside.

Assessing the lack of seats at the two small tables in the room, she turned back to Finlay. "If ye will see to pushing the tables together and securing seats, I'll see what the cook has available." He nodded, and she ambled back to the kitchen.

After discussing the options with the cook, and letting the woman know she couldn't have anything with dairy in it, she returned to the room where the men were all seated, a chair to Finlay's right open for her.

Happy she'd been helpful, she strolled toward the table to join them. Just as she reached her chair, something heavy landed on her skirt. It jerked and pulled then repeated the jarring movements a couple more times. Looking down, she spied Satan's spawn clamping onto her gown.

Big eyes, orange and deceptively adorable, stared up at her until it looked back to the offending material and bit down, clawing, then making more ground by climbing toward her face.

She shrieked.

She danced back, afraid to touch it; the kitten clung tighter and let out little mewls intended to lull her into a false sense of security. She wasn't fooled. The creature would claw her eyes out if she let it get closer.

Finlay was there, reaching down and collecting the little demon, but one claw stuck to her dress, and the animal refused to let go. She became aware of laughter, and her gaze shot from the creature to the Cameron men. *Och*, she'd tried so hard to look competent and take care of them. All her efforts wiped away by a little animal that arched its head into her husband's gentle hand as he stroked it.

After Finlay set it down, the creature stumbled back toward the kitchen, knowing it had made a fool of her.

Brodie was the first to speak through the bursts of laughter. "I keep telling Skye those things are evil, but she won't listen to me. I have to live with one of those furry beasts."

Malcolm chimed in, "I'm surprised Kirstie didn't keep them in the castle with ye."

She closed her eyes and took a breath. Pushing away the irrational fear, she stood up tall, which just barely rose above the men seated at the tables. Cursing her height, she vowed to not look like an incompetent lass who couldn't take care of herself in front of them again.

Finlay placed a hand at the small of her back, and thankfully, she didn't flinch at the surprise. "Come, sit."

"Do ye think there are more?" Her gaze darted around before coming to rest on the reassuring hazel eyes of her husband.

"I'll keep watch and warn ye." Finlay's mirthful smile held warmth and sincerity.

Nodding, she let him lead her back to the table, glad the laughter had died and the men had moved on to talking about the merits of having pets.

She slid into the chair gently, only barely able to keep the wince from her face that should have followed the shock to her rear. She welcomed Finlay's hand as it reached for hers under the table and held on. The reassuring gesture calmed her racing heart.

Finlay focused on the door.

"Are ye expecting someone?"

"Nae. But 'tis always a good thing to be aware of one's surroundings." Leaning over, he whispered so only she could hear, "Ye never ken when a bandit or a wee kitten is lurking in the shadows."

She almost laughed, but embarrassment won out as her cheeks heated.

He squeezed her hand and sat straight, his attention returning to the exit, but his demeanor was relaxed as if he was comfortable by her side. Maybe there was hope they could be partners, work together, and hold each other up as more than just a spouse.

Pleased, her heartbeat returning to normal, Blair glanced at the door, back at him, then scrutinized the men at the corners of the tables who, although they conversed, kept watch as if they could be under attack at any moment. She changed the subject, afraid to know what they were watching for, but also hurt. Were they not trusting her with some threat?

"Do ye come here often?" She hadn't missed the innkeeper's familiarity with Finlay.

"Aye. 'Tis usually my first stop when I go to England."

"Tell me more about yer estate."

"I dinnae ken the place well yet. My father gave it to me last year, and I haven't had much of a chance to visit." He avoided looking at her, and she wondered what he wasn't telling her.

The cook started setting plates of poached eggs, sliced meats, and plums on the tables, one of which wobbled unsteadily, and she thought to suggest setting planks to act as balancers when the innkeeper set down cups filled to the brims with ale. Forgetting her purpose and wanting to quench her dry throat, she clasped a glass and brought the amber liquid to her lips.

"I want to see this house, too," Robbie, the youngest man of the group, proclaimed. "I'm told yer father has favor with the king."

"They are old acquaintances."

"Have ye met King Charles?" She couldn't help the smile that came to her lips.

"Aye."

"And the queen?" Robbie asked.

"Aye, she is a good woman, despite what the Puritans say about her."

After taking a bite of the meat, she sighed as her new husband continued to speak with her as if she were a friend. It gave her hope. How different he seemed from her father. Her flushed embarrassment was fading, but her mind wandered to an unpleasant memory.

She'd probably only been twelve summers when she'd been returning to her room after a riding lesson. Passing by the great hall, she heard a woman wailing and a man yelling. She stopped in the shadows and peered through the side door.

Her mother was down on the floor, a hand clasped to her face in pain, her body convulsed with sobs. Blair was about to run to her until a hulking form stood. Her father. He wore a look of unfiltered rage probably unleashed by a day of drinking. His chair tumbled to the floor behind him with such a *thud* it reverberated off the high ceilings and echoed in the chamber. The room was filled with men who had gone silent, and all she could hear was her heart thumping.

She froze.

"Ye are useless, Sara. I dinnae wish to see ye in here again with me and my men. I'll call for ye when I have need." He yanked her to standing by the meaty part of her arm, which on her frail mother didn't offer much cushion. Her mother tensed, but her father didn't seem to notice or care.

"Now, get out of here."

The cruel words were etched in her memory. It was the moment her world had changed, when she realized women weren't always valued in a man's world.

Her father's next announcement, intended for his men but aimed at her mother, still haunted her. "Women. If they cannae bring ye pleasure and heirs, what else are they good for?"

Sara ran from the room, and as she did, Blair felt tears streaking down her face for the humiliation her mother had endured. It wasn't until that evening she screwed up enough courage to go to her mother's private chamber, where she had locked herself away, to find her in bed despondent.

Her mother confided she'd only that morning lost another child growing in her womb, making Blair wonder if she would have trouble birthing babes, too. Would a husband find her useless if she could not?

She'd made herself a promise then, no man would ever make a fool of her in front of others. Women were worth more than bringing bairns into the world. Even if she couldnae have children, she would educate herself and be indispensable in a household. She would find a husband who would respect her.

She prayed Finlay was that man. Banishing the pain of the past, she concentrated on her husband as the men at the table continued to talk politics.

His hand eased from hers but clasped onto her thigh protectively, like he wanted her there. *Och, please God, let him always respect me.*

Not realizing how hungry she had become, she popped a piece of the warmed meat in her mouth. She'd barely eaten the night before, thank goodness, since she hadn't known what was in the stew, and this morning, she'd only had a couple bites of bread. She'd never been one to eat straight after waking, but if the rest of this journey was going to be similar to today, she might have to change her habits.

As she finished off her last bite of plum, she caught Finlay staring at her. He gently pushed his plate toward her, wordlessly offering the two slices of fruit he had left. It was a sweet gesture, but she shook her head as she fought the mortification threatening to heat her cheeks. She appreciated that he was an attentive husband, but how could she prove she could help him with his estate when she couldn't show restraint at the table?

Finlay polished off his food and reached for her hand.

"Let's see to the horses," he said.

She rose and let him lead her outside as the rest of the men lingered at the table. Her hand felt right in Finlay's, and she leaned into him, wanting to get to know her new husband better. "Are ye always in such a hurry?"

"When I want a moment alone with my wife." His eyes were soft, and he appeared genuinely happy to have her by his side. Her worries that he might not desire her melted away.

"We have no' had much time alone yet."

"We'll remedy that as soon as possible." He smiled, but it was only slight. "Once this business is taken care of in England, I promise we'll have all the time we want."

"We have the rest of our lives to ken each other now."

"Tell me something about ye that I would never guess." Finlay led her through the yard and guided her through the stable doors. They moved down the aisle toward the horses.

"I hum when I'm trying to solve a problem."

"Do ye?" He twirled her around to face him. She actually giggled as he took her other hand. "And what do ye hum?"

"'Tis something different every time. Usually a song from a minstrel or from mass."

"I'd like to hear ye."

"I'm sure ye will catch me doing it many times. Now, tell me something I cannae ken about ye." She squeezed his hands.

"When the weather is nice, I like to go for walks. I always find peace in the woods, especially on Cameron lands." Finlay drew her forward, so there were only inches between them.

She studied his hazel eyes. "Will ye take me on some of yer walks?"

"I was hoping ye would ask. Will ye hum to me while we stroll through the forest?"

"Aye. If ye arenae sick of hearing me by then."

Her breath stilled as Finlay's head dipped toward hers. A thrumming started through her limbs, and she rose up on her toes to meet him.

His lips brushed hers, and it was magic, just as it had been when they'd said their vows. Tingles erupted on her lips and spread down toward her chest. This is what she'd always imagined a kiss should be. His mouth moved over hers, and everything around them disappeared.

Voices from just outside reached her ears and Finlay pulled back. "Wait here. I'll be right back to help ye mount. I have to pay the innkeeper and tell the men our route for the rest of the day."

"Aye, husband."

He released her hands and walked out of the stables.

Her fingers traced her lips, and it dawned on her that she looked forward to her next moment alone with him.

# Chapter Seven

They still had a good distance to go before they reached the inn where Finlay usually stopped for the night, but so far, nothing about this trip had been typical. Although the sky had been dark all day, they'd managed to outrun the rain. But he hadn't overcome the sense that someone was tracking them. He'd pulled the men aside and told them of his apprehensions, but as of yet, no one had seen anything suspicious.

He'd enjoyed how close his wife had sat next to him as they'd eaten at their last stop. Maybe tonight, he would finally feel what it was like to be with Blair. He still couldn't believe she had married him. She must have known she's expecting—her appetite this afternoon had indicated she was eating for more than one. He had seen the deliberation in her eyes when she'd considered taking what he'd offered of his remaining food, but her pride had gotten in the way. He'd almost confided that he knew her secret, but he needed to know she trusted him, and would wait for her to bring the news to him.

He hoped she would one day feel comfortable in front of

him and tell him everything. He had wished she'd continue her chatter from this morning again as they traveled, but she seemed to be tired. Tonight, he'd ask how she was feeling to see if they needed to slow their pace. Despite the rush to get to England, he had to look out for her health.

Relieved to see the ridge in the next hill, which indicated they would be arriving at the next inn shortly, his thoughts turned to the evening ahead. His mouth went dry as he envisioned his wife naked and beside him in a warm bed. He wanted to know what her skin might feel like beneath him and wished for the sensation of her lips once again pressed to his.

Aware of the growing desire between his legs, he shifted in his seat.

Hedwynn let out a high-pitched squeal then bucked. He almost lost his seating, but on instinct, he eased, placing a steadying hand on the center of the saddle, loosening on the reins, and repeating, "It's all right," to the steed.

His horse had never acted in such a manner. Once he was able to calm the beast, he slid from the saddle onto the ground. The animal let out another small squeal but didn't try to forcibly remove him this time.

"What's wrong?" he crooned as he stroked the horse's neck, and it groaned as if relieved. He recalled when he'd climbed on the steed's back as they'd left the last inn, it had shuddered slightly under his weight.

Going on a hunch, he slid his hand under the saddle. Nothing. Sliding his hand around and under the edges, at the rear, his hand hit something wet. Pulling back, he saw bits of crimson on his fingers.

"Is everything all right?" Blair was still mounted but came so close he caught a whiff of her lavender smell just as Heddwyn bucked and squealed.

"Back up," he ordered a little louder than he intended.

She obeyed instantly, moving a good distance away, but he hadn't missed the fear that flashed in his wife's eyes.

After unbelting the saddle, he pulled it off and found a sharp rock embedded under the back of the seat. Having saddled the horses himself, he knew it had not been there this morning when they had left, and the only place they'd stopped was the last inn.

Was someone trying to stop him from reaching the king with news of the imminent threat from Scotland?

After handing the stone to Brodie, who had come up beside him, he took the time to inspect Heddwyn's back, ensuring that he'd be all right.

"That was nae accident." Brodie turned the sharp stone in his hand. "'Twas placed there to cause the most damage."

Finlay had already figured as much but couldn't think of anyone at the inn who would wish to harm him. He'd been stopping there for years, and they had always been kind to him.

"Inspect the rest of the saddles, but dinnae alarm my wife. She doesnae need to be frightened," he muttered.

Brodie nodded.

Blair had enough to worry about. He would ensure their safety for the rest of the journey and keep a guard with the animals at all times. Obviously, this sense that they were being followed had been true. He needed to listen to his gut.

He contemplated heading back to the inn, but he'd lost too much time already. The signed copies of the Covenant were on their way to Edinburgh, and if he didn't act fast, the Covenanter clan armies might join with English forces and beat him to the king. If that happened, he would have failed as a friend and a Scotsman.

Time was not on their side.

Realizing her horse might also have been sabotaged, he hastened toward Blair and ordered, "Dismount," and held out his hand to help her down.

She hesitated, apprehension shining like the stars on a cloudless night, but she took his hand and slid down her palfrey. Hell, he'd not thought to scare her, only protect her from whatever was going on.

Once she was down, he held onto her fingers and started to walk back down the road.

"Come with me." He gentled his tone once she was a safe distance from the horse.

"Where are we going?"

He didn't like the tremble he heard in her usually confident voice. What would cause her to overreact so? Henry had used a sharp tone with her in Edinburgh, the one that had made him want to beat the man, and *och*, Finlay had been terse with her, too. His mind went to something unspeakable.

He stopped, and she skidded to a halt beside him. "Did Henry hurt ye?"

She blushed and glanced away, unable to meet his eyes. No wonder she flinched every time he touched her. That cowardly arse.

His fists clenched before he realized he still held her hand. She inhaled and seemed to shrink. He felt so large next to her. Loosening his grip he said, "Tell me."

Shaking her head, she pulled her hand free and backed away.

"Did Henry hurt ye?"

She didn't answer, but she didn't have to—he saw the truth of it in her eyes. If Henry Graham weren't already dead, he'd kill the man.

"All clear," came the shout from Brodie.

He didn't want to have this conversation in front of the rest of the men. "We will speak about this later."

She didn't acknowledge his words and averted her gaze.

"I promise, if I ever raise my voice to ye, 'twill no' be because I intend to harm ye. 'Twill be for yer protection."

She kept her focus pinned on the earth.

He gently tilted up her chin, so she could see he was sincere. "I will never judge ye for someone else's actions. And I promise to never hurt ye."

She gave him a tentative smile showing she didn't believe him.

Hell, if he had time to reassure her now, he would, but someone might be out to harm them. He couldn't afford to have this conversation out in the open. "Come on. We need to get to the next inn so ye can get some rest."

When they reached her horse, he clasped her waist and lifted her up onto the animal's back. Before climbing back onto Hedwynn, he took a small cloth out of his bag and placed it on the steed's injured spot. He'd have someone see to the animal's injury at the next stop, but it didn't appear to be a deep cut. He'd been lucky.

As they rode on, he kept his anger at bay by trying to figure out who had wished him harm. It was easier than thinking he'd missed the signs in Edinburgh when Henry had laid his hands on Blair.

• • •

What was Blair going to tell Finlay about Henry? She'd let him make her into the very thing she'd never wanted to become — her mother. That Henry had only wanted her because of her connections, for bedsport, and for producing heirs.

She flashed back to that night in Edinburgh. Henry had forced her into his room and, against her protests, had taken his husbandly rights before they were properly wed. His words still haunted her. "Ye'll become accustomed to it."

And when she'd cried, he said, "We need heirs. And ye

will give me more sons than yer mother gave yer father. I'll see to that."

Her chest caved in just thinking about it. She'd witnessed the pain her mother had gone through with the multiple babes lost. It was a heartbreak that her father wouldn't forgive his mother. And she could not shake the feeling that she, like her mother, might not be able to produce many heirs.

She'd been afraid then that all her hard work was for naught, as was all the time she'd spent learning to become invaluable in a household. Henry didn't want her as a partner, he wanted her as a broodmare.

She swallowed and took a deep breath. Telling Finlay she'd chosen poorly wasn't going to change anything. Instead, she asked, "Where is Tristan going?"

"He'll be back soon."

Fisting the reigns, she gave a gentle nudge and scooted ahead of her husband. He was not being untruthful, but he was purposely evasive. She wondered if he would ever trust her enough to be honest with her, consider her an equal partner in their relationship.

A little while later, Finlay cantered up beside her. "What will ye miss most about home?"

"I dinnae ken yet. The only time I've been away from home was the trip to Edinburgh."

"What did ye miss then?"

"My garden."

"But I thought ye didnae cook."

"I don't. I just like the idea of providing something useful and contributing, even if 'tis only a small one. Have ye ever had raspberries straight from the bush?" Her mind turned to the sweet fruit and how the tartness lingered on her tongue.

"Nae. I've never had a garden."

"They are wonderful."

"There is a garden at my estate." His smile relieved the

tension that had been brewing since their stop.

"What's in it?"

"I dinnae ken, but we can take a tour, and if ye like, ye can plant whatever ye want."

*Och*, maybe there was still hope he would value her. "I'd like that."

A short while later, they rode into a large village that was still quite active despite the late hour. They left the horses in a stable, and Finlay guided them to a building where again, the innkeeper knew him by name.

The bottom floor was filled with rambunctious local residents drinking and having some sort of celebration. Taking her hand, Finlay led the group up the stairs. The other Cameron men followed but stopped at a door as she continued on down the hall with her husband.

Brodie was no longer with them.

Why did the men keep disappearing?

Finlay pushed open the door to a room at the end of the hall. Stepping in, her heart started to thud as she realized she was alone with her husband. She'd not even thought of what the night would bring. Would he demand his rights now?

Although it was late and the sky remained filled with clouds, the sun still broke through, lighting the room with its lingering rays and casting an ethereal glow through the window. Finlay lit a candle, and she paced, not wanting to sit on her sore bottom and taking advantage of the opportunity to stretch after riding all day.

He reached around and took the sword from his back, placing it gently on the floor just under the edge of the bed. She busied herself by strolling over to the window and peering out. Brodie was circling the stables then glancing around the town.

"Do ye think someone tried to harm yer horse?"

"Nae." He didn't sound convincing. But she'd seen the

glances he'd continually tossed over his shoulder like he was expecting bandits to fall upon them at any moment. All the Cameron men seemed to be on alert.

Expecting him to continue, she turned, but he only sat and removed his boots, evading the question and planting doubts in her head. "Is someone trying to hurt ye?"

"The only people I can think that would want to harm me are my brothers, and I doubt they'd sully their boots and come all the way to Scotland to do it."

"Will I meet yer brothers?"

"Aye."

A soft knock sounded through the room. Finlay's eyes darted toward his sword, but then turned back to the door. "Who's there?"

"'Tis Mage, sir." Blair recognized the voice as one of the women who had greeted them downstairs upon their arrival.

"Aye, all right then." With two steps, he was across the room in what would have taken her four or more.

After pulling in the door, Finlay moved away to let a hunched woman carrying a tray enter the room. The graying woman smiled at him then her and set her offering on the small table by the unlit hearth. "Welcome missus. So happy to see this one has taken a wife."

"Thank ye."

"If ye need anything else, let us ken."

"Aye," he said as the woman scooted out the door as quick as she'd entered.

Sighing, Blair moved over to the table and slid slowly into one of the padded wooden chairs. She inspected the food and inwardly groaned, hoping to not let her husband see her displeasure at the offering. Stew, looking too similar to what she'd been served at Kentillie last night, and cheese. Neither of which she was going to touch. There was a small loaf of bread, so she decided to go with that. "Are ye going to join me?" Blair asked.

"Aye." Easing in beside her, he took one of the plates.

She felt small next to him, but not fragile. Lifting her cup, she took a sip of the ale. The warm liquid slid down her parched throat easily. She took another sip then broke off a piece of bread. "Do ye ken every innkeeper from Kentillie to England?"

"I've been traveling this route since I was a babe. I ken it well."

"Where in England are we going?"

"Just as far as Middlesbrough. From there, my brothers or father can deliver the message to the king. Supporting Charles is one of the few things my family and I can agree upon."

"Do ye think he will punish my clan if my father insists on sending his men?"

He looked surprised that she knew of her father's plan. "Does yer father keep ye informed on his dealings?"

"Nae, I keep myself informed." She took another sip of the ale.

"I dinnae ken what the king will do to those who rise up against him."

"Can ye attempt to assuage his anger? Ye ken when John takes over 'twill be different."

"Aye, I like yer brother. He's an intelligent man. Loyal."

She found it pleasant talking to her husband, and the tension in her shoulders loosened slightly. She took another sip of the ale.

"Have ye always been interested in politics?" He spooned some stew into his mouth.

"I have educated myself on what I need to ken for the clan."

His eyes lightened, and his lips turned up. She couldn't help smiling back.

They continued to eat in a companionable silence, and after finishing her bread, her body became languid. It was most likely the effects of the ale or the dread of knowing tomorrow would be as grueling as the journey today had been. She found herself staring at his lips and remembering how they tasted. She sighed before she realized it.

Finlay's pupils grew smaller, reminding her that he was a man and had every right to claim her body. It scared her, but at the same time, she didn't feel pressured. She stood and moved over to the bed, thinking it was best if they got the hard part over.

"Are ye ready for bed?" Sitting on the edge, she removed her slipper. He continued to chew, but the task looked harder now. Taking off the other slipper, she placed them at the foot of the bed.

"Aye, shortly."

Blushing, she rose and strolled to the table where he had stilled. "Will ye loosen the ribbons, please."

When he nodded, she dipped to expose the delicate material to his touch. His fingers danced across her back, lingering and taking longer than usual as tingles spread through her spine at the light movements.

"Done." His voice was hoarse and raspy, sending a thrill through her that he'd reacted to her in such a manner. She'd been worried after last night that he'd had second thoughts and didn't want her. His voice and eyes said differently.

Moving back toward the bed, she turned to see his regard hadn't left her. Slowly pulling, the gown slid from one shoulder then the next, as her cheeks stung with embarrassment. Finlay's gaze devoured every move she made, and on top of the shame in it, she felt an odd anticipation as his eyes darkened and his chest rose and fell.

Tearing her gaze away, she moved to lay her gown over the chair she'd vacated and sat back on the bed to remove her stockings.

He rose, bumping into the edge of the table and knocking the tray onto the floor.

"Hell."

He stooped to pick up the dishes, placing everything back on the tray, then stood. Need shone in his eyes when he looked at her, but he walked toward the door, opened it, and placed the remaining food outside. Shutting and bolting the door, he turned back to her.

She stood and waited for him to come closer. His heated gaze trailed from her face down her body. She shuddered.

He came to a stop just in front of her, his mesmerizing eyes piercing hers. His lips landed on her mouth, gentle at first, questioning and seeking approval. Rising up on her toes, she deepened the caress, urgent and needy as her body heated. She welcomed the touch.

It was new and so different from what had come before, like her body had waited for this moment to truly desire a man.

Her husband.

Tentatively, she slid her tongue into his mouth. He stilled, then his tongue started to dance with hers, and a thrill shot through her.

His hands rested on her hips as she rose up to clasp onto arms that were taut and strong, and nearly the size of her waist. She felt safe and desired. They'd barely had the chance to converse on the journey so far, but in this embrace she felt he was saying, "I want ye, need ye, and I'll respect and protect ye." He wasn't a man of words, he was a man of action, and somehow that meant more.

He wrapped his arm around her, pulling her tight, but it was suddenly too much. She gasped and broke the kiss, her body seizing in protest as his hard penis pressed into her belly, proof that he desired her, but also an indication of what was to come. The part she didn't like. The calling that was now her duty.

Would it, too, be different with Finlay?

Not wanting to anger him as she had Henry, she said, "I'm sorry." The words rushed from her mouth as a plea for forgiveness. She hated the twisted emotions that invaded the corners of her mind.

His grip fell as he backed away, releasing her back to the floor. He scrutinized her. "There is nothing to be sorry for. Did I hurt ye?"

"Nae. Just startled me." But that wasn't true, she was terrified and trembling, ready for the verbal assault or a fist.

It didn't come.

Nodding, he went to the chair and sat, removing his boots, then standing to remove his plaid and shirt. She slid into the bed and looked away, shaking as she prepared for him to come at her again.

The light from the candle went out then the bed shifted slightly as he crawled under the blanket next to her. He scooted closer and placed his arm around her. He must have sensed her fear, because he made no moves to further their connection, only held her with his warm body pressed to her back. The reassuring gesture soothed her frayed nerves.

"I'm sorry." She fought back the wave of guilt that enveloped her. For making him turn away, and for thinking he was anything like the brute who had taken her maidenhood. Her husband was nothing like that weasel.

"Nae. 'Tis no' yer fault. We will get there."

After a few minutes of lying cradled in his arms, unable to shut her eyes, unable to stop the images in her head, she confessed, "Henry forced me. I didnae ken it was going to happen. He took me to his room and wouldnae let me leave." Her voice trembled, but she tried to steady it. "I never would have gone with him if I'd known what he intended."

Finlay tensed. "Why did ye no' tell someone? Yer brother or me? I could have helped." His voice took on a low rumble.

He had been in the hall that second night as Henry pulled her from her chamber. She remembered Finlay's tight jaw and clenched fists; she had known he was ready to intervene on her behalf and had almost given in to the urge to plea for help. But, if she called out for assistance, it would have put Finlay and Kirstie's clan in danger. After Henry had forced himself on her the previous evening, she realized she was stuck with him, and there was no reason for the Camerons to feel the weasel's ire. So, she'd gone willingly the rest of the way.

"'Twas too late once he was done. And we were betrothed. No one would have been able to give back what he'd taken, and 'twould only have angered the Grahams for yer interference."

"I'm sorry ye had to go through that. I promise I will never force myself upon ye." He hugged, drawing her in closer, cocooning her in his warmth and assurance.

"I ken, but sometimes my body and my brain arenae in agreement."

"We have plenty of time."

*Time.* Something Henry had not given her. She wanted to roll over, look in Finlay's hazel eyes, and tell him she was ready, and she knew he deserved his rights as a husband, but she couldn't do it.

His head nuzzled up to the back of hers.

A little while later, his arm slackened in sleep. Only then did she relax and shut her own eyes.

# Chapter Eight

Something moved beneath him, bringing Finlay awake. A painful longing between his legs throbbed. One he'd always ignored in the morning, but this time, it was insistent and ached as his body recognized the soft flesh of a woman next to him—Blair, his wife.

Sleep had eluded him most of the evening because unbidden images of Henry putting his hands on her haunted him. How could she have loved a man who had treated her so roughly? He hoped over time, she would come to have some affection for him, but he didn't have all the pretty words and flattery most men did. Hell, he could barely even read.

His thoughts took him to that long-ago, sweltering day when he'd made the decision to keep his deficiency a secret, to work as hard as he could, even if it took him longer than most.

It was on one of his summer trips to England when his stepmother decided he needed a tutor to keep him busy and away from her, since she couldn't escape his presence by returning to London. The tutoring only lasted the one day, but he'd been locked in an attic room with the man and had experienced true fear, one still unmatched to this day.

Finlay couldn't remember the man's appearance, because he'd been terrified to look in his direction, but the instructor smelled of mint, and every time he stumbled over a passage, the tutor slammed a long flat wooden stick across his hands. The pain was intense, and before the lesson was over, his bladder had spilled out onto his seat.

Later, standing outside the drawing room, covered in sweat and his own urine, he overheard the man telling his stepmother that he was ignorant and would never learn to read. Laughter spewed from the two boys within, the ones who were supposed to be his brothers. At one time they'd been kind to him. After that day the relentless teasing started, and he still wasn't sure if it was at the urging of the stepmother or if they'd decided him unworthy of their continued affection on their own. He'd only been ten, but he'd known then he would never earn a place in his father's wife's heart.

His real mother was the only reason he could make sense of the jumbles at all. She'd sat patiently as he'd stumbled through whatever she'd brought for him to read. She loved to read and write, and despite the distance and the void between them, she still wrote to his father.

She was probably the only reason he'd made it through university. More painful memories he didn't want to explore. He shook his head and returned to the present, to the gift that lay beside him.

Running his hand up and down Blair's arm, he wished for another kiss like they'd shared last night. They had connected on a level that had been more than just the need to sate the hunger growing in him—it was like the world had made her for him and like he would burst if they stopped. Of course he didn't push her, but the pain in his member was excruciating, his cock screaming at him for not plunging into her warm sheath. If he were alone, he would take matters into his own hands, but he couldn't do that in front of her.

Stirring, she turned and glanced at him, sultry blue eyes still filled with sleep and an unspoken welcome. Coming up on an elbow, he dipped his head, hoping to link with her again. She sighed into his mouth as her fingers found the bare skin on his side and gently held on as if she needed him as much as he desired her. Her fingernails grazing his skin fueled the yearning that was burning out of control.

As he continued to rest on one elbow, tongue dueling with hers in a dance that had his blood humming, he explored her curves through her shift, her heated flesh calling to him through the material. Going slow so as to not startle her, his hand slid down to her thigh where the undergarment had gathered up. Caressing her soft skin sent tingles through him as he traced circles on her outer leg, slowly moving toward the inner side.

She arched into him. He felt the soft intake of breath as her body melded to his. As his hand slid toward her core, a little whimper escaped from her lips still connected with his, not in protest, but one of encouragement.

Pulling back just to be certain, he whispered, "Are ye all right?"

She only nodded while his fingers continued to trace patterns on her thigh. Her mouth slightly open and eyes dilated, she watched him as if he were the only man in the world and she had complete faith and trust in him.

His mouth returned to hers, hungry and wanting more. This time he didn't let his tongue enter her mouth, he trailed kisses across her soft cheek and down to her neck. Her grip on him tightened as her head tilted to give him better access. As he kissed, sucked, then nibbled on her neck, she gasped.

He whispered into her ear, "Do ye like that?"

"Aye, husband." The word of possession spilled from her

lips and marked itself in his chest, calling out to him. Aye, she already owned him, just as she belonged to him.

He nipped at the small nub at the bottom of her ear, and she moved closer into him. His touch became bold as he tugged at her shift and sought out her core.

At a knock on the door, he stifled the curse that almost burst from his mouth.

"We're up and have the horses ready." Malcolm's voice penetrated through the silence.

He wanted to scream "go away", but he couldn't. He had a duty to get the message to the king. He groaned. Bedding his wife would have to wait.

She looked as pained as he felt—she'd not pulled away this morning, and the trust she'd given him imparted hope. This moment would have him speeding toward tonight's destination, so they could finish what they had started.

"Tristan is back," filtered through the door.

He found his voice, but it felt strained. "Be right down. Can ye see to some food to break our fast?"

"We already have it waiting downstairs."

Argh, he thought that might buy him a few more moments alone with his wife. "We'll be down in a moment."

Boots tramped down the hall, and he was left with the need to finish what they had started, but he wouldn't rush through it. That's what had scared her last night—his over-eagerness. There would be plenty of time tonight.

"Let's dress. I'm afraid we need to be on our way."

She nodded. Pulling back the blankets, he slid from beneath and picked up his shirt.

A gasp came from her lips as she looked at his cock, then her wide eyes rose to meet his. Ah, hell, he'd frightened her anyway. She had lost the sleepy seductive look and now appeared as if someone had tossed cold water in her face.

"I will try no' to hurt ye. I promise to go slow."

She took a breath. "Ye are quite large."

A small moment of triumph rushed through him as he thought at least he had something Henry apparently had not.

He dressed but studied her as she made her way to the bag she'd brought and pulled out a blue gown. It was the color of her eyes. By the time she pulled it on and walked back to him, he was already dressed.

"Do ye mind?" She turned and gave him access to her back and the ribbons that would bind the material to her body.

"Nae." He took his time, ensuring he did it right, but at the same time fantasizing that instead, he was unlacing the gown and pulling it from her shoulders. *Och*, he started to ache again.

Finishing, he shook his head, and they gathered their belongings and headed down to meet the others.

• • •

"Well?" Finlay faced Tristan after his wife rose to look out the window, again not touching her breakfast. She needed to keep her strength up for the journey and the babe—he'd see to it they brought something along with them today.

"They saw no one who shouldnae have been around yer horse."

"Someone put it there. Someone who kenned it would be ye riding that horse," Malcolm said. "Probably someone who kens of yer connection to the king and doesnae want ye telling him the English Puritans have recruited Scots to come fight their battles for them."

"Are ye sure it was meant for Finlay? Our horses are similar." Robbie looked worried, yet defiant, as if he expected an attack at any moment.

"Nae, but I keep having this feeling we're being followed."

Brodie straightened. "I've felt it, too. We'll have to be more vigilant."

Looking to the other men who took shifts watching the animals last night, Finlay asked, "Did anything seem amiss last night?"

Brodie shook his head.

Seamus said, "'Twas quiet after the villagers' celebration last night."

From the corner of his eye, he saw his wife's blue dress swish as she flinched then hid behind the curtain. His first reaction was to jump up to see what she'd been watching, his next was to take in what appeared to be fear etched on her face.

Was she hiding from someone?

The next thought was almost too horrid to contemplate. He'd left Blair alone with the horses. Had his new wife had anything to do with hiding the stone on Hedwynn? Was she truly siding with her brother and the Royalists, or was she trying to gain an advantage for her father? Had she married him so she could stop him from delivering the message to the king?

What did he truly know about her? And why had her father agreed to their union so quickly? Could the Macnab laird have known about his mission and pushed his daughter into sabotaging it? It seemed absurd, but the Macnab laird wasn't known for being stable.

Hedwynn had snorted with displeasure when Blair stood near him. Maybe there was more to the steed not liking his wife than jealousy. And one of the Cameron men in Edinburgh had said, *Ye never ken with the Macnabs, they bend with the favorable winds.* Could Blair be more like her father than he imagined?

The culprit wasn't one of the Cameron men with him on this journey. He knew them all well, had spent years with all except Robbie, and knew their loyalties lay with the Camerons and king. Blair's father played both sides. Would his daughter do the same?

She took a deep breath then rubbed her hands down her skirt and strolled back over to them. But not before her gaze shot to the door then back to them.

"Be vigilant and dinnae say anything to my wife," he whispered before she slid back into her chair. She leaned closer to him as if seeking the comfort of the moment they had shared this morning. He wanted that intimacy again, but maybe he should keep her at arm's length lest she stab him in his sleep. He didn't wish to think the worst of his beautiful new bride. But, she was the only one who had had access to the horses.

· · ·

Rain poured down in thick, unrelenting pellets, assaulting and stinging Blair's skin, but their band kept moving forward, and she didn't complain—she was determined to prove she wasn't a burden.

The men trudged on through the storm, intent on reaching the next inn and not losing any more time. She was growing weary, but she welcomed the exhaustion, because her mind had been churning all day, wondering if she'd imagined who she'd seen this morning.

She'd been on edge since. It could not have been Bruce Graham's contorted, angry face she'd seen. If he was following her to England, what was he going to do? She was wed now, and there was nothing he could do to change it.

Oh dear God, had she made a mistake?

Would the union she'd formed with the Camerons anger the Grahams and pit two of the most powerful Royalist clans against each other? Did Bruce hold that kind of sway with his kin, or was that what he had been hoping for with a marriage to her?

Should she tell her husband?

How would he react to the news she'd married him because she'd been blackmailed? Or would he suspect her capable of pitting the Cameron clan against the Grahams? If Bruce told him that, would he believe the man over her?

*Och*, her father's reputation had tainted them all.

Finlay was a calm man, but that revelation might incite his wrath. And if he set her aside, Bruce would be there to swoop her up, probably at her father's urging, to avoid scandal.

She couldn't risk losing this marriage, so she attempted to push the thoughts from her mind, hoping the image of her blackmailer had all been her imagination.

"Ye are shivering." Finlay spoke after hours of silence.

"'Tis the rain. I'll be all right."

But it wasn't just the weather. It was the fear of everything she might lose and the knowledge that if Bruce tried, he would bring war to the Camerons. Her actions could devastate the Royalists' resistance to the Covenants. Maybe she should stay at Finlay's estate in England. Never go back to Scotland and face the consequences of her decision.

But it would break her heart. She loved the rolling hills, mountains, and streams of the Highlands. Seeing the lavender in the valleys and the thistles on the hills. From what she'd heard of England, she'd probably hate it.

"The rain has slowed us down." Drops trailed down his face, and she studied the hard lines of his jaw.

"I am sorry to be holding everything up." She could tell they'd lightened the pace, most likely to accommodate her.

"Nae, 'tis no' yer fault. We just cannae stop long. I brought some oatcakes if ye would like."

"I'll be all right. How long until we stop?"

"There is a village ahead. Another couple of hours."

• • •

A short while later, they arrived in the village. The rain had continued, leaving Blair and all her belongings soaked.

As they readied the horses for an evening in the stables, Malcolm came out from the inn shaking his head. "'Tis the rain. The inn is full. The only thing they can offer us is the loft above the stables."

"Is it dry?" That's all she cared about.

"Aye, but we will all have to stay up there." Malcom looked to Finlay, whose gaze drifted to her then back to the Cameron man. He nodded.

A short while later, they were climbing up to the loft. She was thankful it was clean, the floors covered with fresh rushes and blankets available. Laying one down on a hefty pile of loose hay, she climbed on then pulled another on top of her to ward off the chill. It didn't work, because with all the men about, she had to remain in her soaked gown.

Finlay had no such inhibitions, taking off all of his clothing and sliding in with her. He put his arms around her and pulled her close to his warm body.

"I'm sorry we couldnae secure a room." The whispered words soothed her worries because they sounded sincere.

"'Twill be all right." But she'd never slept on the floor. Her hips and shoulder hurt, and she couldn't stop shivering. Sleep evaded her as images of Bruce taunted her, and she contemplated how her actions could bring war to the Highlands.

# Chapter Nine

The next morning, the air was still thick, and a fine misting rain clung to it as if another storm might roll back in. His wife had finally stopped shivering, and Finlay hated to take her back out in the weather. He'd been tempted to pull her wet gown from her body last night, but with all the men present, he couldn't risk her being exposed if the blanket fell from her body. The best he'd been able to do was hold her close and attempt to give her his heat.

Pushing up on his elbow, he moved the hair from her face aside. "Good morn, wife."

To his surprise, her eyes were alert as if she'd been awake for hours. He'd kept her pinned to his side all evening not only for warmth, but because of the small possibility she might sneak away and try to meddle with the horses. He just couldn't see her doing it, but he'd been wrong about people before.

"Good morning." She returned and sat up, stretching as some joint popped.

*Och*, guilt wrenched his gut. She deserved better than

sleeping on the hard floor of a stable's loft. And with a babe in her belly, no less. Maybe it would have been best to leave her on Cameron lands until he returned, but he refused to start his marriage that way. Not with how things had gone between his parents.

"Did ye sleep?"

"Nae, but I will be fine." She was the daughter of a powerful laird, one who had barely left her home, and he'd forced her to sleep in a sodden gown in a place fit for no one. Her skin was pale, and she looked to be in pain as she stood and moved around the small space, stretching from side to side. He would make it up to her.

The other men stirred. He was growing anxious to consummate their marriage but hoped the rain would stop so they would have better luck with the next inn tonight. He'd been married for three days, and he still did not know the feel of Blair's naked body next to his. His shaft was tight and uncomfortable, but it was something he would have to live with for now.

She seemed oblivious to his pain and didn't appear to be feeling the lack of intimacy to the extent he was, so he turned his frustration outward. "Do ye ken when yer father is planning on sending his men to aid the English Parliament?"

She froze. Although he'd kept his tone light, he recognized an edge to it.

"Nae." She looked away, which he took as a sign she was unwilling to discuss political matters with him. Could it be because she was hiding her intentions or perhaps that she was uncomfortable with her father's political stance?

"Ye ken if he does that 'twill hasten the Covenanters' plans to force their ways on my clan."

He thought he saw her tremble as she shut her eyes, looking guilty, but he still couldn't believe she would kill him.

"And on mine as well." Did she not count herself as one

of the Camerons now? Would she always be loyal to a clan whose allegiances changed like the tides with the moon, or would she come to be part of his family?

"Ye are a Cameron now." He stifled his anger...or maybe he hadn't, because she swayed as if she'd been dealt a blow. They'd only been married a few days, and she needed time to adjust.

Feeling guilty, he came up behind her, wrapping his arms around her and drawing her slight form into his body.

"I'm sorry." He took a breath, then whispered in her ear, "I'm just angry ye have to sleep on the floor in a stable after I drag ye all over Scotland in the rain. I should no' have taken it out on ye."

She twisted in his arms and laid her head on his chest. She was exhausted, and they had a whole day of riding to go. He hated to push forward, but his loyalty was to clan and king first, then to the wife who might wish him dead.

. . .

The day dragged on as they trudged through a rain that didn't want to end. Finlay's gaze kept drifting to his wife as she peered behind them. It appeared as if she was expecting someone to join their group. Maybe she had an accomplice.

Hell, he hated where his mind was going. She was not treacherous like her father. Blair was a kind soul who was a friend to his laird's sister. She would never betray Kirstie.

Blair started to tilt, her body growing limp. At any moment she might topple over, so he called a halt to their progress. Dismounting, he hurried to her horse and reached up to help her down. Her mouth did this adorable little thing where it quirked to the side as she attempted a grin.

"Let's give ye and yer horse a break. Ride with me." She did smile then as if she appreciated the gesture. Her hand slid into his, and she took his help.

After they were mounted and had started off again, she sank into his chest. Trusting in him, renewing his faith in her.

"Thank ye," she said as one of her hands rested on his leg, her delicate fingers lying there, gently acknowledging she had confidence in his ability to keep her safe. That small gesture spurred him on as another deluge of cold rain descended upon them.

Despite the horrid travel conditions and the urgency of his mission, he was overcome with a sense of peace as her head lolled back into the spot between his chest and shoulder. Snaking an arm around her waist and holding her near, he vowed not to let their journey dampen his mood, and he certainly wouldn't take his frustration out on her again.

By the time they had reached their next stop, they discovered the rain had again driven everyone to the inn, and their party would have to take the stable loft. He wanted to yell, but he tamped it down, asking for extra blankets so he could soften the rushes a little more tonight. After this journey, he vowed Blair would never be forced into such conditions again.

The next morning, the rain had stopped, and the sun rose high on a pleasant July day. The inn was still packed with guests, so instead of seeking a meal inside, he thought to save some time since the merchants were already out in their booths down the street.

"We'll stop at the market for some nourishment before we leave." He turned to Blair.

What he really wanted was to send the men ahead and return to the warm blankets with his wife. The need to touch her, caress her, and finally quench the thirst that had parched him since his wedding night overwhelmed his senses. He restrained the urge because someone would either come upon them, or he'd move too fast and scare her again.

As they walked through the streets, Blair took in the bounty of what appeared to be a very prosperous market.

"Peaches," she squealed and ran for a booth with the sweet-smelling fruit. Whirling back to him, she said, "I've only had them a few times, because we have to import them from farther south."

"How many would ye like?" He was delighted to see her appetite returning.

"Should we get some for everyone? 'Twill be nice to have with us."

"Aye. Anything else ye see?"

She was already inspecting the rest of the fruit when he walked up to the merchant to order two for each in their party. He had peaches quite often in England and would make sure she was well supplied when they arrived. She might even be able to plant some in the orchard. The thought pleased him— if she liked the orchard and gardens, she would be more likely to want to return with him.

After paying, he turned, but Blair had disappeared. He let his gaze drift up and down the street, which had filled with people shopping for their provisions, but no blond lass in a blue dress was visible. Panic setting in, he yelled to Brodie, who was only a booth away, "Do ye see Blair?"

"Nae."

"I cannae find her."

Robbie ran up beside him. "Which way did she go?"

"I dinnae ken. I turned to pay for the fruit, and when I looked around she was gone."

A whizz passed by, and a *thunk* sounded. An arrow landed in the crate between them, only inches away.

"Duck," he yelled to Robbie, and they managed to cover themselves behind a table just before the second shaft skimmed the top and slid to barely miss a woman, a babe in her arms, inspecting the peaches. She screamed, and chaos erupted in the crowded street.

"Brodie," he yelled as he pointed in the direction he believed the projectiles were coming from.

"Aye." Brodie leapt toward the other side of the street, Tristan and Seamus behind them.

No more arrows flew their way. A few moments later, the Cameron men returned, shaking their heads.

"Nothing," Malcolm called out.

"Who were they aiming for?" Seamus asked.

"It could have been either one of us." Robbie shrugged.

"Aye, I cannae say for certain." He saw the fruit he'd dropped and demanded, "Where is my wife?"

Panic gripped him in a vise and squeezed as he scanned the crowd again.

Blair came running up out of breath. Her face was flushed, and a trickle of sweat dripped down her brow.

She couldn't have had something to do with what had just happened, could she? Where would she have even found a bow? But why had she disappeared just before the assault began?

She turned to him and looked relieved, as if she was going to fling herself into his arms, then froze, likely because of his expression. His anger and fear had gotten the best of him; he fisted his hands and was fairly certain he was scowling.

"Where were ye?" he bellowed at her. Those left in the market could see the angry beast he'd become. He took a step toward her.

She shrank away, fear filling her eyes. Stepping on one of the spilled peaches, she slipped and fell flat on her back.

Hell, what was he thinking?

She rose and looked at her hands. They were covered with dust, and blood oozed from her palms. She fought to control her breathing then looked behind her to see everyone watching. Her eyes rolled heavenward, and her body went limp.

# Chapter Ten

A steady rocking and the warm sunshine on her face was a pleasant way to wake. What was even better was finding herself safe in her husband's arms. She felt cherished, well, other than the feeling of pins stabbing her hands. Blair didn't even mind that they were riding along on the big horse that hated her, because it meant Bruce had not found her and what she'd seen was just her imagination mingled with guilt.

She fully opened her eyes and sat up. Funny, she didn't remember falling asleep.

Had she fainted? It had happened only once before, when she'd gotten the scar on her arm. She couldn't come up with another reason for not recalling how she'd gotten there. She felt slightly off balance, and she kenned she had not been eating enough.

She'd seen a monk, but when the robed man turned her way, it was Bruce's face she thought she saw. Panic set in, and the only thing she could think to do was hide, so she sprinted down the street.

After running to the back of the nearest building, she'd

peeked around the corner and waited to see if anyone had followed. No one had.

It had all been her imagination, then, and probably a sign from God it was time to make a confession. So she ran back, looking for the safety of her husband's arms, wanting to tell him of Bruce's ultimatum and beg him for mercy, understanding, and most of all, forgiveness for not telling him sooner. But when she reached Finlay, he'd looked feral, angrier than Henry had when he'd struck her on that second night for refusing to do something he asked.

She'd frozen. Could she trust this man wouldn't hurt her? She'd trusted Henry, and look at where that had gotten her.

Tender hazel eyes met hers.

"Are ye all right?" His voice was calm.

"Aye, my hands hurt." They'd been cleaned, and fabric had been wrapped around them. "Well, and mayhap my head a wee bit."

Her fear eased at the care he'd taken with her. Loosening her spine, she rested her head on him, once again shutting her eyes and pretending she would be safe.

"Where did ye go?"

"What?"

"Ye disappeared from the market."

"I didnae go far. I didnae mean to upset ye." She remembered his cold, accusatory stare, but she'd only been gone a moment.

Silence. She had to fill it, or she might tell him the truth.

"Why did ye yell at me?"

"Ye disappeared."

As if that were enough of a reason. That might inspire worry in him, but not anger, and what she'd seen in his glare had been more than simple concern—it had been another indictment of some kind of guilt. Why was he lying to her?

"Do ye ken how to shoot a bow?"

She marveled at his quick change of subject but was happy for the reprieve.

"Aye, I do."

His muscles tensed.

"Why?"

"Just thought if I was going to teach ye to fish, I could teach ye to hunt as well."

"Nae need. I'm pretty good at it." She was relaxing as the conversation continued, but he seemed to be growing tauter. Maybe he wasn't used to riding with another. Despite his silence she continued, following the urge to confess something to him. "'Tis one of the things my father thought me incapable of doing, so I learned."

"And do ye set yer sights on doing everything ye can to please yer father?" Although he still held her tenderly, she couldn't help but feel his question was more than casual.

"I just want to prove I can be useful."

She squirmed. "I think I can ride on my horse now."

"'Twill slow us. Ye can switch after we stop for a meal." His fingers made little circles on her gown by her ribs, and he nuzzled into her hair. Finlay inhaled as if she smelled delectable.

She must need sleep. First, imagining Bruce would have the audacity to follow her, and now, that Finlay might be angry with her.

"How long have we been riding?" She settled in and relaxed, perfectly content to recline into the strong arms holding her.

"Nae long."

Watching the trees go by, she thought about what would happen when she was forced to tell her husband the truth.

• • •

Stopping for the midday meal, they rested the horses near a stream just off the road in the shade. It was a beautiful day, but they'd been pushing the horses hard, so any break they could give them would be helpful. At least Blair's mare should have an easy time today. Finlay wasn't worried about Hedwynn, with what little weight his wife added to the steed. The horse had protested when Tristan had lifted her up to him but calmed shortly after they were moving.

He would miss having his wife in his arms this afternoon, but at least it would give his cock a break. It had been painful trying to ignore the base urge that was beating at him, and his back was sore from sitting at an odd angle so as to not scare Blair with it. It didn't help that he wanted the feeling to go away until he was certain the lass wasn't trying to kill him.

She'd only been missing a few minutes, which wouldn't have given her enough time to take a position and fire an arrow at him, much less procure a bow. But she kept glancing over her shoulder and peeking out windows as if she knew they were being followed. That made him think, if she were involved, she wasn't acting alone.

He studied her as Blair took out one of the extra plaids he had packed and draped it over the driest spot she could find. The grounds were still wet from the storms, but he hoped the rest of their journey would have weather like this, and that there would be inns with rooms enough so he could have some privacy with his wife. Dangerous or not, she was a lovely lass, and she was his now.

The other men gave them a little privacy, choosing to sit on rocks near the stream, out of earshot and sight.

"Where'd ye get the scar?" A long gash ran from her elbow up to possibly her shoulder—the gown hid the stopping point. He would be sure to trace it later, possibly even place kisses on that tender flesh as he pulled the gown from her shoulders.

Her gaze drifted down, and she frowned. "A cat."

"Ah. That explains the unnatural fear of a wee kitten."

"They are vicious creatures. One minute they pretend to love ye, and the next they do this."

"What happened?"

"I was probably about ten summers when I went to the stables to visit a mother cat that had just given birth. The babies were too small to touch, but they were making a fierce whining noise like the one attacking my skirts the other day."

He stifled the urge to laugh.

"'Tis no' funny," she blurted after he lost his battle, and his chest heaved with amusement.

"Well, what happened?"

"The mother cat came up to me and rubbed against my legs, so I picked her up to pet her. At first she purred and seemed happy by the attention, but John came running in, dogs barking behind him. The cat climbed up my arm, screeching and hissing like I had tried to squeeze her."

"'Tis unfortunate. Cats are verra nice." He handed her a peach.

"I ken 'twas only frightened by the dog, but I bled so much my gown turned red, then Mother took me to the healer, who insisted on stitching it. 'Twas one of the most painful things I've ever done."

"I've never had pets. I wouldnae have been able to care for them with the traveling back and forth I do, but I like animals."

"So why did yer mother never marry yer father? Did she love him?" Blair took her first bite of the peach, sighing; she closed her eyes and savored the sweet, luscious fruit. She looked beautiful.

"Aye, but she hated England. He couldn't stay in Scotland because of his title and responsibilities, but there are times I think he wishes he had given it all up." He had a bite of the bread he'd purchased this morning before they'd come upon the peaches.

"He married?"

"He had to."

"And ye have two brothers?"

"Thomas and Caldwell. Ye will likely meet them."

"Will they approve of me?"

"Nae, but dinnae take it to heart. They never approve of anything I do. Ye'll just learn to ignore them when forced to endure their presence." He handed her a flask, and she took a sip, smiling for the first time since he'd scared her this morning. "But my father will love ye. I'm sure yer brogue will remind him of my mother."

"And what of yer stepmother?"

"She died several years ago."

"How did she feel about ye? It must have been hard for her kenning her husband loved another woman."

"It made my time there difficult when my father wasn't present."

"I'm sorry ye had to go through that. No child deserves to be punished because of who birthed them." Her sincerity soothed him, and he felt reassured he'd done the right thing by marrying her to protect her child. Of course, he'd also done it to build alliances, but had she really been interested in that?

She had a strange fixation on doing things her father thought she couldn't. Would that translate to taking down the king from the inside? Could she be that ruthless? When he'd asked her about the bow, without flinching, she admitted to knowing how to use one. Would she be that open if she had tried to shoot him?

In this moment, he didn't think her capable of harming anyone, even the cats she feared. Her sapphire eyes held no judgment. Leaning in closer, he whispered, "Kiss me, wife."

Her lips parted as her breasts rose and fell. His heart skipped a few beats when her eyes dilated as her head slowly tilted up toward his, inviting and giving him what he'd craved all day.

His mouth fell onto hers as his arm slid around her waist and pulled her up into his lap. There, she was the perfect height to taste and explore as his tongue delved in to mingle with hers. She tasted of peaches and warm ale. He'd never have either again without thinking of this kiss.

One breast pushed into his chest, and his blood heated. His hand skimmed up her side to rest just below her mound—the one he wanted to feel beneath his palm, to lave with his tongue, and to worship. Her arm wrapped around him, so sweet, so tender. If he didn't have her tonight, he would go mad.

Blair's hand rested on his neck, then her fingers burrowed into his hair, sending tingles through his scalp and causing gooseflesh to rise on his arms.

She was willing, wanton in his arms, like a woman who would abandon her inhibitions and fire his blood to boiling. It did so now as his body heated, and he had the urge to remove their clothing and take her on the plaid out here in the open. She deserved better than that, so he pulled back, reigning in the emotions and desire that was swirling out of control. He didn't want to scare or embarrass her with the men remaining somewhere nearby. He would just have to go slow. He looked forward to the nights ahead with this woman by his side. Loosening his grip, he ended the kiss but let her linger on his lap.

When his gaze met her hooded, sensual eyes, he almost groaned and changed his mind. His regard landed on her plump lips, now swollen and a deeper shade of red. It was intoxicating to know he had made her look like this, like a woman desirous and in need of a man's touch.

"Tonight, wife. I promise to no' hurt ye."

A blush crept across her cheeks. She looked so lovely with the green forest behind her, hair disheveled and cheeks pink. He wanted her all to himself, but he heard the rest of their band returning loudly. Making enough noise to purposely warn him of their arrival.

# Chapter Eleven

The ride the rest of the afternoon proved to be pleasant. Finlay enjoyed the warm sun brightening everyone's demeanors and kissing their skin, as if to apologize for its absence the last couple of days. As the inclines of the hills of the lowlands gradually began to decrease, the now dry road became easier terrain to traverse, and they made good time.

He missed having Blair nestled next to him. The way she'd snuggled into him led him to believe she was the woman he thought. How could her gentle caress have any malice behind it? She'd even let her hand drift to his thigh, thrumming her fingers back and forth as if she enjoyed touching him. Thinking she might come to care for him was a balm to his soul.

It was insane that he'd push his fears off on a woman who had given in to his suit in her time of need. He found himself wishing circumstances had been different, that he'd had time to woo her. Hell, he'd thought her magnificent years earlier when she'd barely known who he was.

As they cantered along, his thoughts strayed further

toward the problem he'd pushed away before the trip to Edinburgh.

A troubling letter had arrived from his estate in England. Typically, when he received a missive he would read it and then visit his mother to see if he had interpreted it correctly. But anytime she was reminded of his father, Dwight, her expression became distant and sad. He'd not had the heart to tell her that his sire had named the estate the man had given him after her, Catriona House, so he'd stewed in the news without sharing it with anyone.

He'd only been alerted to the problem because the cook reached out to him. According to the missive, the estate was having troubles maintaining funds for upkeep. The staff was forced to keep minimal supplies on hand, because merchants refused to sell to them and creditors were appearing, asking for money that should have been paid to them months earlier.

The estate manager, who was a childhood friend of his youngest brother's wife, had been keeping the books and had been highly recommended. With the allowance the estate received from the earldom, they should be able to manage upkeep.

Could it cost more to run the place than he had expected? Was someone on his staff stealing? No matter the answer, he wasn't looking forward to examining the books to determine what he could be doing wrong.

He shouldn't have left the place unattended as long as he had. He couldn't let his brothers see that not only could he barely read, he apparently was driving his father's gift into the ground.

The sky had darkened as the sun descended, and so, too, had his thoughts as disappointment in himself clouded his mood. He had people depending on him now, and he would have to do better for them.

Upon arriving at the next inn, he was pleased to discover

they had plenty of rooms.

He doubted the integrity of the owners in the establishments on the next leg of their journey, however. Some had ties to English Parliament, and if it was discovered he traveled to relay news beneficial to the king, they might find their throats slit in the middle of the night. So as much as he hated to put Blair through the trouble and discomfort, they would either be camping beneath the stars or in stables as a group.

With a wife and a bairn on the way, he would have to look for safe places for them to stay in the future, because his family deserved better than sleeping on a tartan out in the elements. A lot of things would be changing now, and he welcomed it.

Once they had the horses settled in the stables and he had discussed the rotation to keep an eye on them with Brodie, they made their way into the inn, settling in at a large table as scents of roasted meats and baking breads drifted in from the kitchens. His stomach growling, while they waited, he ordered a round of ale.

"Brodie, how is it Skye let ye leave? I thought she didnae like ye being away," Malcolm asked.

"She doesnae."

Finlay liked the subtle smile that breached Brodie's lips, as if the recently married man didn't want to be without his wife as well. He was beginning to understand that feeling. He'd never had a companion to trust with his daily struggles, but he was growing quite fond of his wife, except for the little thing that she might be trying to kill him.

"How did Lachlan convince ye to come?" he asked.

When the other men sank back and shifted gazes between one another, he leaned in. So, they had hidden orders he didn't know about—probably something his laird only trusted with a few. He was pretty certain the plans centered around

Robbie, who had stiffened and stared at Brodie, anxiously waiting his reply.

"Och, my wife said I was smothering her and that she wanted a little time to spend with Donella and her babe while Donella's husband was seeing to his ill Fraser family." Brodie was so good at covering his tracks. It was hard to believe that until recently, he'd been considered the Cameron drunk and wastrel.

He didn't miss Robbie's tense shoulders relaxing.

Blair took a sip of her ale, studying the men with a contented demeanor. Pleased, he noticed that despite a discussion he'd had with the group while she lay passed out in his arms this morning that she may have been the wielder of the arrow, they appeared vigilant but relaxed in front of her. It delighted him to know his wife was comfortable with his kin.

Brodie turned the conversation to Blair. "Skye's probably right. I even missed out on all the excitement in Edinburgh because I couldnae bear to leave her side. Did ye like the city, Blair?"

She took another sip of her drink before answering. "'Twas pleasant, but I had Kirstie there with me. All I've done since is travel. I'm ready to get settled somewhere."

"Finlay did tell ye he travels all the time, did he no'?" Tristan asked.

"He did."

A couple of servers brought out plates filled with roasted venison, mushrooms, and potatoes. Mouth watering, he took a bite as the others started in as well.

"'Tis good, but no' as good as Skye's." Malcom looked up at Brodie and winked.

"Aye. I am one lucky man. Now, if I could just get her to stop inviting half the clan over to dine with us every night."

"Do ye cook?" Malcolm asked Blair.

"Nae. Mayhap Skye will teach me a little."

"I can think of nothing more pleasant than coming home to see ye with a babe in yer arms and food on the table," Finlay said, but Blair stopped chewing and almost choked on her meat.

The table got quiet, all eyes on her as she took a sip of her ale to wash her food down and apparently collect her thoughts. Had he said something wrong?

"Is that all ye think a wife should do?" She glared at him.

*Och*, he had definitely said something horribly wrong. He'd planned for her to do whatever she desired, and he only wanted to make her comfortable and happy. "I dinnae wish ye to have to do anything overtaxing."

Her eyes darkened, and she seemed to become angrier.

What the hell was going on? She did look capable of murdering him. He'd have to make sure she didn't have a knife hidden beneath her pillow tonight.

"Ye dinnae believe a wife can do things a man can do... mayhap even better?" Ice dripped from her.

Of course, he knew she was capable of doing amazing things—he'd seen her manage the Macnab household for years—but he was afraid to say anything, because his well-thought out responses were earning him her angry glares and ire. It was like all those times he'd spoken up at Oxford, only to have the other boys shame him.

"I never questioned yer abilities," he said with what he thought was a calm, even tone.

"But ye dinnae see me as an equal?"

He couldn't raise his eyes to meet the gaze of the other Cameron men; for that matter, he could barely meet hers.

What was she doing? He was done with this confrontation in front of his friends. Feeling as if he was under attack, he fought to keep his exasperation from bubbling to the surface, but she'd made him look a fool in front of them all.

"We will discuss this later." Breaking contact with her sapphire eyes, he glanced over to see the men looked as confused as he felt. And for the moment, he didn't care if his words came out clipped and sharp.

"Ah, thank ye," Brodie interrupted as the serving lass brought them another round of ale. He held up his glass. "To the king."

"To the king," the others chimed in.

Brodie's expression became unreadable. "I found this on the ground shortly after ye disappeared today." He pulled out a bow.

Barely glancing at it, Blair appeared as if she didn't recognize it or even care Brodie had it in his possession. "Someone just left it abandoned?"

"Aye. Have ye ever seen one like it?" Brodie smiled, pretending to admire the workmanship. The man seemed to have a way of interrogating someone without their knowledge. He now saw the value in Lachlan's choice to send his cousin along with them.

"Nae, but I've used one before. It looks well made."

He was inclined to believe her. No one was that good at lying, but she might yet have an accomplice. Could they have been followed all the way from Macnab lands without notice? It seemed unlikely with the crew of trained men he had with him, but Blair's furtive glances kept bringing the idea to the forefront.

Brodie placed it on the ground, seeming satisfied with her response as well.

Malcolm chimed in, "Maggie kens how to use a bow, and 'tis rare for a woman. Why did ye learn?"

"Because my father thought I couldn't."

"Do ye do everything yer father says ye cannae?" Tristan was laughing, but the answer was important to Finlay. Why had Blair married him so easily? Did she have an ulterior motive?

"I make it a point to show him that I am capable of doing whatever is needed."

Hell, would she try to bring down King Charles to prove to her father that she was somehow worthy of his attentions?

• • •

Up in their stuffy, overheated room after dinner, Blair flung open the window and inhaled the fresh air then moved to the tub. Still, the confines of the small space with the hulking Highlander who was her husband left her lungs struggling to fill.

She skirted around a screen that had been set up in the room and disrobed to wash herself. As she bathed with the water that had been brought to the room, she wondered, *How little did he think of her?*

And what if she had her mother's affliction and had trouble giving him heirs? Would he turn her out?

Once done bathing, she climbed from the tub and donned her cleanest shift. When she moved from behind the barrier, her husband was glaring at her.

"What?" If anyone should be annoyed, it was her.

"If ye had an issue with me, ye shouldnae have brought it up in front of the others."

*Och*, he was right. Men, well, anyone, didn't like to be confronted in public. Why had she not held her tongue?

"Ye do seem to have too much of an interest in wanting to please yer father."

He was right, but she'd never been called out on it. No one had ever noticed before, and she didn't want to admit how much of a role her father played in who she'd become. "Is it wrong to want to make yer father proud?"

"Nae, it only matters when ye lose who ye are to do it."

His accusation poked her like a needle, and her skin prickled.

"And what does that mean?" Fisting her hands on her hips, she glared at him.

"Would ye support the Covenanters to please him?"

"Have ye gone mad?" Didn't he know how loyal she was to the king and her religion? *Och*, she couldn't hold her tongue, but damn if he'd just accused her of the one thing she would never agree on with her father. "How dare ye accuse me of such a thing?"

His face reddened. "What am I supposed to believe if ye wish so hard for his approval? He hasnae shown any kind of loyalty."

"Are ye questioning my loyalty?" She was shaking, and her fury came to a boil. The only person who had ever made her this angry was her father, and now, she was being accused of being just like him.

Finlay took a step toward her.

She held up her hand and backed toward the bed. "Dinnae come near me."

He looked for a moment like he wouldn't listen, like he wanted to shake her or pull her in for an embrace. She wasn't certain of which. "Did ye put that rock under my saddle?"

"What?" The accusations just kept getting worse.

"Ye were the only one near Hedwynn before we left. Tristan returned to the inn and asked. They saw no one near my horse but ye. And every time ye go near him he acts as if ye are the devil."

Did he just call her the devil? Did he just accuse her of trying to kill him?

She was certain her mouth fell open, and she didn't even have the energy to snap it shut. Dropping down on the bed, she shook her head. "If I wanted to harm ye, I wouldnae do it through an innocent animal." She let her hurt and disbelief pour into the words. "Ye think me capable of harming yer horse in order to try to hurt ye?"

"'Twas just a theory." He tried to move closer, but she held up a hand up. She had no words. His horse's opinion rated higher than hers.

"Why did ye marry me if ye dinnae trust me?" She found the strength to hold up her hand. "Nae, wait. Dinnae tell me. I dinnae think I want to ken."

Tears stung at the back of her eyes, but she was not going to let him see what he'd done to her. Turning away, she fought the rise and fall of her breath.

"Why did ye accept my offer?" He looked as if he already knew her answer, just like he'd expected her to admit to treachery.

Instead of telling him she thought him kind and admired the way he made her feel protected, even cherished, or that they had been a good match because of their beliefs, she gave him the ugly part of the truth. "I married ye because I was being blackmailed."

His face drained of color.

Out of anger, she'd only given him the most hideous part of her reason for marrying him. He deserved to know she would have chosen him had she never met Bruce Graham. She trusted Finlay and wanted to be his partner; she knew no better man to call husband, but she'd just destroyed his faith in her. She rose and reached out to tell him she was sorry, but his lips thinned, and he pulled away. Her breath seized.

"Sit," he instructed in a ragged voice she didn't recognize, pointing to the bed.

Plopping down on the soft mattress, she studied Finlay as he crossed the room. He focused on something in front of him as his shoulders expanded then contracted, then he took hold of the chair situated at a small dressing table. Picking it up, he pivoted back toward her like a solider about to interrogate a criminal.

After placing the seat in front of her, he sat, muscles tense and hard. His jaw ticked. Reclining, he crossed his arms, and his breathing slowed.

"Tell me everything." His voice was steady, but not harsh. It didn't appear to be anger staring back at her, but determination, like a commander on a field taking charge. He'd also somehow pushed away his hurt. She could tell it still lingered, but he didn't want her to know he had been so affected.

She told him about Bruce's demands and claims. The whole time, Finlay remained silent. She finished the story with Bruce in the village and how he'd glared at them as they'd passed.

He stood and returned the chair to the table, leaving her wondering what he was thinking. He glanced her way briefly then said, "Ye need some rest."

Heart heavy, remorse eating at her, she nodded. Moisture stung at the back of her eyes, but she held the tears at bay. She didn't want to cry in front of Finlay, and in all their moving about, she'd lost her favorite Macnab kerchief. Maybe, when they returned to Kentillie, she would have Kirstie work with her on embroidering a new cloth. Blair thought she would like one with an emblem from the Cameron clan.

The rest of the evening was torture as they moved about the room to prepare for the night ahead. Neither spoke.

She unbound her hair, thinking it might help the headache that had come on, then undressed down to her shift without asking for assistance.

Finlay did the same, but she kept her eyes turned away and climbed into the bed. He slid into bed and stretched out on his back, not moving to gather her in his arms as he had the other nights. She pretended to fall to sleep.

. . .

The next day they rode on in silence. Her husband set a pace as if the devil were chasing them. Blair kept up without complaint. Several times, she caught him eyeing her, but when she met his gaze, he would look away. Finlay obviously had something he wanted to say to her but either didn't want to start an argument in front of his men or couldn't get past his anger to let the words out.

Late in the afternoon, as the sun started to dip behind the trees, her arms became heavy, and her shoulders sagged. She shook herself to alleviate fatigue. Finlay inched closer to her and called, "Halt."

The men stopped in unison.

Before she could figure out why they'd stopped, he jumped to the ground and reached for her hand. "Come, wife. Ye'll ride the rest of the day with me."

Too tired to protest, and still feeling guilt over her confession, she slid down into his waiting arms. A burst of security ran through her as his arms lingered around her waist, and she found comfort in the small gesture. Shortly thereafter, they were mounted again on his horse and moving.

"How are ye feeling?" His mouth was close to her ear so only she could hear.

"I'm well, husband."

"I need ye to tell me if we are moving too fast. I dinnae wish to cause ye any discomfort." His voice was smooth, reassuring, giving her hope he could forgive her deception.

"I will," she said as she rested her head into his chest. He nuzzled close, and the hand wrapped around her waist held her a little tighter, causing gooseflesh to rise on her arms as her body warmed to his touch.

"I am no' angry with ye. Ye were right to no' give in to Bruce's commands. I was angry ye didnae have faith in me and hadnae told me sooner."

"I am sorry. I should have trusted ye." She remembered

Bruce's twisted face as he'd given her the ultimatum. The fear threatened to return, but locked in her husband's arms, she felt as if they could weather anything.

"When I saw Bruce in the village, I became afraid I had made a mistake, and that I had put ye and yer clan at risk of the wrath of the Grahams." A shiver ran through her before she could hide it.

"Nae. 'Twill no' be a problem. Montrose will hold the Grahams back. He willnae be willing to lose the Camerons or my connection with the king."

"I've been so worried. I thought Bruce was following us." A small laugh sounding like a hiccup escaped her lips. Maybe now that she was free of the knowledge of her misdeed, her mind would stop playing tricks on her.

Hugging her, he said, "'Twill be all right. Let yer worries go. I cannae blame ye for yer actions. I had not proven myself to ye yet, but I want ye to ken from here on out that I will do whatever is necessary to protect ye. Ye have nothing to fear from me."

Her lungs filled for the first time since imagining she'd seen Bruce in the village.

He laughed in her ear. "I'll even protect ye from the wee kittens if need be."

She melted into him.

That night, they camped beneath the stars. The skies were clear and calm, but a slight breeze kept them huddled together under the blankets. Brodie sat at the fringes of the group keeping watch, but she felt at peace as Finlay's breath evened out, and she soon followed.

The next few days followed a similar pattern. Anytime they met another group or passerby on the road, the rest of the men flanked Robbie in a protective position. She wondered what it was that had the men so rattled.

The silence was starting to weigh on her nerves, so she

pulled up next to the lad. "Do ye go to England often?"

"Nae. I've spent most of my life in Scotland."

"What takes ye there now? My husband said he normally travels alone."

"I have some business at the chapel near Finlay's home." He did have the bearing and reserve of a priest, but also the build and steady eyes of a battle-hardened Highlander.

"I heard ye were raised by a priest. Do ye seek to one day join their ranks?"

"If I must." Despite his devotion to the symbol around his neck, an elaborate cross, he didn't sound too eager.

"Mayhap ye can serve the king one day."

Nodding, Robbie changed the subject. "He didnae mean to offend ye."

Confused, she wondered what he was talking about until Robbie tilted his head toward her husband.

She remembered her outburst from dinner at the inn.

"I believe he wants ye to do what makes ye happy, and as with most men, he just assumes that raising a family and doing the typical wifely duties are what ye want. If 'tis different, ye must tell him."

Biting the inside of her lip, she considered his words. The boy, no, almost a man, was insightful. "How do ye ken so much for being so young?"

"I'm good at watching and assessing." He smiled.

"Ye will make someone a fine husband one day."

"Nae. I wouldnae do that to anyone." Suddenly, he appeared sad.

"Och, a lass would be lucky to catch ye in her web."

"If I were the only spider in it, 'twould nae be a problem."

# Chapter Twelve

It would be the last evening before reaching his home in England, and dread settled in, clinging to Finlay like a leech and sucking the peace from his soul. This part of the country possessed divided loyalties that pitted men against their neighbors. Accusations were being hurled daily as old friends accused each other of treason against either King Charles or Parliament. The printed press had done little to assuage their fears, having them believe the king's nephew would slaughter their women and children in their sleep. If it were known Finlay held vital information for the king, their party would be attacked.

He also dreaded facing the usual disdain of his brothers and possibly the Roundheads in Middlesbrough, who supported Parliament. The thought of sparring with his family already exhausted him. At least his sister-in-law, Prudence, brought levity to the atmosphere.

Finlay didn't know how his younger brother had lucked into finding a woman as intelligent and kind as her. She was a Puritan and quite religious. He'd not expected Caldwell to marry outside their Catholic faith, but perhaps some of Prudence's virtues would bestow themselves on him by proximity. She seemed like a good person, so Finlay couldn't hold her faith against her.

And apprehension assailed him at the thought of looking at his account ledgers. He suspected that somehow his estate was being sabotaged. It was a constant shame that curled in his gut when he attempted to make sense of ledgers. According to the conversation he'd had with his father, his income should be able to run three homes the size of Catriona House.

He swallowed. After relaying his message to the king, he'd have to find the culprit, but duty came first, then his home.

When the last inn of their journey came into view, he sighed, thankful the owners were sympathetic to the king.

It was one of the more impressive English inns, possessing clean and well-furnished rooms for all of their group. After seeing everyone situated in rooms, he returned below to order a meal and some items for the morning, along with a bath, to be brought up. Along their journey, they had been bathing in cold rivers and streams, but he wanted his wife to have a warm and comfortable wash before they made their way onto his land.

After hearing her tale of Bruce, he'd doubled their pace and warned the men to be on lookout. But if the Graham man was following them, they might never see him. Finlay had overheard tales of his hunting skills and ability to track while they'd been in Edinburgh. Blair was already frightened of Bruce; he didn't want to scare her over an assumption that might not be true. The Cameron men were making sure she was well guarded.

Upon walking into his chamber, his gaze was caught by the sight of his wife peeling her dirty gown from her shoulders. She stopped and held it together. His mouth watered as the need for her resurfaced.

Stepping over to the satchel he'd carried up, she reached into her bag and pulled out a compress of some sort to place on the chair before sitting on it. He'd seen her do it many nights now but not thought anything about it, assuming it was some tincture that women used.

"What is that ye've been sitting on?"

"'Tis a compress made with lavender and cypress to help with the bruising from riding all day. Maggie made it for me before we left Kentillie."

Freezing, his guts twisted as he realized he might have made a tremendous error.

His horse had once eaten too much lavender and become ill. Ever since, the beast had hated the flower. Bucking, moaning, and complaining whenever the scent was near. Exactly what he'd done anytime Blair ventured close.

The second mistake he'd made was forcing his new bride to ride for weeks on end when she'd not been accustomed to traveling at all. She was probably exhausted, lonely, and missing her former home. The new understanding didn't, however, explain her absence in the village when he'd been attacked.

A knock sounded at the door. Still contemplating his mistakes, he stepped toward the door and pulled it in to admit several men carrying a tub. Servants ran in and out with buckets, filling the bath with warm water.

"Cook is preparing the meal. It should be up within the half hour." He nodded at the servant and gave the lad a coin.

After the door clicked into place, he bolted it then pivoted to see his wife contemplating the bath. Her cheeks flushed a shade of pink to rival the prettiest roses in England.

"I hoped ye would enjoy it after our journey."

"It looks lovely."

"We will arrive at my estate tomorrow, and I thought it

might make ye more comfortable to bathe before we arrive."

"Aye." She blushed.

"Dinnae be ashamed." Approaching her, his hand fell onto her small waist. Circling behind her, he felt her shiver beneath his palm, but instead of pulling away, she leaned into his touch.

He pulled the strap binding the tip of her hair free. "I ken why ye've been pleating yer hair for the journey, but I prefer it down."

"I can do that," she said, but she made no move to pull away as he deftly unbraided the plaits.

"Nae. I've wanted to feel these silky strands run through my fingers." Once the waves fell free to her waist, his fingertips roamed upward as the smooth tresses slid through his hands. He massaged the tender flesh of her scalp. Her head tilted into the movements.

He drew her hair to the side and let his hands trail down her back, savoring the feel of her fevered skin beneath her shift. The material was already loose. He reached up, pulling the gown from her shoulders and placing gentle kisses on the newly exposed skin up the curvature, along her neck.

She leaned into him for support. He continued to caress her skin, and she moaned.

"If I dinnae stop, ye will not make it into that water while 'tis still warm." He nibbled at her ear, and she arched into him.

Tonight, he would do more than just sleep with Blair, but he was determined to do this right after the mishandled opportunities and resentments.

"Hmmm," was her only response, as if he'd set her at ease and she was looking forward to him ravishing her. It didn't help his self-control.

Pulling away, he instructed, "Bathe. We will have all night for me to teach ye how a woman should be cherished."

She sat in the chair and removed her slippers. Watching as she slid the stockings from her legs, he imagined his fingers gliding down her calf then back up again, all the way to the center of her, the part he ached to touch and taste.

Noticing the dust on her stockings, he frowned. She only had two changes of clothes for their journey, and she'd taken care to hang her garments each night, but it hadn't been enough.

"I need to see to something, so I'll give ye some privacy for yer bath. Lock the door behind me."

• • •

A short time later, Finlay found himself outside the chamber he was sharing with Blair. Anticipation coursed through his veins. Inserting the key into the lock, he turned the handle and pushed open the door to see her sitting at the dressing table wearing only her shift and brushing her long golden hair.

Was she humming? He couldn't place the tune, but it was pleasant. Quietly pulling the door closed behind him, he locked it and moved toward her. Reaching out, he touched her shoulder. She flinched then turned, but when she saw it was him, she smiled.

"Ye smell nice."

"Lemons."

"Hmm," he said as he lifted a strand of her wet hair and brought it up to his nose.

"They have molded soap. It smelled of lemons." Her eyes lit with a childlike amusement.

"Do ye like it?"

"Aye. I didnae ken that it could be put in such an easy form."

"I'll keep ye supplied in it, if it pleases ye."

"I'll bathe before they bring the meal." Before he could

push her too fast, he hurried over to the tub, where he undressed and climbed in.

Blair called over her shoulder, "I hope 'tis no' too cold for ye."

"Nae, 'tis fine." Truly, it had chilled, but he welcomed the cool, because it gave a slight relief to the part of him that had sprung to life upon being near his wife.

She rose and meandered toward the bed, her hips swaying through a material he noticed was quite thin. The cold water's effects dulled as he again started to yearn for the lass as she sat lazily on the bed. "Do ye always stay at this inn as well?"

"Nae. I think 'twill have to reevaluate our route for future trips. I feel like a negligent husband making ye sleep in some of the places we have."

"The bed does feel soft." She fell back on it and spread her arms out, sliding her fingertips over the bedding.

Upon climbing out of the tub, he started for his wife, who had tempted him by laying out like an offering on a tray at English teatime. Hell, he'd lost his mind. She had her eyes closed, peace and contentment on her face.

He was stopped by a knock on the door.

Her eyes flung open.

Cursing, he grabbed his plaid, wrapped it around his waist, and vaulted toward the door, drops of water sliding down his legs, reminding him he'd not taken the time to dry.

The same lad he'd given coin to earlier was holding a platter overflowing with filled plates, cups, and a pitcher. Another lad accompanied him holding a bundle of something else. Stepping aside but attempting to block the men's view of Blair, he let the servants enter and set down the tray and bundle.

Once he'd shut the door behind the servants, his wife bounded toward the table. "I'm so hungry."

Their meals had been sporadic on the trip. Something

else he would have to work on in the future. Worry stabbed at him as the cook's message sprang into his thoughts—the pantry at his home might be empty upon their arrival. What was he taking his new wife to?

"It smells delicious."

Sitting, she glanced up at him and smiled, the gesture pushing away his fears and giving him hope. She made no move for the food. "Are ye going to join me?"

"Aye." He picked up a pin and fastened the tartan. Not bothering with a shirt, he returned to the table.

"Ale?" Blair asked as she held his cup out for him.

"Aye."

She took a sip of her own as his gaze lingered on her over his cup. She'd gathered up her long hair and had it draped over one shoulder. He wanted to feel it now that it had dried some.

Glad to see she appeared at ease, he said, "I'm sorry."

Blair's head tilted. She took another sip of her ale.

"I didnae mean to doubt yer loyalty or assume I knew what ye wanted."

She appeared shocked. Then, a small smile curved her lips.

"Can ye forgive me?"

"Aye." She beamed, rising and closing in the short distance between them to place a quick kiss on his lips. "Thank ye."

She kissed him again, but this time he coiled his arm around her waist and drew her down onto his lap. His breath became ragged.

He'd gone too long without his mouth moving on hers, without the touch he'd been craving for days. She sighed and tilted to give him better access, and that set his body on fire. Her surrender, the way she leaned into his body, spoke of a trust he'd only dreamed of gaining from her.

As his tongue delved between her lips to find hers, they became one, twirling and caressing. His fingers curled around her waist, tightening his grip and ensuring she not flee this world-shattering kiss. They had kissed a couple of times, but in this moment, there was something new, a bond that couldn't be broken, faith that had been earned, and surrender that tasted like honey and ale.

Their mouths still joined, he rose, holding her, and veered toward the bed.

# Chapter Thirteen

Blair's body burned, blazes bursting to life on the sensitive areas of her skin where Finlay's hands slid down her as he eased her feet to the floor. He backed away, and she shivered at the loss of his warmth until his heated gaze returned to her with a longing so intense she thought she would ignite.

Swallowing, she shuddered and averted her eyes.

"Look at me," came the gravelly order that sent awareness down to her core.

He lifted her chin, and she met those multicolored eyes.

"I'm going to go slow."

She thought she felt herself nod but couldn't tell if she'd made the move or if the room was tilting.

His hand circled her nape, fingers cradling her head as his mouth came crashing down on hers. Lips tingling, she felt another odd sensation as her chest rubbed against his. Her breasts felt tight and full, like they'd swelled under her shift, which now felt impossibly tight.

Her hands reached for his side, and she was rewarded with taut flesh. She explored from his hips to his back then pulled herself on her toes and up onto his solid form to deepen the connection.

Vaguely aware of him moving as his mouth worshipped hers, she felt a light brush of air as his hands drew her shift up to her hips, revealing her bare skin and bringing back that feeling of being vulnerable and exposed. She shivered and dropped to the balls of her feet, severing the connection.

His eyes had dilated, and his body had become tense and rigid like the walls of an impregnable fortress. His breathing appeared labored, or was that hers?

Licking his lips, he stilled, seeming to ask permission.

Her heartbeat accelerated, but she took a breath and nodded.

Thumbs hooked the outside of the thin material while the rest of his fingers dipped to the inside and lifted. The backs of his knuckles skimmed her hips and then her waist, causing gooseflesh to rise on her flesh at the feather-light touch. The quickening of her pulse and tingles that lit in her body felt right. This was what being with a man was supposed to be like, or maybe this was better, because she wanted each caress to go on forever.

"Lift yer arms." Then, his mouth was on hers again, drowning any reservations she had as his tongue moved over hers and stole her inhibitions. His lips dipped to her neck, where he nibbled and sucked until she barely felt the slow rise of her shift and forgot any embarrassment as the sensations took her away.

He trailed slow, warm kisses up her neck. Reaching her ear, he nibbled at the lobe. Once, fire shot through her, twice, a need took hold in a way she'd never experienced. Heat pooled at her core as her body recognized that she shouldn't fear what she was feeling but should embrace it. Arching, she rose on her toes again, laying bare her desire for him and admitting that she had succumbed to his touch.

"Trust me, wife." And that one word pulled her under—the word that said she belonged to him—for truly in that moment she did. The outside world had washed away as if only her husband and she were alive. She nodded.

Continuing with his attentions, he drew her shift up. Her body followed his will and that of the fabric. She wasn't sure what had happened with her undergarment, but his arms had returned to circle around her. Her breasts tightened and felt full as his hard chest rubbed against her.

A slight movement backward had her thighs hitting the soft surface of the bed. His hands lowered to her hips, guiding her down, giving her instructions with his movements. Stepping away, his heated stare trapped her eyes in his. What she saw there awoke the primal woman in her, and she felt as if she held all the control, not this powerful man who towered over her with the authority of a stone fortress.

Feeling confident, she started to back onto the mattress, an invitation for him to join her. He withdrew the pin from the plaid still wrapped around his waist.

Her mouth watered, and she was certain her eyes rounded as her pulse raced. He put one knee on the bed and climbed on after her. Lowering onto his side, his hand reached out, fingers forking into her hair as he drew her in for another kiss.

As their mouths danced in a tangled bliss, his leg gently rested on top of hers and wedged itself between her thighs, spreading them apart with a slow, deliberate ease. His stiff rod poked her upper leg, and instead of it scaring her, she moved into it, welcoming the part of him that might give some relief to the pressure building in her center.

His mouth continued to devour hers as his palm slid from her nape, down her shoulder, to her breast, where it stopped. He cupped the engorged flesh and she bucked into his touch as new sensations awoke inside her. His lips broke free from hers as his dilated hazel gaze watched her. He worked to control his breath, then a small hungry smile curved up before his head dipped again.

Those tempting lips didn't land on her mouth but the peak of her breast, kissing, then sucking. She gasped, and he nipped at the tender skin as his hand dipped lower, reaching the spot where her core met her leg. He drew lazy circles on the spot as his mouth continued to work magic. She tilted her hips into his touch, seeking more than the tingles that had erupted at his teasing.

"Finlay." The rasping plea came from somewhere deep inside.

His hand stopped moving.

Nae, she didn't want him to stop.

And the ravenous stare he gave her proved he didn't want to stop, either. He joined her mouth with his in an intensity that had not been there before. It was as if he, too, was feeling this all-encompassing desire that threatened to leave her forever wanting if he didn't sate her torturous desire.

Suddenly, strong fingers glided up and down her passage, and to her surprise, they slid back and forth as if they were in the water. When his finger circled the nub above her slit, teasing, it drove her mad with a need she'd never felt before. Gasping into his mouth, she reached up and clutched his arm, pleading for more. He removed his hand just as she felt something was about to burst.

Shifting, he rose, leaving her cold and wanting. Wishing for his lips back on hers, his touch to soothe the sweet ache between her legs. He positioned himself between her legs and moved his rod up and down like his fingers had, and she found the slickness was still there. The friction of the flesh at her most intimate area heated her even more.

His gaze steady on hers, he guided his swollen staff slowly into her passage. It didn't hurt. Quite the opposite. The pressure massaged her channel and felt nice...no, that wasn't the word for it. Heavenly, because surely this pleasure was more than anything she'd ever imagined, at least until he buried himself deep inside her and rocked his hips back and forth.

She gasped as her fingers dug into his hips, drawing him farther in. A pulse burst through her, a delicious warning that there would be more. Another, and her mouth fell open.

Then, they assaulted her, one sinfully pleasurable wave after another. And she was panting as she fell into a sweet oblivion where nothing existed except the ecstasy that had devoured her.

He cried out, continuing to drive harder. Then he slowed, but his breath became ragged as he collapsed onto his elbow, just barely stopping before putting the whole of his weight on top of her.

Shifting onto his side, he lay beside her, tracing the curves of her flesh. She'd had no idea being intimate with a man could feel so right.

. . .

Maybe it was that he'd spilled his seed inside Blair, but Finlay had never longed to stay so near a woman after being intimate with her. He found himself in new territory, not wanting to move from his wife's side and wishing for nothing more than to fall asleep and wake in the same position, to start all over again.

After a few moments of blissful silence as they lay cradled in each other's arms, he thought she had almost drifted off until her stomach rumbled.

"Come, wife." *Och*, he enjoyed calling her that. Sliding his arm from under her and placing a soft kiss on her forehead, he rose. "Ye need some food in yer belly. I cannae have my servants thinking I've starved ye upon our arrival tomorrow."

What he left unsaid was that she might need her strength to deal with the potentially dire straits of his estate.

Blair inched from the bed, holding the blanket to her bare body as she searched for something, possibly her shift. He considered kicking it under the bed so she never found it—he thought he might like to dine nude with her.

And maybe one day he would, but for now he wanted her to be comfortable. Reaching down, he picked up the garment. "Blair."

She pivoted toward him, and when he threw it over, she dropped the blanket to expose the creamy expanse of her pale, petite form, and he wanted to toss her back on the bed to plunge into her once again.

He refrained. Peeling his gaze away to give her a moment of privacy, he walked back over to the table, where the food still sat cooling on the tray. Sitting down, he picked up a cup of ale and took a big swig. It was smooth and hearty, better than the watered-down ale typically found in England.

Blair joined him and took a sip from her own cup. "I didnae realize how thirsty I'd become."

She picked up a fork and started moving the food around on her plate as if she were a child, making hills and trenches to ready little toy soldiers for battle.

He laughed. "What are ye doing, lass?"

"I have to get the cheese out of the way. Everything else looks fine."

"And what did the cheese do to offend ye?"

"It makes me ill. I've never been able to have it."

"I thought ye liked cheese. 'Tis why I've been trying to feed it to ye." He took a gulp of ale.

"Nae, it makes me feel unwell."

"Well then, I willnae order it for ye anymore." Taking her plate, he turned it sideways and used his fork to push it onto his plate.

"Do I need to send for a new plate?"

"Nae, 'twill be fine."

Nodding, he took a bit of the meat and savored the roasted flavor.

"Thank ye for apologizing before. I ken 'tis a hard thing for a man to do."

"Well, get used to it. I'm sure I'll do plenty wrong."

She laughed, deepening the blush on her cheeks, still flushed from their exertions.

"I'll have to find something to apologize for everyday, if it is a prelude to what we just did."

"Does it always feel like that?"

"Let's hope it does."

"Ye have done it before?"

"Aye, but no' many times, and I have only spilled my seed inside ye."

"I didnae think I would ever enjoy bed play, but I think I would like to do it again."

His cock jumped at her confession. That was good to hear, because he didn't think he ever wanted to stop.

• • •

The next morning, sun shone in the window as Finlay woke his wife in the way he'd wanted to for the last couple of weeks. He lifted her shift, took her in his arms, whispered what he was going to do, then watched her blush. Then, he'd proceeded to claim her, and once her willing body shattered beneath his, he let his seed once again fill her.

As she lay nestled in the crook of his arm, contentment washed over him, along with an overwhelming need to keep her safe. He breathed her in now; the lavender scent of her was a heady and calming balm.

His thoughts drifted to Bruce Graham. The man was a

snake. Bruce had deserted his cousin, Henry, in the midst of the battle that took the life of the man who would have wed Blair. Finlay was thankful things had played out the way they had and she would no longer have to worry with either of the blackguards.

It struck him then why the snake must have given his wife such an insidious ultimatum. Before Finlay had left Edinburgh, he'd heard the Graham men discussing Bruce's fate as a deserter. He was to be exiled from the Graham clan. The arse no longer had a home. The vile man must have been seeking a way to redeem himself with his clan, and securing the loyalty of the Macnabs might have earned him that boon.

There was a soft knock on the door. Pulling the covers over Blair to hide her, he rose, wrapped a plaid around his waist, and pulled open the door. A bevy of servants carried a tray with the breakfast meal and the other items he'd requested the evening before.

He noticed immediately the cheese on both plates. "May we have another plate brought up without cheese? And a small basin with some fresh water and a cloth."

A man nodded and hurried away.

The other servants came in and placed the requested items on the chair.

"'Tis all for now. Thank ye." After shutting the door behind them and latching it, he strolled back over to the bed.

"Are ye hungry, wife?"

"Aye, but I feel as if I could stay in bed all day."

*Och*, if only they didn't have to get home and finalize delivering his message—he would be happy to spend the entire day having her make those delicious noises as he drove into her. "There is nothing I'd rather be doing as well, but we have to get moving."

Sitting up, she stretched and gave a sleepy sigh. She was beautiful in the morning, her hair falling around her shoulders, slightly mussed from sleep and their bed play.

Sliding from under the covers, she stood and strolled to the table to join him. If England weren't on the brink of war, he would turn her around and march her right back to his quiet little cottage on Cameron lands. He wanted to spare her from the jealousy and plots of his brothers. But all he could do now was hope his family would be on their best behavior.

# Chapter Fourteen

After they broke their fast, Blair was pleased to discover a bundle for her on the dressing table. Finlay had taken one of the dusty gowns she'd worn on the trip down to be measured and had a seamstress prepare from ready stock a gown suitable for meeting the residents and servants of her husband's estate.

It was beautiful, made of the softest silk to ever touch her skin. With the dress, along with a new shift, slippers, and stockings, she felt truly cherished. Her father had never bothered to purchase anything for her, only her mother had with a meager allowance Father had given her.

The material was cream, with blue brocade in swirling designs of vines and flowers. Blue ribbons crisscrossed the top in the front to lace it up and hold her small bosom in what she hoped was an appealing fashion. She held matching ribbons and braided them through her hair.

Finlay came up behind her in his plaid and a clean shirt he'd had delivered to the room. "Do ye have a maid? Ye didnae say anything about one when we left."

"I did, but she is my mother's as well, and I didnae wish to take her away. She is also aging and doesnae get about well, so I thought 'twas best if she could stay near her family."

"Well, ye willnae need one when we are in Scotland, but mayhap we can go into the village tomorrow and find ye one for here."

"I would like that. How long will it take to get to yer home?"

"We should be there by the midday meal."

What would his estate be like? Would she be as close to the servants as she had been at home, and would they have enough on hand to feed the group once they arrived? She was about to ask when a pounding jolted her, and she looked to the door.

"We have the horses ready when ye two want to join us." It was Malcolm's teasing voice. She blushed, thinking the men must know what they had done, twice, since coming to the room.

"We will be right down." Gathering the rest of their belongings, he placed them in their bags.

Before walking to the door, she said, "Thank ye."

He smiled but didn't seem to understand. "For the gown and everything else. Ye didnae have to." She waved a hand up and down to indicate the accoutrements he'd purchased.

"But I wanted to," he said, shrugging and pretending it was nothing. But to her it meant he cared, even if just a little.

• • •

The road was wide and well trodden here as if it were the thoroughfare to a large village. Blair was struck by the beautiful white flowers that fringed the edges of the seemingly man-made drainage canals lining the perimeter. As the new plants swayed in the gentle breeze, she was reminded of the purple and blue shades of the heather and thistles at home, and she became anxious.

Finlay seemed more rigid and reserved the closer they got to his home. She wished she could put him at ease but didn't know what to say, so she watched the lovely countryside and thought about how different it was from home.

There was a war going on here in England. Last she'd heard, the king had fled London and had retreated to Oxford for fear of his own safety.

The rest of the men had grown solemn, too. Over the last couple weeks, she'd come to know them quite well, and they always seemed to be slinging barbs at one another, joking and laughing. They did none of those things now as their gazes darted about as if looking for threats from all directions. They'd settled with Robbie between them, while Finlay and she took the lead. Occasionally, the young man rubbed at his shirt, where he wore an ornate cross beneath.

She shouldn't have worried about her overactive imagination and Bruce, because if he had followed her, these men would have seen him.

A cluster of three children frolicked in an open field down the road. The group laughed as if they had no cares in the world. The children came to a halt, said something to each other, pointed in their direction, and then ran off into the woods as if hiding from someone.

What would their children look like, and would they be gallivanting in the fields of England or the mountains and glens of Scotland? She pictured a brown-haired boy with hazel eyes running in the field, followed by a blond girl, and then a redheaded lad.

"Did ye play in these meadows when ye were a child?" It was hard to imagine the reserved man beside her as a playful youth.

"Nae here. A little farther south near my father's house."

"What do yer brothers do?"

"Thomas has an estate a little larger than mine. It's to the east." Finlay pointed in the direction. "He is the oldest of my father's legitimate heirs." No bitterness or jealousy escaped in his tone, just acceptance.

"Caldwell's home is at the far south of Father's lands. He married last year, a woman named Prudence. I'm hoping her influence has evened his temper."

"And they dinnae treat ye as brothers should?" She couldn't fathom a world where John and she weren't as close as the twin trees at the entrance of her father's castle, even if one of their parents had been different. They had always been able to count on each other.

"My brothers never forgave my father for not loving their mother. They take it out on me when he's no' looking."

She couldn't imagine going through life with a sibling who resented her.

"Their mother never liked me. She was a duke's daughter and never expected to have to deal with the illegitimate child of her husband. 'Twas an arranged marriage, and neither were ever happy."

Blair imagined it would be hard for such a woman to accept that her husband's heart had been claimed by another woman. While Finlay and she were not yet close, it would be devastating to think his affections belonged to another. But that hurt should never turn into the ill treatment of a child.

"Does yer father miss yer mother?"

"Mayhap, but I havenae heard him say so. I think he would have gone after her if he thought there was still some hope she would join him in England."

"But yer mother loves him as well?"

"Aye, but they both have loyalties and cannae see past them to make it work."

"'Tis a good attribute, but loyalties can make ye choose

poorly sometimes."

His lips pursed at her words, and he inspected her as if she'd made an awful admission. Finlay guided them down a thoroughfare that broke off to the west. As they continued on the smaller path, she was struck by the trees uniformly lining both edges. They loomed over each side of the road, creating a cool, dark tunnel that made her think of a portal to a realm where faeries might live.

Halfway through the trees, a massive structure came into view, a house so large that two of her father's castles would have fit in it. The estate grew to three stories, and the breadth of it was wider than the entire bailey of the Macnab stronghold. One turret tower rested in the center of the magnificent estate, the only thing reminiscent of the stone fortification of her youth. A chapel with a tall, ornate cross at the tip of the entrance was attached to one side of the property. Its flying buttresses lent the visage an air of permanence and stability, while the pointed windows made it appear as if God himself had commissioned the lovely edifice.

"This is yer home?" Her eyes widened, and she gaped.

"Aye. But I've seen it only once before."

She wanted to jump down, run through every part of it and explore, but she held back. That was not what ladies should do. Especially a Highland lass who would be dealing with the English, whom she had heard were stuffy and followed rules to the letter. She hoped Finlay would show her his home once they were settled.

"Will ye give me a tour?"

"Aye, but it may no' be until tomorrow. After we have some nourishment, I need to send word to my father and brothers I have a message for the king."

They reached the drive just outside the door, and no one came out to greet them. She'd imagined with this big of a house, the servants would be rushing to help their master with his horses. Finlay seemed confused, as if he'd expected to be greeted as well.

"Wait here," Finlay said as he dismounted. She didn't argue, didn't know that she could do anything to help.

After a moment of knocking, the door swung in. A man dressed in English livery answered the door. Shock registered on his face as Finlay said something to him, but the man composed himself and disappeared behind the stately wooden door. Finlay strolled back down to where they waited.

"'Twill only be a moment. They were not expecting us, so most of the staff is engaged elsewhere." His speech had become more formal, more English. Unease crept in—she didn't like the stuffy Finlay. She wanted her Highland warrior back.

A couple of nights ago, as he'd nestled into her back, he confessed, "I'm happy ye will be there with me."

"I will be certain to make myself useful."

"Nae, dinnae worry much about what needs to be done." His hand slipped lower, and his fingers gently thrummed her belly. "I only wish for yer company. I always feel so alone there."

Then he became silent. It was as if he'd revealed a part of himself he was ashamed of. She'd twined her fingers with his and said, "I will be wherever ye need me." And she meant it. She would do her best to make certain his home in England was as much a true home for him as the little cottage back on Cameron lands.

Returning to the present, she slid down from her horse's back. She glanced up at the beautiful house, noticing the ivy growing up the sides, which lent it a rustic charm, but also the untended grounds and the windows in desperate need of a washing. This place needed a lot of work. It had obviously been ignored for years, even before Finlay had come to live in it.

Several lads bounded around the house and took the horses. The group of stable boys appeared too young and untrained.

Once the children had gathered the horses and led them toward the stables, their group made their way up the stairs and walked into the most luxurious entryway she'd ever seen. Beautiful paper with white, flowing designs and a lavender background hung on the wall. The entryway was appointed with a magnificent mirror bordered with a gold trim. In it, she could see the portrait of a woman on the opposite wall. An ornately carved table rested beneath the looking glass, balancing the visual effect and grounding the room.

But at the same time, the space was cold and dark as if it had been abandoned by time and its occupants. She shivered.

"I knew who yer father was, but I never imagined ye in a place like this," Brodie whispered to Finlay, but the sound carried in the cavernous space.

"I havenae had it long. Until recently when I've come to England, I stayed with my father."

The butler, a tall graying man with pale gaunt features, as if he, too, had been locked away for decades in the neglected estate, appeared again. "Shall I show you to the drawing room and bring some refreshments?"

"Aye," Finlay said. "But first, Andrew, this is my wife. Blair Cameron."

"Pleased to meet you, my lady. Welcome to Catriona House." Bowing, he sounded genuinely pleased to have guests in this long-ago forgotten place that inspired thoughts of a mausoleum.

"Thank ye," she returned.

As he pulled the butler aside, she overheard Finlay ask, "Did my estate manager no' send ye staff and the things we had suggested?"

She didn't like the worry that had crept into his tone.

"He sent word that he was working on it, but no one ever appeared. I'm sorry I didn't write to you sooner, but he kept insisting he was taking care of it."

Finlay gestured for the man to lead them to the drawing room. It was dark in the hallway, but she could just make out a hint of red coloring Finlay's cheeks, along with the tightening of his jaw and possibly his fists.

They followed Andrew to a large room furnished with plush velvet covered chairs and a sofa the color of the English forest. Thick, heavy drapes covered the windows, and before they had a chance to sit, a servant rushed in to pull them back; dust fled from its crevices and spurred a coughing fit from Seamus.

Another young servant bearing a remarkable likeness to Andrew, in fact he might have been one of the lads who helped with the horses, tromped in. He held a tray with tea and some sort of pastries. She took one, along with a cup, and sat down on one of the chairs. As a stale taste hit her tongue, she realized they must at least be a day old.

Before the butler left the room, Blair made her way over to him and inquired, "I ken we are unexpected, but can the cook prepare a meal for us this evening?"

"Yes, my lady, but it will not be much. There is not staff to support a full kitchen, and I am not certain what Cook has on hand." The man blushed, and despite the admission, he stood tall and proud.

"That will do for now. We will see about hiring some more." Finlay's voice sliced through the air, sounding more disgusted with the situation than the servant, whom he seemed to have a fondness for.

"What about someone to prepare rooms for us?"

"There is not much of a staff, my lady." The butler peered at her, looking as bewildered as she felt.

"Do ye no' have anyone who can prepare rooms?" She was starting to worry she would have to do it all on her own.

"We do, my lady. Jenny." Andrew straightened as if proud of the girl in question or at least thankful to have someone around.

"Is she the only one?"

"Yes, my lady."

"Please send her to me, and she and I will see what needs to be done together."

Jenny appeared only moments after the butler left. A lass probably about fifteen years her senior, with pale cheeks and light brown hair. The woman looked as if she were ready for inspection and expected to fail—Jenny's blush and painfully evasive eyes kept shifting up and down as if seeking approval. It endeared the woman to Blair immediately.

"Pleased to meet you, my lady. I'm Jenny, and I'm at your service."

"Happy to meet ye as well, Jenny. Could ye show me to the rooms we need to prepare for my husband, myself, and these guests, please?"

"Yes, my lady. Right away." Jenny fled through the doors.

Following behind, Blair glanced over her shoulder to let her husband know what she was doing, but he was engrossed in conversation with the men and didn't seem to notice her departure. It made her feel neglected, just like the home she found herself in now.

• • •

The house looked the same as when Finlay had stopped by on his way back to Scotland last year. He'd hired an estate manager based on the recommendation of Prudence, his youngest brother's wife. The man had been instructed to hire a staff and see to it the house was brought to a manageable state, along with caring for the estate's property and managing the books.

Although Everly Gerrick had admirable recommendations, so far, it appeared the man had done nothing. Was the estate manager responsible for the problems Catriona House was facing? If not, the man was still guilty of negligence for not letting Finlay know his estate was in dire straits. As far as Finlay could tell, the only staff present were the ones who had been in place when he'd left. The cook who had written to him and the family of servants who had maintained the property for the years it had remained vacant.

The thought of telling Blair that he might lose this home due to his inability to understand basic numbers and letters wrenched at his side any time he thought about it. It was a physical pain which made his stomach burn. They were just developing a friendship, and he couldn't let her know there was a possibility that, at least in England, he couldn't provide a home and safety for her.

He'd pulled the men aside and discussed walking the estate this afternoon to make certain if someone had been following them, they would have a plan. He also gave strict instructions that until they'd discovered what the threat was, his wife should be accompanied anytime she left the house. As he'd done so, Blair had slipped from the room with the housekeeper.

"I feel the need to visit the sanctuary. Is there a priest in residence?" Robbie paced around the room. He appeared more nervous than he had the whole journey, which was saying a lot, because the lad always looked as if the devil were after him.

"Aye, but I'm afraid he is only here for mass for the few servants on hand."

"Is he in the village?"

"He should be. But if ye want go to check the chapel,

mayhap he is here now. The rest of ye may explore until Blair has some rooms ready for ye. I need to pen a missive to my father and brothers to inform them that I have arrived.

As Robbie departed toward the chapel, the men followed, and Finlay found himself wandering toward his office and sitting at the large mahogany desk his father had picked out for him. Finlay's hand glided across the smooth surface, but then he coughed as dust flew into the air.

Anger assailed him. What the hell had been going on while he was gone? This place was supposed to be running itself, but nothing had been done.

Banging his fist on the desk, he tightened his resolve and got to work. Upon sticking the quill into the inkpot, he discovered the ink had dried. Cursing, he wondered how he was going to manage in this place without help.

He called for Andrew and requested a new pot of ink. It took only moments for the butler to track one down and return.

"What excuse did the estate manager give for not procuring the help ye need?"

"He said it was because the war had taken many able-bodied men from the villages to the battlefield."

"Even though the battles have stayed to the south?"

"Yes, my lord, but there is talk of spontaneous skirmishes about the countryside. It might be best to keep your new wife close to the estate until she knows her way around."

"Ye are probably correct. I'll have the Cameron men stay a while and keep watch." He'd heard awful stories of neighbors turning on neighbors. "Have ye had any problems with the Puritans coming onto our lands?" He ran his fingers through his hair to relieve some of the stress that made his temples ache.

"No sir, it has been peaceful out here in the country."

"Good. Thank ye for the ink, Andrew."

"My pleasure, sir." The butler moved seamlessly through the door, shutting it without a sound.

Settling back in, Finlay began the missive to his father. He kept it short, but it still felt as if it took hours to write it out. He'd thought about asking Andrew to do it for him, but he didn't want to appear ignorant.

*Dearest Father,*

*I have returned and brought a wife. Please join us Friday for dinner. We have much to discuss.*

*Your devoted son,*

*Finlay*

He then penned two similar letters to his brothers. Once they were all assembled they would discuss the best way to get the news to the king.

The next letter, to his estate manager, took the longest.

*Mr. Garrick,*

*I am in residence at Catriona House. I request your appearance tomorrow, Thursday. Please be prepared to review the account books so that we can determine what needs to be done to get the house and its holdings in order.*

*Finlay Cameron*

The thought of poring over mixed up, jumbled numbers and letters with Mr. Garrick gave him an awful pounding in the head. Standing, he strolled over to the well-stocked cabinet that seemed out of place, considering the condition of the rest of the estate. Shaking off the notion the house was cursed, he poured a serving of whisky, thankful that at least something in this forsaken place had not spoiled.

# Chapter Fifteen

Blair followed Jenny up the ornate steps to find herself standing in a corridor only slightly smaller than the one downstairs. Each room off to the side had massive wooden doors whose frames were intricately carved and decorated. Rugs lined the floor. They'd at one time been beautiful, but under the darkness of the closed doors, drawn curtains, and dust, she wasn't certain if they could be salvaged.

"This is the way to the master's bedroom," Jenny said and led her to the back of the house. She'd expected it to be toward the front, so that any guests arriving could be seen from the room.

"How long has it been since someone has used it?"

"To the best of my knowledge, it has never been used." The woman must be mistaken.

"How long have ye been here?"

"My father came to work here when I was just a wee thing."

How was it possible this magnificent house had remained empty for so long?

Jenny pushed in the door, and Blair followed. Not able to see much because of the thick drapes that blocked out the sun, she moved into the room cautiously.

"Can we open up the curtains and see what kind of shape it's in?"

With the thick material drawn back, light filtered into the room, but motes of dust danced in the freshly disturbed air. Coughing, she said, "I think we should also open the windows. This place needs fresh air."

The massive Venetian window didn't budge. Jenny stepped beside her, and they heaved together. Blair almost fell when the window flew up, exposing a terrace she might have seen sooner, had the windows not been covered with years of grime.

Stepping out onto the balcony, she was astonished to see an artfully arranged garden similar to one she'd seen in Edinburgh, but on a much grander scale. It looked in need of pruning and shaping, but the bones of it breathed in her a new hope that maybe not everything was beyond repair.

Her attention riveted to the gentle rolling hills extending as far as she could see, wild lavender growing on them in purples and blues. It was breathtaking and reminded her of home. She caught a hint of the scent of the fragrant flower in the breeze that tickled her skin.

"Are you all right, my lady?"

"Oh, aye." She hadn't realized she'd been staring. "Let's get the other one open."

Once they had the room airing, Blair turned her attention to the bedding. "Well, there isnae much we can do on short notice, but at least we can strip the beds. Beat the bedding to clear the dust and put them back on."

Jenny looked at her with pleased, eager eyes, seeming happy to have a purpose.

"How many servants are on hand?"

She blushed. "Not many, my lady. They were supposed to be hired, but none have shown."

"Hmm. What about the lads I saw earlier?"

"They are my boys." A hint of pride twinkled in Jenny's eyes.

"Well then, they can help us. We will open all the windows, take care of the bedding, and have them wipe down all the surfaces with a damp cloth."

Several hours later, Blair walked into the dining room exhausted, but pleased they had been able to make accommodations fairly presentable for their large group, at least for tonight. Jenny and she had a lot of work ahead of them.

. . .

Finlay was on his second dram of whisky when his wife strolled into the dining room. Tendrils of her soft hair tumbled loose from the elaborate braid she'd pleated this morning, and dirt smudged the edges of her new gown. Her face, bonny as ever, was drawn and tired.

*Och,* he should have stayed longer last year to ensure the estate manager had done his job and hired a proper staff for the place. Blair was with child and hadn't even had a chance to rest after their long journey.

At least he'd had a chance to walk the grounds with the Cameron men, and there was no sign that anyone had followed them. He'd also alerted what few servants were on hand to be on the lookout for anything suspicious.

Letting out a long, frustrated breath, he took another swig of the amber liquid as she walked toward him and eased into the chair to his right. "Where is everyone?" She looked worried.

"There didnae seem to be much in the kitchen, so they've

gone into the village to eat at the tavern tonight."

That was another thing that cut to the bone. This was supposed to be his house, but he couldn't even manage to offer his friends a meal.

She frowned. "With yer permission, I can go into the village tomorrow to see to it ye have the proper staff. I managed the help at my father's castle. I cannae imagine 'tis too different here."

The idea of her going into the village without him was preposterous. What if the war really had reached this area? He didn't want his wife out of his sight until he knew the countryside and village was safe. So he said, "I was hoping to be able to show ye around tomorrow, but we do need more people. I'm expecting company in the afternoon, so we cannae be gone long."

"It shouldnae be too hard to find those in need of a good job."

Andrew strode into the room holding a tray containing two plates. There was a twinkle in his eyes Finlay had never seen before—the servant seemed pleased to finally have a family in residence. The man had occasionally filled in at his father's house when the butler there had health problems. Over the years, Finlay had somehow managed to form a bond with the older man.

"'Tis what I thought, but mayhap there is a drought of able-bodied people in the village."

"We shall see tomorrow."

Andrew set a plate down in front of him then, Blair.

"Thank ye," she said and smiled at the man. He nodded, pleasure evident in the tilt of his head and the confidence in his step.

"I have rooms prepared for everyone. Will they return tonight?"

The butler placed cups of a red liquid in front of both of

them.

"Aye."

"I'll have Jenny wait up to show them to their rooms then." Blair smiled at Andrew, and the butler dipped his head.

He lowered his spoon into the stew—a kind of meat, likely venison, with root vegetables and a broth. It was fair, but nothing compared to what the cook at his father's home could do, or perhaps it was the lack of supplies that dulled the taste. Maybe after things were settled and during their time in Scotland, the man could train some with his father's cook. The distance wasn't so great that he couldn't afford to go a couple times a week for a lesson.

Blair eyed her spoonful then brought it up to her nose to smell before taking a sip.

"I spoke to the cook earlier. I let him ken ye cannae have anything with cheese."

"Thank ye. I havenae had the chance to meet him yet. Does he seem competent?"

"Aye, he will do."

"Ye will need a gardener as well. Ye have the most marvelous start to a garden behind the house. Beautiful shrubbery. It just needs some pruning and care."

"Did ye spy a place for yer peach tree?"

"Nae, I had forgotten. Oh, but there are also the most wonderful meadows filled with lavender."

That reminded him. "There is a story behind this estate."

Her eyes lit. "What is it?"

"My father built it for my mother in hopes that one day she would come to England to live with him."

"That explains why no one has stayed, and why there is no' much staff. It must have cost him a fortune."

"'Tis why my stepmother hated me. I reminded her of the woman who held my father's affections."

"And ye say yer mother loved him as well?"

"Aye."

"But she wouldnae join him?"

"Nae. She wouldnae live as a mistress."

"Why did he no' ask her to marry him?" Blair took a sip of what he'd discovered was a pleasant spiced wine.

"He couldn't. A contract had already been signed promising that he and my stepmother would be wed, but my father always held out hope that one day she would bring me down and join him."

"And now that yer stepmother has passed? Will yer mother join him?"

"Apparently, he wrote to her and she refused. 'Tis why he finally gifted the estate to me. He gave up hope."

Blair's eyes saddened.

"They are both very stubborn, but because of it, ye and I have gained this." He waved his arms to indicate the home.

"I am quite looking forward to exploring."

"I havenae even seen it all yet."

"Mayhap we can tour it together?" Her eyes sparkled again, and he found himself enthusiastic for the first time to explore his new home. Eager to lay his wife down in each room and plunge into her warm body, claim every space as his hands roamed up and down her curves while she made those breathless, panting noises beneath him. Truly make this their home and no one else's.

His blood pumped faster, and he licked his lips. "Mayhap we can."

"Mayhap after yer guest leaves tomorrow. Och, how long will we need to entertain the men who came with us?"

"My guess is they willnae stay long, but I think we will need to stay longer than originally intended. Once we get a proper staff hired and make sure everything is in order we can go back to Scotland."

"Aye. I have yet to meet yer mother." At least she didn't say she wanted to leave right away.

After she set her cup down for the last time, he rose and took her hand. Thoughts of lying in bed with his wife had been plaguing him all day. It was time he took her to their chamber and spent the night exploring her body.

# Chapter Sixteen

Finlay locked the door as they strolled into their bedroom for the first time together. Blair blushed with anticipation as she thought about what the night might bring.

"Wife," came his husky words.

"Aye, husband."

"I've thought of much today, but the only thing that has kept me sane was knowing I could hold ye in my arms tonight."

Suddenly, his hands were on her, unfastening her clothes, then removing his; the clothing was scattered and left discarded in a pile on the floor. Having backed her to the bed, he laid her down and spent what felt like glorious hours touching and teasing her, driving his hard body into hers until they were left in a tangled, satisfied mess.

A storm had moved in, but as the pounding rain hit the window in a steady rhythm, his body relaxed and his breathing slowed. He drifted off to sleep. Wedded life had its benefits other than alliances and heirs. She was starting to feel close to this man, as if they could be friends. He might even come to view her as a partner.

Sated and sleepy, she heard Jenny show the Cameron men to their rooms. Thankful they were in for the evening and had been cared for, she felt she could finally fall asleep. But then she saw a flash through the edges of the curtains, followed by a large *boom*.

Glad Jenny and she had closed the windows in all the rooms before heading down for dinner, she snuggled deeper into the blankets, seeking the refuge of her husband's warmth. The soft sounds of dripping alerted her to a leak. She lit the candle by the bed and rose to try to find it before more damage could be done. She hurried into the adjoining room then on to a room intended for a nursery, where she discovered a large puddle of water near the window. Drops were landing on the hardwood floor, soaking the edge of the rug centered in the room.

After running back to the main room, she grabbed the basin she'd brought up earlier for cleaning and returned to the leak. She slipped, falling backward and bumping her head on the uncovered ground. The basin clanged to the floor. Her candle sputtered, the flame dying as it joined her and the pot.

Seconds later, Finlay rushed into the room, a sword in his hands. She was only able to make him out because the curtains were open, and a flash of lightening illuminated the room.

"'Tis only me," she called before he mistook her for an intruder.

"What are ye doing?" He sounded angry, as if he didn't trust her. Why would he still doubt her loyalty?

"I slipped. There is a leak, and I thought to put the basin under to catch it."

He placed his sword on the dressing table then returned to stretch out his hand and pull her up. Once she was on her feet, his arm circled her. "Hell, ye are soaked."

"Aye. I told ye 'twas leaking."

"Wait here," Finlay instructed and darted from the room.

"Here. Hold this." Breaking into her thoughts, he handed her a new, lit candle, and she held it out to illuminate the wet spot. He muttered under his breath, and although she couldn't make out the words, he was clearly angry. She imagined he had not anticipated all the issues that might come with the house once his father passed it along.

After placing the basin under the leak, he moved to the small bed set aside for a child and yanked the blankets off. He used the material to sop up the wet mess on the floor.

"Let's go back to bed. We'll see to it in the morning." Taking the candle, he placed his large hand on the small of her back. His touch was warm through the wet material as he guided her through the chamber.

"Hell," he said and left the room.

She pulled the shift from her body, tossed it in the direction of the nearest table, and climbed back under the covers. It was not worth fumbling through the dark to find another.

When he returned, he once again carried his sword, placing it reverently on the floor by his side of the bed. It must be a habit. What threat did he fear which would cause him to sleep with a weapon like that?

His arms around her, he drew her into the space between the crook of his arm and his shoulder. He was rigid, taut with either anger or disappointment.

"We can find some men to inspect the roofs tomorrow."

"Aye." But he sighed again. After a moment he continued, "I never wanted this place."

"Well, we are here. We can make it our place."

He seemed to relax a little. As she snuggled up against him, the bone-deep weariness of the day and her activities caught up with her. She felt her eyes shutting as she thought about the stress her husband was under.

*Will he trust me as a partner and let me help get the house in order?*

• • •

As the sun peeked in through the drawn curtains, Finlay woke. Blair still slumbered with his arm cradled around her side. He reluctantly withdrew his hold from his wife's soft form. Sliding to the side, he made as little movement as possible. She needed her sleep after the work she'd put in yesterday and for the day they had ahead.

Dressing, he snuck from the room and plodded down the steps to the breakfast room. Robbie and Tristan were already there, taking advantage of the meager portions of eggs, cheese, and bread that had been left out on the sideboard.

"Did ye sleep soundly?" He grabbed a plate, only taking enough to satisfy his hunger. It was important to ensure the other guests and his wife would have food when they broke their fasts. Thankfully, he'd brought plenty of coin from Scotland with him. He only hoped it would be enough to see them through until he could decipher what had gone so terribly wrong here.

"Aye," Tristan said. "The rain always lulls me into a deep sleep."

Robbie only nodded, staring out the window as they waited for Finlay to take a seat first.

"Were ye able to find the priest?" he asked as he slid into the chair at the head of the table, the one that was supposed to belong to an earl, not his bastard son.

"The men at the tavern said Father Thomas would be here Saturday eve. He comes in for mass on Sunday mornings." Tristan scooped a spoonful of eggs and plopped them on his plate.

"He keeps up yer chapel and invites those from the village to come on Sundays."

"Good. Hopefully one part of the estate is not in ruins, then."

Tomorrow, he would have to take a good look around the property and see what needed to be done and who he needed to bring in. Today was about getting some staff for the house and answers from Mr. Gerrick.

"And what did they say of the war?" He shoveled a bite of eggs into his mouth.

"Thus far, it appears the north has been unaffected. Most of the fighting is south."

"I pray it stays that way."

"Is the king still ensconced at Oxford?" He looked at Tristan.

"Aye. Do ye plan on going to see him?" Robbie's gaze pinned him, and Finlay realized for the first time that the lad's accent had grown stronger. He didn't sound as English as he had when he'd first arrived at Kentillie all those months ago.

"I dinnae ken yet. It depends on whether my father and brothers are willing to deliver the news to him for me. They will be here tomorrow to discuss it."

Talk of war and politics halted as Blair strolled into the room wearing one of the gowns from their journey down. He'd promised to get her what she needed, and so far, he'd failed miserably, only managing to procure the one she'd soiled yesterday putting to right his house.

He'd lain awake last night thinking about the leaking nursery. He had planned for the babe to stay in that room. How could he expect anyone, let alone a child, to live in such conditions? He'd been furious after seeing his wife sprawled out on the floor covered in rainwater. What if she had been hurt?

"Good morning," Tristan said as she drifted into the room.

"Aye, 'tis that. Were the rooms comfortable?"

"Aye," Robbie and Tristan chimed in at the same time.

"I'm glad to hear. We found a leak last night. Do either of ye ken how to repair them?" Finlay had not even thought to ask the men for help.

"Nae, but Brodie might," Tristan said.

After filling a plate, Blair threaded her way through the two men who still stood beside the table and eased into the chair beside him. Andrew walked into the room, a tray with a pitcher in hand.

"Would ye like some tea, my lady?"

"I would like some coffee, if ye have any."

Tristan took the seat next to Blair and Robbie the one on his left side.

"No, my lady, I'm afraid we do not have coffee." He reddened.

"'Tis all right then, I'll take tea."

The butler poured her a cup then did the same for the others as they sat. He then inspected the sidebar and left the room.

Malcolm, Brodie, and Seamus strolled into the room, and the greetings began all over again.

Once they were seated, Blair spoke up, addressing the Cameron men. "I dinnae ken what yer plans are, but if ye will be about and have nothing else to do, we could use a little bit of help."

"We are just waiting on the priest to get here."

Why had they come all the way from Scotland to see the priest who tended the chapel at his home? His suspicions were growing by the minute. He was afraid when he pried their answer from them, he wasn't going to like it.

"'Tis settled then. If ye gentlemen would accompany me

this afternoon, we will take a tour of the grounds and see if there are tasks ye can help with."

Their conversation faded as Finlay groaned internally. He felt it as a physical punch to the gut that because of his neglect, others would have to stand in for him on something he wished he could do with Blair. He would be meeting with his estate manager and couldn't even give his wife a tour of the home he was offering her. Hell, he'd not been able to give her a chance to see his cottage back on Cameron lands, either.

After a lengthy discussion on how Highlanders were better workers than Sassenachs, he determined to salvage part of the day with his wife and said, "Whenever ye wish to head into the village, I am ready."

She smiled at him and rose then pushed in her chair. "I can be ready shortly. Shall I meet ye in the foyer?"

"Aye. I'll be waiting for ye."

She hurried from the room, and he couldn't help but smile at her eagerness. At least this morning, he would be the one with her undivided attention.

# Chapter Seventeen

Finlay sat across from his estate manager who talked down to him like the professors and headmaster at Oxford had. Worse, Everly Gerrick smelled of mint like his long-ago tutor. Mr. Gerrick reminded him of all the people who had tried to make him believe that because of his brogue and upbringing, he was beneath them.

Why had he hired this man? Surely his younger brother, who had also hired the man, had planned this. But he knew why—the advice had really come from Prudence, and she'd always been kind to him. Perhaps she didn't know the man as well as she thought.

"Did ye even try to find staff?"

The man sat as if a rod extended from his ass up to the top of his arrogant, bulbous head. It seemed like an attempt to make the estate manager taller so he could look down on Finlay. It didn't work—he felt no threat, just willful indignation.

"Yes. All the men have gone off to fight for the king or Parliament. There was no one left."

"I've heard our area has no' been as hard hit by the war."

"Ye have been away and have heard wrong." Mr. Gerrick pinned him with a blank stare, but there appeared to be some hint of malice beneath the man's cold regard.

"How is it that within a couple of hours in the village this morning, my wife was able to find someone to tend the gardens, a foreman to oversee repairs, and several maids?" Not to mention that she'd spent half their morning in with a seamstress who had promised to bring Blair some gowns tomorrow and continue fitting her for whatever else it was women needed.

The man actually appeared flustered after being caught in his lie. Face reddening, Mr. Gerrick started to stutter his words. "They—they are not of good quality. I thought you would only want the—the best for this precious estate your father has given you. I thought you wanted it run properly." Before the diatribe was done, the arse's tone turned condescending.

"Aye, I do, but I don't see ye running it at all."

Mr. Gerrick straightened his shoulders but stayed silent.

"Ye brought the books?"

"Yes, I did." A sly smile passed the man's lips. He unfolded the satchel at his waist, pulled it into his lap, and drew out two thick leather volumes. Standing, looking down at him, the man placed them squarely on the desk in front of him.

Without opening the books and attempting to make sense out of them in front of this arse, Finlay asked, "How is it that I am spending so much when I'm not paying for anything? I have no' even been here, and creditors are knocking on the doors looking for coin owed them."

"It's all there." The stiff Sassenach pointed in challenge, without taking his place back in the chair, obviously attempting to intimidate. "Take a look, and you will find I am handling things properly."

"I suspect ye are correct, but now that I will be spending more time in residence, I should ken what's going on." He expected there were more errors in the books than he would be able to find, but he couldn't confront the man based on a gut feeling and the man's inaction alone.

The man only stared at him.

"How fares Caldwell's estate?"

Everly Gerrick smiled, appearing as if he had made a fortune for his younger brother and Prudence, possibly ensuring the stability of his position with them. What if the man weren't at fault? Could it be Finlay's lack of attention that caused the problems at Catriona House?

"Funds are being allocated exactly as they should be, and everything is running smoothly."

Finlay couldn't help but turn the words over in his mind as the hint of some double meaning eluded him. It was as if the man were jumbling his thoughts, just like the markings on a page misaligned themselves.

He leaned back, running his hands through his hair as he prepared to open the books and dive into the puzzle.

"My mother has been called to London, and I must accompany her. The roads aren't safe these days." Mr. Gerrick appeared truly worried about the welfare of his mother.

"When will ye be back?"

"I plan to return within the month."

That gave Finlay time, because he had to ensure the king was alerted to the danger headed his way before he could stop to make sense of what had transpired here. "When ye do, we should sit down and plan out how we need to proceed going forward."

"I will send a message when I return."

"Please do." Finlay considered relieving the man of his post immediately but thought it prudent to examine the books before making the decision. After all, Prudence, who had never looked at him with disdain but kindness, wouldn't have steered him wrong. He would question his brother's motives, but Prudence had always been gracious to him.

"Good day, sir."

With that, Everly Gerrick pivoted and strode toward the door as if he couldn't move fast enough without running.

Settling back into his seat, Finlay picked up the first leather-bound book. He thumbed through the volume. As expected, numbers and letters swam and swirled, moving around the page, reversing themselves and causing his head to ache.

• • •

Blair believed the morning had been a complete success, and now as she toiled around the house making lists of what needed to be done. Jenny followed with bright, eager eyes.

"So when do they all start, my lady?"

"Tomorrow. Although the new gardener said he may bring a couple more able-bodied men for me to interview to work the stables as well. 'Twill be nice if we donnae have to rely on yer little ones."

"They are hard workers."

"I ken, Jenny, but they should also have the opportunity to be children. We will find tasks for them. Believe me, there are plenty. Now, before we tour the west side, let's stop by the kitchens. I'd like to meet the cook and find out what he plans to prepare. 'Tis almost time for the midday meal, and we need to pass by, anyway."

After entering the kitchen, which was twice the size of the one at her father's castle, she stopped in place. It was empty, though the smell of warm bread and meat carried through the room. "Where's the cook?"

"I don't know, but I'll find out for you." Jenny darted out to look for the butler.

While the housekeeper was gone, Blair took the opportunity to stroll around the large room and take it all in. Although the pantry was almost bare, at least the cook had done a good job of keeping the room clean, and unlike the rest of the house, it appeared well cared for. With renewed hope the man would be up to the task of running the kitchen of a large estate, she made her way into the dining room.

The Cameron men were already present, and the food had been set up on a sideboard similar to how it had been for breakfast this morning. As she entered, they stood.

"Am I late?" Time had flown by after a busy morning in the village and a tour of the east wing.

"Nae, we havenae been too long."

She strolled over to inspect the food and filled a plate with sliced warm beef, a sauce for the top, some summer squash, bread, and fresh berries. The cook had done a nice job.

Sitting, she got to business straight away. "Brodie, I hear ye are good with roofs. Do ye mind checking the estate's roofs to see where it needs repairs? There was a leak in the nursery last night."

"Aye. Finlay mentioned it. I'll be happy to take a look."

"Thank ye. I'm sure Finlay will be pleased. He's in with the estate manager now trying to come up with a plan for taking charge of this place."

"I can check the stables to see what needs to be done there," Malcolm chimed in. "I've spent enough time in them helping my sister out and have learned my way around them."

"I can make a plan for the garden and grounds," said Seamus.

"Once they have plans, I can go into the village to secure supplies and any additional help we still might need," Tristan weighed in.

Robbie was last. "I'll take charge of the chapel and see what needs attention in it."

Her heart burst with happiness. She'd never had so much help back at home, but then again, she'd not needed it. And the men seemed to regard her as capable of leading the charge to repair the neglect of the estate.

Hours later, after she'd made more lists then cleaned, she waited alone at the dining table, her husband nowhere to be seen, the Cameron men again choosing to go into the village for the evening meal.

Once Andrew filled her cup of spiced wine for the second time, she became bold. "Have ye seen my husband?"

"Yes, my lady. He is in his study and has asked not to be disturbed."

"Thank ye."

Things must not have gone well with the estate manager. "Is the man with the books still here?"

"No, my lady, he left hours ago."

Surely her husband could have spared a few minutes to dine with her. Unbidden, her thoughts turned to the many nights her mother and she were alone at the table, her father and brother holed up in the study and ignoring them and the possibility they might be able to help.

Taking a fortifying drink of her wine and pushing her plate aside, she rose, grabbing her husband's untouched glass and plate. If he was not going to join her, she would go to him.

When she reached the solid wood door of the study, she remembered the verbal abuse her mother had endured when she interrupted her father. Blair almost turned around, almost decided she should let Finlay guide what their relationship would be like. But no, she was determined their marriage would be different from her parents'. She would not be something to be forgotten until it was time for him to take his pleasure on her.

She pushed the door in with her hip then squared her shoulders as she strode in. Finlay crossed his arms and studied her.

"I brought ye something to eat."

"Thank ye." Then he just stared at her as she attempted not to slink over like a scared mouse.

Setting down the plate and cup, she smiled at him, but he didn't move from the defensive, tense pose he'd taken up upon her entry.

"Did the meeting go well today?"

"It went as expected."

"Did ye get any answers?"

He closed his eyes briefly and shook his head.

"Are those the books?"

Finlay nodded.

"Is there something I can help ye with? I helped with the account keeping at home."

"Nae. I can do it." He closed the books with a *thump* and pushed them to the other side of the desk, away from her.

She beat down the hurt that settled in her chest. "Can ye no' take a break to eat?"

"Nae, I cannae."

"I can help if ye need it. I'm good with numbers. We can do it together."

"I dinnae want yer help. I dinnae need it. Go to bed, Blair. I have work to do."

The ground out words surprised her. He'd shown nothing but kindness toward her, except for the time in the village, after she'd imagined Bruce stalking her. He'd been truly angry with her then as well. Was there a side to her husband she didn't know?

Backing from the room, she didn't let another word fall from her lips as she closed the door and meandered aimlessly down the hall. She didn't know where she was going until she was outside, walking in the moonlight through the garden and into the soothing fields of lavender. She tried to tell herself that she meant more to Finlay than a pretty face to warm his bed.

But she bet at one time, her mother had thought the same about her father.

# Chapter Eighteen

*Hell.*

Finlay drove his fingers through his hair as he looked up at the ceiling that needed a fresh painting.

Why had he yelled at her? She'd only been trying to help. But letting her do so would mean admitting she'd married a man undeserving of her strong will and intelligence, a man who could barely read. He couldn't let her know the truth.

He was supposed to take care of his wife and expanding family, but how would she have faith in him if she learned his secret?

He'd been looking at the numbers all day, and as soon as he thought he'd found a problem, his gaze became unfocused, and he wasn't sure if he'd imagined the errors or if they were real. It all appeared to be written in another language, and he wished he'd opened the books and asked about it before Mr. Gerrick left.

Standing, he walked around the room and stretched. He'd hoped to have this figured out by the time his father and brothers arrived tomorrow. *Och*, he'd forgotten to tell Blair or the cook they would be coming tomorrow. He'd have to inform them in the morning.

After settling back in at his desk, he took a sip of the wine Blair had brought to him. She had such a kind heart he couldn't disappoint her, so he examined the second book, hoping it would be easier to read. It wasn't. If anything his head ached more.

• • •

Pushing the door in hours later, Finlay was pleased Blair had left a candle burning for him on a side table. Undressing quickly, he threw his plaid and shirt onto a chair and advanced toward the bed. It was nice to know her warm, willing body waited beneath the covers. But when he reached the mattress, she wasn't there.

Panic hit first, then fear, then anger.

Where the hell was she? Lifting the candle, he looked around the chamber. She had been here—her gown was hung neatly near the open window, most likely to air in the breeze of the open panes. When he didn't find her, he hurried through the dressing area and into the connecting bedroom.

He almost didn't see her, the small lump beneath the covers.

What was she doing? They had never discussed it, but he wanted her in his bed every night. This wouldn't do.

After marching back to the main room, he set the candle down, then pulled back the covers. Quietly, he negotiated his way through the dark and back to her side, but he had to let his eyes adjust before drawing back the covers. When scooping her up in his arms, he caught the scent of lavender and wondered if she'd used the packs Maggie had made her for the journey.

Making his way back to their bed, he inhaled and

breathed her in. Mixed in with the lavender was the slightest hint of something else, something exotic, something purely Blair. She didn't stir except to lean into his chest and nuzzle her head against his biceps.

He'd have to talk to her tomorrow about his expectations for their marriage, but for now he'd let her sleep. He was beyond exhausted himself. So he lay down with her, pulled the covers up, and wrapped his arms around her. Despite the comfort and warmth of Blair's nearness, he had trouble falling asleep.

In the morning, he woke with a stiff ache between his legs, his wife still beside him. He turned into her, waking her gently with soft kisses on her neck as his fingers slid down to tease at that sweet spot between her legs. When she was fully awake, wet and arching into him for more, he settled between her thighs and filled her until she cried out from the pleasure, and he once again spilled his seed inside her.

He gave her a final kiss before rolling over onto his side so that he could study the sleepy, thoroughly ravished woman who lay beside him.

Which reminded him, he never wanted to wake a day without her.

"Ye willnae stay in the other room."

"Why?" Her gaze, which only moments ago had been warm and soft with rapture, became icy and cold. She rose up on her elbows and turned away from him as her brow crinkled.

"Ye are my wife, and ye belong here in this bed." Why was she having such a problem with this?

She blinked a few times as if his words were soaking in, but then she pinned him with a determined gaze. "Ye can come get me whenever ye like."

"Nae. Ye will stay here." He sat up, his ire starting to rise along with her stubbornness.

"Why?"

"Because we are partners, and I want ye by my side."

Sitting up completely now, she drew the blankets close to her chest, covering the breasts he'd yet to examine in the daylight.

"We weren't partners when ye didnae show up for the midday meal." She threw back the covers, no longer shy, her flushed skin bared to his view. His mouth watered until he thought about what she said and took in her angry stance. "We weren't partners when ye hid in yer study without speaking to me all afternoon." She rose from the bed and turned her back to him. "We weren't partners when ye left me sitting at the dinner table alone last night."

Had he done all that? Aye, he had. Sighing, he shook his head at his mistake.

She pulled on the shift he'd stripped from her body this morning. "And when I came to yer study and offered ye my help, ye turned me away. If that is what a partner does, I'll be taking my own room."

Stomping through the dressing area, she pivoted and slammed the door to the adjoining room. The only other sound was the *click* of the lock as she shut him out.

• • •

Blair waited a good quarter of an hour after she heard Finlay leave the room before venturing back in to pick out a gown for the day. She went with the blue one she'd worn on the journey, the one in the worst condition with the torn hem and stains on the bottom from the grime of the road. Jenny and she were only going to be cleaning rooms this morning, and if time permitted, she would sneak into the cook's vegetable garden to see what he had planted.

Before exiting the room, she peeked out. She was furious

with her husband, and if she saw him again, she might say other things she would regret. As it was, she'd probably crossed a line. She hadn't even thought about what had been bothering her until the words tumbled from her mouth.

She considered heading straight for the kitchen to break her fast there but decided that would be hiding, and she wouldn't do that. Instead, she held her head high and proceeded into the breakfast room, pushing over to the sideboards and loading a plate. Inspecting the table, she was surprised to see Robbie was the only one in the room.

Thankful she wouldn't have to face her husband, she floated over and eased into the chair on the opposite side of the table.

"Good morn." Robbie spoke first.

"And to ye. How is yer room?" She took a bite of the eggs and sighed at how good they tasted after barely touching her meal yesterday.

"It's quite comfortable."

"Today is the day the priest arrives?"

"Aye."

"Do ye have sins to confess that a priest in Scotland couldnae hear?" *Och*, that was rude of her. It was time to let go of last night's resentments. But she hadn't been able to grasp why he'd made the journey here and everything seemed so secretive.

Robbie's finger flicked at the cross he wore beneath his shirt. "Sometimes I feel as if I'm cursed. It doesnae hurt to have blessings wherever I may find them."

He'd found a way to evade her question. If he didn't want to confess to her, he was going about it the right way.

Andrew placed a cup in front of her. "Your coffee, my lady."

"Thank ye. Och. The cook was able to find some. Please tell him thank ye as well."

"Yes, my lady." He turned to go, and she picked up the cup, holding it to her nose, savoring the rich smell.

"Still, ye came all the way to England to seek out another priest?"

"Ah, that is something I must unfortunately keep to myself." A glint of mischief lit his gaze, but also something that looked like sorrow.

She nodded. He didn't have to share his secrets.

Jenny walked in just then. "My lady, I'm ready and will be waiting for you outside."

"Yes, Jenny. I'll be right there." Taking another bite of the eggs, she turned back toward Robbie.

"I'm going to see what the chapel needs before he gets here. If ye want any other help, please let me know." Pushing his chair back without making a sound, he rose and bowed his head toward her.

"Thank ye, but I believe we are starting to get things under control. Especially with all of ye Cameron men here to help."

She was left alone again, finishing the eggs and enjoying her coffee for a few blessed moments of peace before the work began. When she emerged, Jenny was waiting outside, just as promised.

"I think we will start with the lady's chamber today." She'd peeled back the blankets last night and regretted climbing in with the dust, but she had needed space. Tonight, the room would be clean, and she would work on making it her own. Aye, she wanted to sleep with her husband, but she also had pride.

Strolling into her chamber, she smiled at the space she would have all to herself. The purple hues were pleasing and reminded her of the lavender fields she could see from the balcony off this room, too.

"Let's start with the bedding. We can get it down to wash,

and mayhap when the new maids arrive this afternoon, they can help ye finish."

"Yes, my lady. I'm thrilled I'll have a staff to work with."

"Ye will be in charge. I am making ye the head housekeeper and increasing yer pay." Once she got her hands on those ledgers.

"Will ye open the windows to bring in the fresh air? I'm going to see what's in this trunk."

Lifting the lid and expecting to see linens, she was surprised to find letters bundled up neatly in organized stacks. A few odd items stuck out, as well. A sprig of dried lavender, a red ribbon, and another small box. Picking up one of the letters, she read on the outside.

*Dwight*
*From: Catriona*

Her heart lurched. *Och*. Finlay's father had saved all of the correspondences with her husband's mother. This was private. She shouldn't look.

"What did you find?" Jenny came up behind her, and she nearly flinched.

"Nae, 'tis nothing we need. Let's move on to getting the curtains down so we can clean them as well." Placing the letters back in the trunk, she shut it gently and stood to help the housekeeper.

After what felt like hours of cleaning, she found herself wandering through the poor excuse of a vegetable garden. The cook had kept up the herbs, but he was only one man. Frustrated, she strolled a bit farther into the fields of lavender and picked several bunches. These were a little bit past peak, but they would be good for drying and putting into sachets to keep in the guest rooms, hopefully keeping away the musty smell until all the leaks could be repaired. She and Jenny had found two more and Brodie was even now in the village getting the materials to do the work.

Heading back to the house, she swiped at the hair that had come unbound and tickled at her nose, unaware until she felt herself smear it on her cheek that she had dirt on her hand. *Och*, she would have to bathe before the dressmaker arrived. Would that give her time to make it to the midday meal?

Not wanting to trail dirt through the house, she slid out of her slippers as she entered through the kitchen door and spied Jenny having a bite to eat. "Jenny, could yer boys bring up some water for a bath?"

"Yes, my lady. I'll put them to it straight away."

"Thank ye."

She almost dropped the lavender on the counter to come back for later but decided it would be nice in the tub, so she continued out into the hall, inspecting the bounty. Absently, she turned the corner into the main hall and took two steps before a sophisticated English accent reached her ears.

"Your servants are filthy, brother. You should be ashamed of how you care for the hired help."

She gaped and turned to see what was wrong with Jenny, but there was no one there. The lout was referring to her. Her cheeks flushed, although she wasn't sure if it was from embarrassment or anger.

The man, who appeared to be the same age as Finlay, continued in a crude manner as his stare drifted from her face down the length of her body. "Although, I would not be adverse to taking her off your hands."

"No, brother." The second word was enunciated with unbridled fury. "This is my wife, Blair Cameron."

"Blair, this is my father, Dwight Quinton, the Earl of Middlesbrough, and my oldest brother, his heir, Thomas Quinton."

# Chapter Nineteen

There were two things that stopped Finlay from pummeling his brother right then. First, there was the deep cherry red Blair had turned at Thomas's insult. He held back only because he didn't want to cause her any more distress. Hell, if this wasn't his fault—he'd forgotten to tell her his family would be here early this afternoon.

Second, he was fighting the urge to scold her for going out on grounds without a guard. The more he thought about it, the less comfortable he felt with her roaming about when either Bruce or someone determined to stop him from reaching the king may have followed them. He'd pull her aside this afternoon and talk with her.

"Bloody hell," his brother continued. "That chit married you?"

The *you* was said with such derision Finlay had to hold his breath and count to five before answering. "'Tis too hard to believe a bonny lass might want to marry me?" Blair was paralyzed; she studied the three of them.

Stepping forward, his father bowed, took Blair's free

hand, and brought it to his mouth to give her a small kiss. "I am pleased to meet you, Blair."

Regaining her composure and putting on the breathtaking, self-assured smile that was only made more devastating by her disheveled appearance, she replied, "'Tis a pleasure to meet ye, too."

"Oh, Finlay, you've brought home a lovely Scottish lass." The grin his father gave him was akin to the one he'd given him upon his completion of his studies at Oxford. "Why didn't you let me know?"

"I didnae have time. I planned to tell ye today, however, I neglected to inform her ye would be arriving so soon. 'Tis my carelessness that leaves her unprepared to greet ye."

"Nonsense. This is the perfect greeting. Welcome to the family, Blair." Thank heaven his father had decency.

"Thank ye. If I could have just a few moments, I'll clean myself up and meet ye for the midday meal. I smelled something wonderful when I passed through the kitchens just now."

His brother wheeled his way in and took the hand the earl had just released. His head dipped, and he placed a kiss on her hand then held it too long while gazing into her eyes. "Do accept my apologies. There is no excuse for my behavior."

*What?* Thomas actually seemed remorseful for something he'd done.

"I believe, sir, that ye may owe an apology to my husband and all his servants as well." Blair held her head high, facing his brother with no fear. She was becoming the mistress of the house, just as she had been back on Macnab lands, and Finlay had never been prouder she'd chosen him. Well, she'd been blackmailed into choosing him, she hadn't really wanted him, but she was here. And she was taking charge.

"If you wish, I will get down on my knees and beg."

Once he finally released her hand, she backed a step but gave him a tilt of her chin that indicated she'd already forgiven him.

"I promise, just a few moments and I'll make sure the cook has everything ready." She glanced to his father, ignoring Finlay. She couldn't still be angry, could she? Nodding to the earl, she swept by them without giving him a second glance, then ascended the steps, his brother and father gawking as she disappeared.

"We can talk in the study." His father gestured, knowing the way better than he did.

When the door thudded shut behind them, Finlay pivoted and planted his fist squarely on Thomas's jaw. His brother fell back, letting his hand come up to inspect the sight of the shot. He dropped it, straightened, and said, "I deserved that."

"Dinnae even think of touching my wife." His breath came in short bursts.

Raising hands palm up, Thomas backed as Finlay continued, "She is the one thing that belongs to me ye cannae have."

"Do you think I would try to steal your wife?"

He wouldn't put it past the arse who had tried to sabotage his life from the moment he understood what a bastard was.

"Enough," his father chided in the imperious tone of the Earl of Middlesbrough. Moving farther into the room, the earl motioned for him to take the seat behind the desk, which didn't feel quite right in the man's presence. Finlay moved in that direction as his father moved over to the liquor cabinet and pulled out a decanter and three glasses. "Sit," the earl ordered.

His brother and he obeyed as their father poured a generous dram of whisky, handed it to them, then returned to dispense another for himself. No one spoke until the earl took the seat next to Thomas.

"So what is this urgent news that Charles needs to know?" his father asked.

"The Kirk is about to accept the Solemn League and Covenant."

"Why does it matter if the Scottish Parliament wishes to ensure their reformed religion is made law?" his brother asked.

"Because the English Parliament has agreed to back them if Scottish troops are sent to help defeat the king."

"Are you certain this is imminent?" His father closed his eyes, shaking his head.

"Aye, 'tis on their docket for the seventeenth of August."

"That gives us a little time to prepare."

"It hasn't been approved yet, but it has already been circulated around some of the clans who have agreed to sign and pledge men. They will be prepared sooner than expected."

"Yes, Charles needs to know straight away. We will all leave tomorrow," his father declared.

Calculating the time it would take to get there and back, approximately two weeks, Finlay considered crying off and asking his father and brother to go without him, but he couldn't do that. King Charles would want to hear it from him, and his father appeared to want him there.

It tore at him to leave his new wife, but at least the other Cameron men and Andrew were here. They would keep her safe.

• • •

As soon as the boys had filled her tub and left, Blair stripped her clothes and climbed in. If she'd known they were having company, she wouldn't have wasted the time in the gardens. She'd only barely remembered to add a little of the lavender to her water. The scent of the flowers had a pleasant, calming effect that had her lingering a few minutes longer than she should have.

Finished, she rushed into the nicest gown she had, the one Finlay had purchased where they consummated their marriage.

"Och. I still need a lady's maid. My hair is a mess." Brushing at the long, clean mess of tangles, she realized she'd never be able to style it in a fashionable English way in time for the meal. Turning toward the housekeeper as she returned into the room, she asked, "Do ye ken how to fix it?"

"No, my lady. I've only had boys to take care of."

Oh well. She left it free, thinking to let it dry a little before braiding it.

"Will the earl like me?" Suddenly nervous, she turned toward Jenny.

"Yes, my lady. I've known him all my life, and he likes almost everyone. More than that, he'll be pleased his son wed and has brought you here."

Taking a deep breath, she glanced back to the mirror. Not wanting to wait any longer, she pleated her hair and added ribbons to match the blue in her gown. It would have to do.

Trusting Jenny to take care of everything, she rushed out and down the steps to join the men. They were already sitting as she scurried into the dining room and skidded to a halt. Straightening her shoulders, she gave Finlay's father her best smile, then his brother. She was feeling gracious enough to give one to her husband, even if he didn't believe her a partner in all things. Over time, he would see how capable she was.

Standing, each of them returned her smile. Finlay's looked relieved, the earl's eyes seemed pleased, and Thomas appeared to be curious. Strolling to the table, she said, "Sit, please," but they waited until she eased into the seat next to

Finlay, the one his brother had left between them.

"How was your journey to England?" The earl gave her his full attention.

"*Och*. We came so fast there was no' time to enjoy the countryside on the way here, but 'tis bonny."

"Brother, how is it you did not send word that you were taking such a lovely wife? I'm sure Father would have wanted to be there." Thomas's eyes pinned her husband with accusation.

"There was no time."

"A rushed marriage then?"

She caught his implication at once. To dampen the tension, she jumped between the two with, "Nae, we have kenned each other for several years, but 'twas no' until recently that his hazel eyes pulled me into his web." It was the truth.

"He's a lucky man," Thomas stated.

"Are you a Cameron?" the earl asked.

"Nae, a Macnab."

The earl frowned, and his gaze shifted to Finlay, who shook his head as if to say, *dinnae bring it up*. The men must have discussed her father's duplicity.

What would they think of her when they discovered she had pitted two clans against each other?

Finlay had confidence that his sway with Montrose was enough to keep the Grahams from attacking the Camerons, but what if Bruce was still looking for her and pushed the issue? And *och*, she hadn't even thought of it, but if her father discovered the Grahams and Camerons fighting because of her, he would surely reject her altogether and swear his loyalty to the Covenanters. She groaned inside but somehow managed to keep her lips curved upward.

"You are loyal to King Charles."

"Aye, I am." It was true. She put all the conviction she could muster into it because one day soon, if Bruce had gone to his cousin, they might all be questioning her loyalty.

"Well, then, there is nothing more to be said on it. How do you like Catriona House?"

"'Tis grand and beautiful, but it has been neglected." Dwight's gaze darted to the window and fogged. She could see he was mulling her words, not just ignoring her.

"Can it be salvaged?" His voice was rough and off in the distance.

"Aye, with the proper attention and care. It will be magnificent."

"That reminds me, Thomas," Finlay chimed in. "The estate manager Prudence recommended hasnae followed through on getting things in order. His books are quite difficult to follow as well. The estate seems to be taking all my allowance and not producing anything. Have ye and Caldwell had much success with the man?"

Was that why he'd stayed in the study all day yesterday? Was he being cheated? She had to get a look at those books.

"I usually do my own books. When Prudence suggested him, I declined." Funny, but that almost looked like amusement in Thomas's eyes.

Changing the subject, she asked, "Will ye be staying with us tonight?"

"No, we are close enough there is no need. Caldwell is a little farther, so when he comes for a visit, he may take you up on the offer. You'll get along nicely with Prudence, too. He would have come today, but he is currently in London."

"I'm sorry I didnae get to meet him."

Andrew appeared at her side. "My lady, the dressmaker has arrived. I put her in the parlor."

"Aye, thank ye, Andrew."

"Ah, yes. We will need to be on our way as well." They all rose and strolled toward the front door together.

Surprising her, Dwight pulled her in for a warm,

welcoming embrace. "I am pleased Finlay has brought you into the family and am looking forward to conversing with you again."

"Thank ye." She nodded at him then looked to Finlay, who had a soft smile on his face.

"And again, dear sister. I apologize for my earlier behavior." She wanted to forgive him, but there was still something there she didn't trust.

"I will forgive ye when ye apologize to all the servants in England." Winking at him, she laughed.

"I will set out doing so with great haste." After kissing her hand, he dropped it slowly then backed toward the door.

Once Finlay shut the door behind them, he said, "I am sorry I forgot to tell ye they were coming. I meant to warn ye, but I got so caught up in going through those journals last night I couldn't see straight when I came up to bed."

"Ye are forgiven. They are my family now, and I guess they will forgive me for not welcoming them."

"I did tell them that I neglected to let ye ken."

"Can I help ye with the accounts? I'm good at it." His gaze darted away as if he were ashamed of her. Why would he not let her help? He was shutting her out again, but perhaps he needed a little more time. She would find a way to prove herself.

"We'll see about it later. For now, ye have a guest."

He took her hand. Tingles shot through her arm as he moved to wrap his arms around her, and her disappointment faded. It was the first time since they'd been intimate that he had reached for her outside of the bedchamber. Drawing her close to his long, lean body, he dipped his head, giving her a soft, searching kiss as he held her. He didn't ask for anything or move to deepen the embrace, just held the contact for a moment, as if he was seeking the reassurance of her presence.

The touch had been comfortable, familiar. Something

more than just duty or desire. It was companionship. Maybe he wanted it, too, needed it the way she did.

"I will be in my study, but I promise to no' leave ye alone for the next meal. Please come get me if ye ever feel I am neglecting ye." His attention lingered on her, and she was off balance and looking forward to the next time she would see him. Contentment washed over her, along with anticipation of their next meeting. Could her husband actually care for her?

# Chapter Twenty

After poring over the books all day, Finlay realized something was still wrong. When he returned from Oxford, he would invite Prudence and his youngest brother for a visit. Then, his sister-in-law could give him more information on Mr. Gerrick. What had she found trustworthy about the man when all he saw was a lying weasel?

Frustrated and not quite able to find the answer, he looked forward to the welcome distraction of dinner with his wife. She'd seemed to have forgiven him despite his Herculean feat to mess things up. He was hopeful she would join him in bed tonight without his having to go in search of her.

Maybe he should make sure he had a key to her room. Better yet, close it in and forget about its existence. Why would his father build such a thing?

He was almost to the door when he spied her coming from the back of the house. Waiting for her to draw near, he noticed she was wearing a gown he hadn't seen yet—it was the lightest shade of pink. It looked good on her, and he finally felt at peace knowing he was providing for her.

When she reached him, he threaded his arm with hers as they strolled through the already open door. "Ye look lovely."

"Thank ye."

"Did ye order some new gowns?"

"Aye, I did, but only a few. I dinnae ken what my budget would be, and I didnae want to spend too much." Ah, she had heard what he'd said earlier about his allowance disappearing.

"Dinnae worry, ye can buy whatever ye like."

They were about to sit when Brodie strolled into the room, followed by every other Cameron man who had joined them on the journey. He'd not been aware they weren't going into the village tonight.

"The gardener came today." Tristan glanced to Blair as he took the seat next to her.

"Do ye think he will do?"

"Aye, he seemed competent, and better yet, he agreed with the plans I drew up. He's brought a man who works with vegetables and herbs as well to help Cook with his garden."

Brodie said to Finlay, "When I was returning from the village today, I met yer father and brother. Is it true ye are going to Oxford tomorrow?"

Finlay glanced at Blair, who stared back at him blankly. "Aye, 'tis true. He wants me there when he seeks an audience with King Charles."

"I didnae ken." Blair's blue eyes frosted over, possibly angry with him, yet again, for his poor timing.

"Nae, I havenae had the chance to tell ye."

"What do I need to pack?"

"Ye will be staying here."

Shock registered in her gaze before she averted her eyes and studied her plate.

*Hell*, this hadn't been the way he'd wanted to tell her, but he couldn't explain it all in front of the men. They were going into an area where men were killing each other because of their allegiances. She was safe here.

The meal went by with Blair barely speaking as the men talked about their day and what they had done.

He longed to pull her into his arms, carry her up to their bed, and tell her all, but just as everyone was shuffling through the door, Robbie pulled him aside. "I need to speak with ye."

"Can it wait until the morning?"

"Nae. It must be now."

Groaning inside, he remembered the promise to his laird that he would do what Robbie asked without question. He tilted his head to indicate the direction. "In my study."

By the time he looked up, his wife had fled.

Malcolm, his laird's brother, followed them into the study, shutting and locking the door behind him. Hurrying over to the decanter, Finlay poured a serving of whisky for each of them then took a seat at his desk, trying to ignore the books taunting him.

Robbie started, "I need to ask something of ye."

"Go ahead."

"I need ye to take the priest to Oxford with ye."

"Won't he miss mass tomorrow if he goes?"

"I can lead it for him."

"I don't like it— It will probably slow us. But my laird has instructed I do whatever ye wish, so 'twill be done."

Robbie nodded, relief washing over him as he took a large gulp of the amber liquid in his hand. It was the first time he'd seen the young man with a stout drink.

"Can ye trust me with what ye are doing here?"

"Ye are loyal to King Charles?"

"Aye."

"Would ye lay down yer life to protect him and his family?"

He answered without hesitation, "Aye, 'tis my sworn duty."

Robbie stood and squared his shoulders. "My true name is Robert Stuart, son to King Charles Stuart and his wife, Henrietta Maria."

"How?" Finlay was certain his eyes were as round as the moon and his jaw was slack.

"You ken my mother is Catholic." Robbie waited for him to respond, so he nodded. "My parents made an arrangement when they wed. Their second son would be raised in my mother's faith. I am the twin to Charles II. I was born three minutes after him."

How could this be true? He glanced to Malcolm.

"Aye, 'tis true," Malcolm backed the words of the youth who stood before him.

"My mother's faith is not welcome in England, so they sent me to where they believed I would be safe. I have not seen them in years, but they saw to it that the church cared for me until it was no longer safe."

Finlay gulped.

Robbie continued, "There are a few who have discovered my existence. Do ye remember the day Lachlan found me?"

"Aye." Finlay was with Lachlan when they came upon the charred remains of a church. They had discovered Robbie holding a priest who had been left for dead in the assault that had taken place before their arrival.

"The priest was killed because he didnae divulge where I was hidden away. If Conall had known who I was, he would have waited for me to return to take my life, or worse, hold me as leverage against the king."

The man who had attempted to kill Lachlan was in league with the Covenanters.

"Ye were fortunate to no' be home the morning of the attack."

"I have found a home and safety with the Camerons, but I miss my family. Please have the priest deliver the message for me? It's too dangerous to put my request in writing."

"Aye." He knelt. "Yer Royal Highness."

"And ye must never call me that again. It puts us all in danger. No one can ken who I am. Not even Blair. She is safer if she doesnae ken my true identity." Rising, he nodded. Robbie told the truth—if word of his presence and his religion got out to the people, they would swarm his estate and kill anyone in residence.

He wanted this whole journey over. He wanted Robbie back on Cameron lands, and he wanted his wife out of danger, because they were all at risk with his presence here.

"Can the priest be ready to leave after breaking his fast?"

"Aye, I will be certain he is."

Once the men were gone, Finlay finally breathed again and calculated what needed to be done to complete this mission. Then, he poured another dram of whisky before settling at his desk to try one more time to make sense of the letters and numbers in the journals before him. Just ten more minutes, then he'd seek out his wife.

Two hours later, his study door slowly creaked open.

• • •

After stomping into his bedchamber, Blair slammed the door. She'd thought they had made progress today, but her husband still thought it not necessary to tell her he was going to desert her in a place she knew very little about, where everything kept going wrong and she had no access to the accounts.

Pacing the room, she wondered what she could do.

It was too early to go to bed. Besides, she was so angry she couldn't have slept if she wanted to. She was not going back down to see her husband when he didn't have the decency to tell her what he was up to. Their relationship would only become strained if she closed herself off. She didn't want to end up living separately like his mother and father had.

A knock sounded at the door.

"Enter," she called out as she continued to pace the large master bedchamber.

Jenny walked in. "Good evening, my lady."

"Good evening. How did it go with the new servants?"

"They are going to do nicely, and one has a sister who is trained as a lady's maid. I told the lass to send her tomorrow so you can see if she will suit."

"Wonderful."

"I heard Mr. Cameron won't be in tomorrow. I'll have Father cancel the interviews he had scheduled."

"I didn't know he had made appointments."

"Oh, yes. He had several lined up to go over repairs for the house with the Cameron men and a fellow from the village."

"Do not cancel them. I can work on it with them. I've overseen some work at my father's castle, and 'twill no' be a problem."

"Yes, my lady. Do you need anything else tonight?"

"Nae, och, well, may I have a glass of that spiced wine brought up, please? Thank ye."

A little while later, she was pulling off her gown and hanging it. She'd been hot all day, and it still seemed quite stuffy inside with no breeze blowing, so she switched into the lightest, softest shift she had then picked up a candle and the glass of wine Jenny had brought.

Slipping through the dressing area and into the lady's chamber, she ambled to the nightstand to set down her wine then slinked over to the trunk. She pulled open the lid, and the scent of the long-ago lavender wafted up. Despite its age, the plant sprigs had been well cared for. She took out the first letter and carried it to the bed.

Carefully, she peeled open the page to find a lovely,

scrolling text. She felt a tinge of guilt for interloping, but maybe his parents' relationship would give her more insight into the man who was now her husband. How was she to prevent the same thing from happening to them if she didn't read it?

*My dearest Dwight,*

*Ye are in my thoughts every day. 'Twould have been easier if I had no' met ye on yer recent visit, but I am happy we had the chance to ken what love could be.*

*I ken ye will be married by the time this letter reaches ye, and I have tried to force myself to no' correspond with ye, but I feel 'tis my duty to let ye ken that I am with child. I dinnae expect or want any help, my laird will look after me, but I felt it dishonest no' to let ye ken ye would have a child born soon.*

*Please dinnae worry for me. I am happy to have a precious life to remember what we shared.*

*Always,*
*Catriona*

After placing the letter on the bed, she took a sip of her wine as a tear trailed down her cheek. Despite how hard the confession must have been for Finlay's mother—knowing nothing could change the course of events—she still had told the earl the truth.

Folding the letter and placing it back in the trunk, Blair returned to Finlay's bedchamber, brushed her hair, and decided to let go of the resentment. She wanted to know that kind of love for her husband, and if it was to happen, she needed to tell him the truth.

If he didn't know how important it was to her that she be

useful, he would never give her the chance.

It was late enough that everyone should be in bed. She didn't bother changing into a gown, because she had to do this before she lost her nerve. She didn't even stop to don slippers before she was navigating the dark hall and descending the steps.

As she pushed in the door, she almost stopped, panicked by the sudden fear Finlay might laugh at her like the men and her father had at her mother that day in the hall. But she had to do this now, before he left.

Finlay looked up from his desk. She averted her gaze and noticed he'd been studying the books again. If she was able to take a peek, she might be able to make a comment and show him how competent she was.

"I thought ye were in bed." His ragged voice traveled over her.

"Nae, I have something I need to tell ye." After sliding fully into the room, she shut the door behind her and moved toward the big wooden desk that made her feel miles away from Finlay.

"Wait." He indicated she should sit as he rose and came around the desk, easing into the chair next to her. "Let me apologize. I didnae want ye to find out the way ye did that I would be leaving. I wanted to tell ye myself."

"Why didnae ye?" She scrutinized the hands she'd folded in her lap, afraid of what he'd say, but then thought herself silly and reinitiated contact.

"I thought we would be alone tonight, and I could tell ye over the meal."

"Why do ye no' want me to go with ye?" Her heart lurched, and she realized she was hurt that he'd want to leave her. Not only did he not trust her with his books, but he didn't have faith in her to be a good ambassador to the king.

He took her hand. "I do want ye to come, but ye cannae.

'Tis no' safe in Oxford. This area is relatively peaceful, but the English are in the midst of a civil war, and 'tis raging on to the south."

She didn't say anything—she was torn between feeling cherished and too sheltered.

"I want ye here, where I ken there are people to take care of ye if something happens to me."

But what if something happened to him? Her pulse quickened. "Why do ye have to go?"

"My father and the king wish it, but I promise I will be there and back quickly. I willnae dally anywhere, because I have ye to come home to." Tugging her hand, he drew her toward him, pulling her out of her seat and into his lap, his arm coiling around her to pin her to his chest. His free hand landed on her thigh. His head nuzzled hers. "I dinnae want to leave ye, and I've got so much here that needs to get done."

Warmth radiated from his hand into her leg, and she shivered at the feeling that began to take bud in her core. "Promise ye will come back to me soon, and I'll promise ye to take care of things here for ye."

"Aye, 'tis a deal." His smile was genuine.

"And before I forget," he continued, "please dinnae go out on the grounds without someone with ye."

"Why?"

"I dinnae ken our neighbors yet, and with this war going on 'tis hard to ken who is friend or foe. I just want to ken you are safe until I return." His brow creased, and she found herself wanting to erase the worry that had settled into his eyes.

She was about to tell him she could manage the estate in his absence, but his head tilted and his lips claimed hers, and she turned her whole body into the embrace. Her chest tightened. The peaks of her breasts became engorged and full, seeking out the friction of his hard muscles. Everything but his touch receded from her mind.

Their tongues met in a clash of need and something more than desire—it was stark and tangible, a feeling of trust and an odd acknowledgement of a new fear…being without each other. It was as if they had to soak up this moment because any time apart was too long, like they wouldn't be able to breathe without each other until they were joined again.

As his tongue swirled around hers, mingling and stealing her senses, Finlay's hand drifted down the soft material of her shift. When he reached the hem of the material, his fingers slipped beneath, and she sighed at the connection, but it wasn't enough.

He broke the kiss.

When she opened her eyes, his gaze immersed in hers. She was captivated by the rapture his dilated hazel eyes promised in their depths.

"I want to be inside ye, wife." His husky words sent need coursing through her, and all she could do was nod that she desired the same.

Without releasing his hold on her, he stood then gently slid her to the floor. Unbelting his plaid, he let it fall, then kicked off his boots and removed the rest of his clothing while she stood and watched the sculpted body that had taught her true pleasure could be had between a man and a woman.

But they were in his study. "We dinnae have a bed."

His grin was slow and mischievous, making gooseflesh rise on her fevered flesh. "'Tis nae need."

"What?" she asked, but his hands were on the material at her waist, pulling up and drawing the shift over her head. He tossed it to the ground. She really had to do something about how careless he was with their clothing.

His mouth was on her neck as his hands closed around her waist, pulling her up and against his body. Their flesh touched, igniting the part of her that didn't give a damn about what was on the floor.

She felt as if she were falling into him until she realized he was sitting back in the chair, pulling her along with him. She was in his lap, but this time nothing separated their skin as it touched so intimately. Prying her legs apart, he let his fingers slide up her thigh and delve up to her apex. One finger moved in circles on the sensitive nub above her slit. She bowed into the touch as his lips came crashing down on hers.

His finger dipped into her slick opening, coaxing that odd mewling sound from her that she couldn't control. He pulled out, slow, once, then in and out again. Then two fingers were inside her, pumping ever so casually as his thumb came up to touch her nub and circle again.

Sensations of pleasure bursting from his attentions, she was about to fall into oblivion when he removed his hand, and she was left wanting while he continued to caress her mouth with his.

Drawing back, she let her heated gaze fall on him. "Please," she whispered.

His smile indicated he knew what she needed, but instead he loosened his grip, and she wanted to cry.

"Put one leg on each side of me." He lifted her with both hands as she swung a leg around to straddle him. He drew her close once again, her wet passage flush to the base of his penis. She was almost eye level with him in this position, but he still had to dip slightly when his lips sought out her neck, closing down on the sensitive flesh and sucking.

She felt the sigh in her throat as she buried her breasts in his chest, seeking more, seeking everything. He bit down, scraping his teeth lightly against the place where her pulse throbbed and heated, then he sucked again, and she moaned aloud.

Hands tightened on her hips, and suddenly he was lifting her. His cock sprung out, and he lowered her slowly onto it, stretching and filling her until she rested in his lap, and he impaled her so deeply she thought it might be too much.

Instead of moving, his hands pinned her on him. His eyes met hers, and what she saw there was a need that must be reflected in her own gaze. Something deep in the core of her heart called out "yes," said that this was where she belonged and her husband owned her in a way no other ever could.

His hips rocked from side to side, and as he moved inside her, the sensitive spot above her opening rubbed against him. Then she was rocking, too, her hips circling his as she held onto his shoulders. The ride pulled her under a tide of desire, making the world blur, and then it went black until colors and sensations burst in her head. Flinging her head back, she inhaled sharply as the ecstasy peaked, and she screamed, "Finlay."

The waves still crashed around her as hands grasped her rear and pulled her closer and closer. He continued to pump into her, and then he was panting and gasping like she had been. His staff throbbed inside her as her channel clenched, milking him and sating them both.

Resting her head on his chest, she was boneless and spent. She hugged him with one arm, while her other hand slid through the dark curls on his chest.

"I've become accustomed to being beside ye at night."

A contented sigh escaped her throat at his heartfelt words. "I dinnae want ye to go."

"I don't want to leave ye, but I promise, 'twill no' be gone too long."

She nodded, but she couldn't shake the apprehension the thought of his absence brought.

# Chapter Twenty-One

Waking in the early dawn hours with Blair in his arms, Finlay claimed her body once more before whispering, "I'll make all due haste."

He pulled her in for a last kiss, before reluctantly letting her go and climbing from the bed. He thought he saw a mist in her eyes as she said, "Be safe."

He smiled and kissed her again before dressing and rushing out the door.

The journey took days and was miserable, he and his brother taking turns throwing barbs at each other. His father questioned him about Blair then his mother with a curiosity that said he was still haunted by the lass who had stolen his heart all those years ago.

The closer they got to Oxford, the direr the situation appeared. Businesses were shuttered, and men hung from ropes on the sides of the roads, some with signs that read *roundheads*, indicating they supported Parliament, and others that said *he chose the king*.

A wall stood around the school, one that had not been

there when he'd been forced to attend. Upon getting closer, he could see ragged men and boys carefully hefting rocks in place to bolster the king's defenses.

"Who goes there?" a guard with dark circles under his eyes shouted as they drew closer.

"Dwight Quinton, the Earl of Middlesbrough, and my sons. I request an audience with King Charles to give him news he would wish to hear."

The guard looked to another, that one nodding his approval, and they were allowed to pass. Inside, bodies were piled high near one edge of the fence, with men digging next to the heap. An unhealthy smell permeated the area. A man with a death mask, one with a long beak to preserve a physician's health, entered a home. Wailing escaped from the inside before the door could be shut.

"The less time we are here, Father, the better. Let's deliver our news and be on our way," Finlay said.

His father bobbed and looked away from the gruesome scenes. They'd heard that the fighting to the south had escalated, but no one had warned them of diseases.

Once they saw the horses stabled, they made their way into the narrow halls of the school, while the priest headed for the chapel. At one time this place had been a torture to him, now King Charles was sequestered here with sick men, overcrowded rooms, and dwindling supplies. The scene was horrible, and he hated that he was bringing even more bad news.

They were guided down the halls to a chamber that boasted an elaborate scrollwork desk and walls lined with old tomes. A large southern-facing window drenched the room in light. Likely, the office had belonged to the chancellor prior to the king's residence.

When they stood before the king, everyone else was shooed from the room. "Ah, Dwight. It is good to see you, old friend."

"I am happy to see you as well, Your Majesty." The men clasped each other on the shoulder and hugged. Years of the king visiting their dinner table came rushing back, along with the time his father had taken them to London to dine with the king.

"Oh, and you have brought two of your sons to see me."

"Yes, Your Majesty, I have."

The door burst in. A flurry of skirts rushed toward the king. Finlay made to block the path and protect him, but recognition dawned just before he stepped in front of the queen.

"Give us a moment, please." Grabbing the king's hand, Henrietta Maria of France pulled her husband into an alcove and whispered something in his ear. They had an animated conversation then embraced tightly. The king nodded to his wife and gave her a kiss. Paying them no heed, she rushed from the room.

It was said Charles and Henrietta were madly in love, and the rumors appeared to be true. It was one of the reasons the Puritans had turned on the king—his wife was Catholic, and they were terrified of her influence on him. That was the reason the couple had chosen to hide the birth of Robbie, since they were raising him Catholic. What a tremendous sacrifice.

Finlay couldn't imagine giving up a child, especially after what he'd gone through as a youth. He felt a kinship to the young man who had accompanied him from Cameron lands, the prince without a proper home.

Returning to his desk, the king gave the earl a brighter smile than he had moments earlier. "So we were talking about sons."

"Yes, Your Majesty. One of them brings news of Scotland. Do you remember Finlay Cameron?"

The king gave him a pleased smile. "Of course I remember him. And did I hear that you recently married?"

"Yes, Your Majesty."

"Who is the lucky lady?" King Charles leaned back in his chair, a broad grin on his face.

"Blair Macnab."

The king's brow tightened. "The Macnab laird's daughter?"

"Yes, Your Majesty."

The king mulled the news. "Good choice, good choice. I approve. You never know what her father is thinking, but I hear he's in poor health and his son has sworn fealty to me. It is good to shore up alliances with the Macnabs."

Finlay bowed, relieved the king was happy with his marriage.

"Let's hear the news. What are our neighbors in the north up to while the people in England throw themselves on each other's blades?"

"I'm afraid it is not good news." Finlay fought to keep his Scottish brogue in check, possibly just from being in these horrid halls where he'd been ridiculed during his most impressionable years.

"I have heard rumors but nothing of real substance, so go on. I am prepared."

"The Puritans are working with the Scottish Parliament to draft a Solemn League and Covenant. The Scottish Parliament plans to ratify it and make it law next month."

The king nodded. He seemed familiar with the treaty.

"The English Parliament has agreed to sign it and help enforce the provisions if the Covenanter clans of Scotland send troops to help support their cause."

A sharp intake of breath greeted his news. "So far, to the north we have been winning. If the Covenanters are successful and send reinforcements to the English Parliament, they could cut off all supplies from that direction." Sitting straighter, Charles folded his arms then pulled at his beard. A tired gaze roamed the room, apparently looking for solutions. "How long do you think we have?"

"After it's signed in Scotland, if my sources are correct, in a couple more weeks the English Parliament will stamp their approval on it. I would say troops could be leaving Scotland as soon as the end of September."

"This news is most distressing but will be useful. When my nephew Rupert returns, we will discuss strategy."

They discussed the war for another hour. Once the sun started dipping low in the sky, the king stood to dismiss them.

After giving the earl an embrace, he shook Thomas's hand then turned to him. "May I speak with you alone, Mr. Cameron?"

"Yes, Your Majesty." Shock registered on his brother's face, but Finlay couldn't blame him. He was just as stunned the king asked for an audience with the bastard son of an earl.

Finlay waited as they shuffled from the room. His father looked back over his shoulder. "We'll be retrieving the horses."

Finlay gave the king his full attention.

"Please, sit," King Charles instructed, and he obeyed. "I would like to pen a letter to your laird. Please assure me it will arrive to him safe and unopened."

"Yes, Your Majesty. I will make it my priority. I must stop in Middlesbrough to retrieve my wife and a group of Cameron men who need to return to Scotland as well. The letter will be safe in numbers."

"You may do so, but do not tarry too long. The Lochiel *must* receive this message." He'd never heard anyone in England address Lachlan by the same title the people of the Cameron clan did.

The king pulled out a sheet of paper and went to work. While he sat, keeping his eyes averted from the message, he wondered if the king knew his son was one of the men at Catriona House. He assumed, based on the queen's visit and the king's subsequent show of pride, the priest had shared the news.

After sealing the letter, Charles stood. "Do not tell anyone you have this. It is best kept secret."

"Yes, Your Majesty. I swear to deliver the message, and not another soul will ken it exists."

"Good. You may go, and may God be with you."

"And also with you, Your Majesty."

Finlay bowed and left the room, understanding the King of England had a common bond with his laird from the Highlands of Scotland because of a young man they both cared for, but whose very existence could destroy the monarchy.

• • •

Blair blotted at her eyes. At first she'd tried to stop herself, thinking it was an invasion of privacy, but with the thought of facing the lonely bed without her husband, she found herself reading another one of Catriona's letters to Dwight, glass of wine in hand. They seemed to have been kept in the trunk in stacks by year order and then the oldest on top.

Tonight's letter had her imagining what it had been like for her husband's mother.

*My dearest Dwight,*

*Ye have a son. I have named him Finlay, and he shall bear the name Cameron because he is one of my clan. He has yer eyes and smile. Ken that he is healthy and well taken care of.*

*Nae, I willnae come to England. It would break my heart to join ye only to be looking in on something my son and I cannae have with ye. Please understand why I must stay here and guard my heart. If ye choose, I will let ye see yer son whenever ye wish.*

*Always,*
*Catriona*

It became her nightly ritual—each evening climbing the stairs with a glass of wine to read one bundle of letters. The only thing that changed was that she carried them into the master bedchamber to feel close to Finlay.

*My dearest Dwight,*

*It broke my heart to let ye and Finlay both go this time, but I think ye are right. He does need both of us. It would be selfish for me to always keep him here.*

*Please take good care of him and write to let me ken how he is and if yer other sons play with him.*

*Always,*
*Catriona*

Years of letters went by in the evenings, but it was a week and a half before she read the letter that had her jumping up, nearly spilling her wine, and running for the study.

*My dearest Dwight,*

*Upon his return, Finlay told me about all the wonderful things ye did together. He also said that his brothers played a cruel trick on him. They sent him on a hunt but wrote the message in code to purposely confuse him. Are they aware that he has a problem with reading, and those tasks are harder for him than most?*

*I missed seeing ye this time and was sad to hear ye had been detained on business. Please ken ye are never far from my thoughts.*

*Always,*
*Catriona*

Once she'd pulled open the book, she saw it right away. The words she had believed to be an unknown language were actually substitutions for letters that should have been there.

His brothers—the arses—were trying to destroy Finlay's chance to make this estate profitable. How could brothers be so cruel?

Over the next week, she worked to decipher the code and rewrote the figures into another journal. It was a painstaking process that had her eyes blurring so much by the time she made it up the stairs, she could almost resist reading the letters.

Almost.

*My dearest Dwight,*

*I thought of ye today as I walked through the lavender on my way to our special spot. I'm reliving old memories now that business keeps ye from coming to visit us. I go there when something is troubling me. Usually, the memory of our special times wipes away any worries, but today that was no' the case.*

*Our son has become distant. I believe sending him to Oxford was a mistake. Each time he comes home 'tis becoming more apparent that something or someone there is hurting him, and the thought of sending him back steals my breath.*

*He respects ye and only continues at the university to please ye. I havenae ever asked anything of ye, but I do ask that ye try to ease whatever is paining him.*

*Please,*
*Catriona*

Tears stung her eyes as she folded the last letter of that bundle and put it away.

• • •

The next day, Blair sat at Finlay's desk, new journals in hand, putting the accounts into her own words, using the method she had used back home to carefully track every coin as it came and went from the estate. It was a tedious task, like solving a puzzle. She dove into the task with a fervor similar to that of a woodpecker carving out its home in a tree or looking for its next meal.

A light rapping sounded at the door. She glanced up to see Jenny peeking in from the hall.

"Pardon, my lady, but ye have a guest."

"Aye, send him in." She was expecting a man to speak with her about the cultivation of the fields behind the estate and how best to use them.

"Oh no, my lady, it's your sister-in-law, Prudence Quinton. Caldwell's wife."

"Och, show her in then." Standing and leaving her work, she straightened out her skirts as the door swung in.

A girl close to her age, wearing a muted gray gown of a Puritan, strode into the room. No one had told her that Finlay's brother had married a Protestant. Blair tensed at first but then relaxed at the prospect of having a sister of a different faith. The world might be a better place if everyone took such a view.

"'Tis so nice to meet ye. I'm Blair."

"I am pleased to make your acquaintance and was happy to hear Finlay had found a wife." Prudence's dark hair was pulled up in a severe fashion that stretched her cheeks and made her appear older than she was.

"Jenny, will ye have some refreshments brought, please? We can take them out on the terrace since 'tis so lovely out."

"Yes, my lady." The housekeeper rushed from the room.

Blair moved closer to Prudence and considered embracing her new sister, but she thought better of it. Protocol in England for greeting someone you'd just met might be different, and she had ink stains all over her hands. Still, she'd never had a sister and wanted the lass to like her. She missed her talks with Kirstie—she would have her friend to return to on Cameron lands, but it was nice to know she might have a companion in England as well.

Holding her palms up, she apologized, "I'm so sorry. Do ye mind? I'll go wash off and come back straight away."

"Oh, one of the great pleasures in life is being able to write. I can wait right here."

The comment put her at ease. The lass's smile was infectious, despite her reserved appearance. Prudence sat, smiling, her dark eyes enthusiastic as if she was happy to be here. Blair already liked Caldwell's wife.

After hurrying from the room, Blair washed quickly and returned to find her new sister standing over the desk, inspecting the books. *Och*, maybe they had even more in common. "Does Finlay let ye manage the accounts? Caldwell is so guarded with ours."

Her cheeks turned hot. "Well, he doesnae ken I've been working on them, but I'll tell him when he returns. I used to manage my father's accounts."

"It is astounding that a man would turn over his control. You must be good with numbers."

Blair thought she heard a hint of censure hidden in the words, and she wondered if it was against Puritan beliefs for women to take interest in such matters. She brushed aside the concern.

"I quite enjoy it. 'Tis like a puzzle waiting to be solved."

"Do you think he'll be angry? I would hate to see my new sister-in-law banished to Scotland. I want you here so I can get to know you." Maybe Prudence was looking forward to having a sister as well. The concern Prudence had for her warmed her heart, but at the same time, brought back the fear Finlay might not want her help.

"Nae, I'm hoping he'll be pleased."

Jenny appeared, tray in hand. "Och, let's sit on the terrace."

Once they'd settled outside, Blair asked, "I havenae met Caldwell yet. What's he like?"

"He never sits still. He's in London but due to come home soon."

"I'm sure ye miss him. I cannae wait for my husband to return."

"I was visiting my sister in the village when I heard Finlay was back. I rushed over, but to my surprise, he'd already left and I have more family." Prudence laughed. It was a lovely sound. Any suspicions the woman before her was involved in Finlay's brothers' attempt to sabotage her husband fled. Prudence seemed like most typical married women she'd met, uninterested in men's affairs.

"He'll be back soon. Mayhap we can have ye and Caldwell over for a visit."

"I'd like that. We will have you over, too."

They spent the next hour with Prudence offering her gossip on the locals and teaching her more about Finlay's family, until the clouds turned darker.

"I must be on my way. It's a long ride, and I'd like to not be caught out in a storm."

"I agree, but I'm so thankful ye stopped by. 'Tis nice to have someone to call sister."

"I'm pleased that I did, and I am so happy for Finlay that he found a woman as kind as you."

She hugged Prudence, not caring about decorum. After all, she was family, and this had been a bright spot in her tedious tasks of cleaning and working on books.

After the lass had departed, her other guest arrived, and it was hours before she settled back at the desk to continue sorting out the mess Finlay's estate manager had made of the books. Although she now felt pangs of doubt that Finlay would be pleased with her work on the accounts, she was proud of the plans that had been discussed with her second guest. And now she had a friend, a sister. The only thing she still needed was for her husband to come home.

• • •

Finlay had been gone two weeks, and while Blair's days were spent repairing some area of the house or deciphering the journal, her evenings still found her climbing the stairs, glass in hand, to their room alone. Picking up the last bundle of letters, she was surprised to see the weight of the paper was different, thicker, and smoother.

The first one showed her why.

*Catriona, my love,*

*I miss you, I miss your letters. I'm sorry. You know I have our son's best interest at heart. His education will be what prepares him for independence and the ability to provide for his family in the future. I want him to be able to have the choices we did not.*

*My biggest regret in life is that I didn't throw away this damned title and come to you. If there had been someone to take my place I would have.*

*Still, after all these years, I go on loving you,*
*Dwight*

The rest of the letters were from the earl, and all spoke of his undying love. They all remained unsent, and the words tugged at her heart.

*But the letter that hit her the hardest was the last one.*

*Catriona, my love,*

*My wife went to God last week. I am released from my obligation, and all I want to do is pass on my title and run to you, but I fear you gave up on me long ago. It has been torture these last few years not hearing from you. I never told you, because I knew you wouldn't come, I built a house for you, for us.*

*When my heart has ached to be near you, I sit on the balcony and look out upon the fields of lavender I planted to make it feel like home for you.*

*Our son is a grown man who now needs to make a life of his own, and I'm an old man who needs to stop believing that hope exists where there is none. I will give the house to him soon because the ache grows deeper still, but maybe he can make a life and be happy here.*

*Still, after all these years, I go on loving you,*
*Dwight*

Sobbing, she folded the letters and returned them to the trunk. She now felt an obligation to her husband to right the wrongs done him and a new duty to this house, to make it the home it was meant to be.

She slept peacefully for the first time since her husband had left, knowing that by the time Finlay returned, she would have solved his problem and proven her worth.

# Chapter Twenty-Two

The sun was high on a hot, cloudless day, but even the heat couldn't dampen Finlay's mood as Catriona House came into view. Each time he'd seen it before he was filled with dread, but now his wife was in that house. He'd missed falling asleep next to her and waking to the feel of her petite, lithe body next to his.

The journey to Oxford and back had taken almost three weeks instead of the two projected. Days of rain on the return journey, along with the nun who had insisted she accompany the priest back to his lands, had brought one delay after another, but soon he would be home. Unfortunately, they would have to leave immediately to deliver the king's message to Lachlan.

He smiled when he thought of what he'd always considered his true home, the Highlands. He'd never looked upon England as a place he could grow attached to, but as long as he had Blair with him, it would be home, too. Whether they were in this massive estate or his small cottage on Cameron lands, he could be content.

The gnawing started in his gut as it had for weeks. It was time to discover what was going on with the allowance the earl was giving him. The coin wasn't going to the upkeep of his home, and he'd come to the conclusion, Mr. Gerrick was possibly never coming back and that may be for the best. Finlay committed to finding the error and making Catriona House self-sufficient.

Perhaps he would even ask Blair for her help. It was one of the reasons he'd wed her, because he'd seen over the years how capable she was and had admired how she'd run her father's home. Could he entice her to do the same here without her finding out his secret shame?

Pulling to a stop in front of the estate, he was surprised that two men came to greet them. "My lord, welcome home. I am George, your new stable master. This is Abe. He will be my assistant."

"Welcome," he said as he passed off the reins. The men moved to help the priest, nun, and the large contingent of the king's soldiers who had ridden along to ensure their safety on the trip. Charles had instructed that they only accompany him to Middlesbrough and then see the nun back to Oxford. He'd not gotten a good look at her face beneath the robes—she kept it well hidden—but based on the way she had been guarded, he had a suspicion the woman was no nun at all.

When he turned to face the house, a flurry of cream and pink skirts appeared as Blair rushed toward him. A smile bubbled up as something inside him warmed. He loved that she didn't stand on ceremony and wait for him like a tin soldier like he'd seen his stepmother do for his father. The joy on Blair's face at his return tugged a place in him he didn't know existed.

She ran right into his waiting arms, nearly knocking him back with the force. Scooping Blair up, he breathed her in. The mix of exotic flowers and lavender eased his tired soul and woke parts of him that urged him to carry her up to their chamber and never leave.

"Welcome home, husband." She squeezed her arms around him, paying no heed to the others in the group.

"Aye, wife, 'tis good to see ye." Her grip slipped, but as it did, her hand slid down to grasp onto his.

"When ye didnae show, I started to worry."

"I have brought more guests." He indicated the group.

She bowed her head to the priest and nun.

"This is Sister Margaret. She'll be staying with us a few days. Ye have already met Father Thomas, and these are king's men who have joined us to ensure a safe journey home."

"I'll have Jenny prepare rooms straight away. Please, everyone is welcome in the parlor, I'm sure Andrew can find ye some refreshments."

Threading her hand through his arm, she pulled him toward the house. "I have so much to show ye."

Andrew was waiting at the top of the steps. "Welcome home, my lord."

"Thank ye, Andrew."

Stepping into the foyer, he noticed the changes immediately—the musty smell was gone, the hanging art and surfaces that were previously covered in dust were now polished and shining. Everything smelled of lemon, and there seemed to be a glow about the place that wasn't there before.

Blair whispered a few words to the butler, who guided all of the guests in, while she continued to pull him down the hall toward his study.

His office even smelled of citrus and had been cleaned. It was almost like a new room, but his eyes were drawn to the chair in front of his desk. A smile crept up his cheeks as he remembered his last night in here with his wife.

After shutting the door, he locked it, picked her up, and strode toward the chair. She squeaked but then gave a giggle.

His lips were already on hers before he was fully seated, enjoying the honey sweetness of her tongue as she arched into him. Her laughter melted into a content sigh.

Pulling back, he rested his forehead on hers while he caught his breath. "What did ye want to show me?"

She blinked as if he'd completely thrown her off course, and the knowledge that he had kissed her senseless made his heart yearn to do it again.

A frantic knock sounded at the door. "Just a moment," he called out as he rose and gently let his wife slide from his body. He groaned as he realized his cock was already hard and hungry for his wife. "We will finish this later."

Taking a step away from temptation, he announced, "Enter."

Robbie rushed into the room, his gaze flying about. "Did the priest come back with ye?"

"Aye."

"Do ye ken where I can find him?"

"In the parlor, but I had Andrew bring him and the guests some refreshments. If ye wish to speak with him in private, ye will have to ask him to join ye in the chapel."

"Did he come alone?"

"Nae, a nun accompanied us on the return."

"Thank ye," he said, bolting from the room as if he didn't confess his sins to the man soon, he'd be pulled into the pits of hell by the devil himself. He suddenly realized why the woman had kept her face hidden, and why so many of the king's men escorted them home—the nun was the queen come to visit her son.

He glanced toward the door Robbie had left ajar in his hasty departure. Another figure appeared. Brodie watched them with a knowing smirk on his face, as if he understood the need for a man and woman to reconnect after a long absence. "Och, I cannae wait to get back to Skye."

"Ye willnae have to wait long. We must leave for Cameron lands within a couple days."

"Why the rush?" Brodie asked.

"I promised my wife we would only be in England for a short time. I fear 'tis time I took her back to meet my mother." It was all true, but he could tell no one of the king's message to his laird. As far he knew, he shouldn't even share the information with Malcolm, the laird's brother.

"Well, ye may be pleased to ken yer roof is fixed, along with other minor repairs that needed to be addressed. The estate is in good shape. Blair also found ye a good man to keep on for an emergency." Pride surged in his heart. This little woman had managed well without him.

"How was yer visit to the king?" the Cameron man prodded as he moved into the room and took the other seat.

"Things are dire there. I fear for his health closed up in that place. There is a sickness spreading around the people. He took the news I brought seriously and will be talking over strategies with his nephew."

"Ah, Prince Rupert. Although he's brilliant, since he sacked Birmingham, even the king's people can't stomach his cruelty."

"Aye, his anger got in the way, and he made a tragic mistake. It may cost Charles this war."

Tristan, Seamus, and Malcolm appeared in the open door. He was happy to see them, but he preferred time alone with Blair.

"Ah, yer back." Malcolm pushed past him to take a seat on the sofa, near the fireplace.

Another area of the room he needed to try out with his wife.

Shaking his head to refocus, he retold the whole story of his time with the king for the rest of the men. While he talked to the men about preparing to leave, Blair kissed him on the cheek and left to ensure their guests had been accommodated.

"Did ye find any signs of trespassers?" Finlay was hoping the feeling they were being watched would disappear after his visit with the king, but the worry still niggled in the back of his head.

"Nae. Nothing while ye were gone, but we kept close watch on Blair. She was never outside on her own," Brodie said.

Andrew called for dinner, and they strolled into the dining room. Blair came in shortly after them, flushed as if she'd been involved with some task, the color on her cheeks reminding him of what she looked like beneath him. He wanted dinner to be over so he could carry her up to their room and alleviate the ache in his cock.

When the other men were engaged in conversation, Blair turned to him. "I'm pleased I'll be able to meet yer mother on our return."

"Aye. She'll probably be angry with me for stealing ye away before she could even meet ye."

"Will she like me?"

"Of course she will. She likes whatever makes me happy."

"Why did she no' come to see yer father after his wife died?"

"I dinnae ken. She stopped speaking about him as I grew older. I had always hoped one day they would find a way to make things work out, but they never did."

"I have to admit that I like it here, but I'm looking forward to seeing yer other home and the Highlands again." Her gaze drifted to the boisterous men at the table. "'Twill be nice to be just ye and me for a while."

His heart burst with pride and a heady feeling that must be pure joy—Blair was what he'd always wanted. A woman who cared for him enough to share both of his worlds. Now, if he could only figure out how to keep this one from drowning in debt.

After the meal, he tried to pull her toward the stairs, but she shook her head and guided him back to the study. "I have to show ye something."

"Nae, it can wait. I cannae." With his grin, he hoped he had enough charm to lead her off course, but she continued to tug him along.

"We have all night. Ye must see this first."

She hurried over to his desk while he stopped and locked the door. No interruptions this time. After opening a drawer, she pulled out two books he'd never seen, along with the journals from the estate manager. He groaned. It was the last thing he wanted to be doing right now.

"Och, put it away, Blair. I dinnae want to look at books tonight. I wish to carry ye upstairs and show ye how much I've missed ye."

"But this is important."

He pushed the books aside then twirled her to face him. "Not now, Blair. Ye shouldn't be looking at these, anyway."

Blair stilled, and her eyes glazed over. *Och*, he'd upset her. "I'm sorry. I'm tired from the journey, and the last thing I'm thinking about are these damn books."

Her head bobbed, but the happiness was gone from her eyes.

He was about to give in and let her show him the books when there was pounding on the door.

"What?" he called out.

Malcolm's voice called from the other side, "Come, quick, the stable is on fire."

• • •

"Stay in the house," Finlay ordered over his shoulder, already running toward the door.

"But," Blair wanted to protest. She followed the men down the hall, stopping only when she'd reached the edge of the kitchen. There was already a large group of men seeing to the fire.

After a few more minutes had passed, one of Jenny's boys ran up, and she asked, "How is it?"

"It's under control, my lady. All the fire is out."

Her shoulders relaxed. She took a step outside and started to hurry across the grounds to the stables.

Tristan came rushing up to her, blocking her path. "Nae. Finlay wants ye back inside."

"But the fire is out."

"Aye, 'tis, but they're inspecting the structure, and he will be in shortly."

Of course he didn't want her to help. She was nothing more to him than her mother had been to her father. A wife to slake his needs and do his bidding. Her insides twisted.

*Nae*, Finlay was different. Perhaps he was truly tired from both the journey and now this fire. She'd give him the night to rest before telling him how important it was she had a role in running the estate.

Reluctantly, she made her way back into the house and moved through the kitchen without her nightly glass of wine. She had her husband to keep her warm tonight. She smiled, thankful that her courses had come again last week and her husband would not be put off by them.

Passing back into the hall, she noticed Finlay's office had gone dark. Although she didn't remember doing so, she must have extinguished the candles before following her husband from the room.

When she reached their chamber, she stripped to her chemise and bare feet, then sat at the dressing table. Removing the pins from her hair, she thought about what he'd said. She had faith he would trust her to manage the estate, and he'd be pleased when he learned she had taken it upon herself to figure out the accounts.

When Finlay finally walked in, a resounding calm washed over her as she waited for him to join her. He sat and took off his boots as he seemed to roll something over in his thoughts. As he slid his shirt over his head, she asked, "Was anyone hurt?"

He paused for a moment as if weighing what to say but then said, "Abe's head was struck, but 'tis all. No one is seriously harmed." Finlay's plaid fell to the floor, where he left it as he moved closer to the bed.

"And the fire is out?"

His hands and knees sank into the bed as he moved toward her.

"Aye." His gaze was filled with desire and longing, a need so stark it called to the deepest feminine part of her. It screamed out *take me.*

Maneuvering onto his bottom next to her, he took her hand in his and brought it up to his mouth. He turned it over and slowly closed his mouth around the point where her pulse beat. Her insides clenched at the unexpected desire that shot through her.

"I cannae wait another minute to hold ye."

His mouth returned to that spot, and he eased her back on the bed. He sucked, and she was arching into the exquisite feel. Fire exploded at her center and called to her, saying she'd been without this man for far too long. Nothing else mattered but letting her husband take her to that place that only he could.

Clutching Finlay's arm, she pulled herself closer to him, seeking his touch and the connection that moved her to her soul when she looked into his hazel eyes.

The part of her that had thought love didn't exist had

been wrong. Surely, the need to never be parted from this man, the one who stole her breath, was love.

Hands grasped her shift, and he pulled. The material tugged beneath her rear, and she rose to let it slide farther. He drew her to sit then shimmied the garment over her head. "Ye dinnae need this when we are in bed together."

As he tossed it to the side, her gaze remained fixed on his taut chest as the material landed somewhere on the ground.

His arm coiled around her waist, and his lips touched on her shoulders. They explored the slope of her neckline, sending waves of desire through her. Did he feel the same way, did she do that to him?

Twisting, she put her hand on his chest and urged him down on the bed, before turning onto her knees and leaning over his chest. Lowering her head, she kissed and licked as the smell of musk and woods and smoke all blended together. His scent called to her senses and drove her onward.

A thrill of approval shot through her when she noticed he'd angled to expose his neck. His mouth was open, waiting for her next move, raptured by her efforts. She trailed her fingers along his bare skin, savoring the feel of his chest rising and falling while she explored the peaks and valleys.

Finlay's hand slid up her thigh to cup her rear and squeeze. The sensations spurred her on. She returned her mouth to his flesh and started inching upward, stretching out on top of him as she moved. Reaching his nape, she kissed, taking her time, enjoying every second of the throaty groan that escaped from her husband's lips.

She slid her teeth across his sensitive flesh and was rewarded as his body arched into hers. A pleased grin broke across her lips. Everything he made her feel, she could do to him, and he liked it as much as she did.

She lavished attention on his neck as she worked her way up to his ear. When her mouth closed around her husband's earlobe, she was pleased with a soft moan that escaped his throat. "I like the noises ye make," she whispered into his ear, her breath warm as the raspy sound left her lips.

"Ye are going to destroy me, lass."

"Do ye like it?"

"Och, yes, but I dinnae think I will be able to control myself much longer. I've gone too much time without ye."

Biting down, her teeth pulled gently as her breasts rubbed against his shoulder. The sensation of flesh on flesh seared her nipples with pleasure, and her chest seemed to become engorged, full and seeking the relief that would come when he plunged into her.

Her husband's hand slid from her rear, down the back of her leg, then around to the inside of her thigh, seeking her wet core and finding it. His finger ran up her slick folds then rested on her sensitive nub, circling while her hips moved into his touch, and she gasped in his ear.

"Och, wife. What ye do to me." Finlay broke all contact, quickly turning and guiding her body farther up the length of the bed. His gaze pinned her—intense, dilated, and hungry for more than just her tentative kisses.

This time, it was his head dipping to her mouth. His lips covered hers, urgent, needy, as his tongue dove in to search out hers, and a hand clasped onto her breast. Her body moved into the touch as if she couldn't get close enough. His fingers kneaded and massaged, then two of them pinched her nipple. Shock at first, then a slight trickle of pain that turned into pleasure as her core throbbed, begging for more. He did it again, and she moaned into his mouth.

His hand skimmed across her rib cage, her waist, then hip until it was at her leg. It slid across her wet, waiting channel, flicked at the sensitive nub at the top, then moved to her other thigh. He relinquished her lips and stared at her with a heated, needy gaze.

He moved again, and he was on his knees between her legs. Instead of thrusting into her, he scooted down and dipped down toward her private area. Panic assailed her.

"What?" She started to say something else, but his hot mouth was on the bud at her center, clasping it and lapping as she inhaled and bucked.

He sucked harder, and she thought she would explode as the tension built, driving her to that place where the world around her disappeared and sensations carried her into oblivion. She was almost there when he pulled away. He stared at her from between her thighs, grinning as she gaped at him.

His eyes grew darker. His fingers returned to her core, one sliding into her while his thumb teased and played at the top of her. She started to fade into the place of ecstasy. A soft cry of "Finlay," might have escaped her lips, but she wasn't sure, and then he drew back again, just before she could fall.

Her husband guided his staff into her waiting passage. As the fullness enveloped her, he wrapped his arm around her to hug her closer. Her head fell back as his rod massaged her insides and his pelvis rocked against her outside.

She broke.

The dam of sensation that had twice been held back crumbled as her insides pulsed and throbbed and robbed her of everything except for the pleasure. Shock waves crashed against every corner of her body as she arched and gave in to the feelings.

Consciousness started to return, and she refocused to see her husband staring down at her, his soul bare, open, raw with emotions.

For her.

She knew then, she loved him. Loved him with her body, loved him with her mind and soul, but most of all, loved him so much that her heart might stop beating in his absence.

He would forever own this piece of her she'd not known she could give, this part of her that wanted to implode with just the knowing.

His thrusts became uneven as his head fell forward. The sweetest of ragged moans escaped from his mouth as his grip tightened. It was beautiful to watch him fall into that same abyss that had claimed her and to know she had done that to him, made him lose himself as she had to the perfection of their joining.

Relaxing, his sleepy, sated gaze roamed from down where they were still joined, then back to her face. It sent shivers of awareness and vulnerability spiraling through her. She'd never let anyone close enough to see her deepest yearnings before, and it terrified her that he could lead her to hell and she would follow, that she had opened herself up to hurt. But Finlay was worth it.

Sinking, his lips came down to caress hers gently, moving slow, one kiss, then two, three, then his tongue swept in to claim her. She returned the embrace, not caring he could be her undoing, welcoming it and matching each stroke. She tilted her head to get closer and sighed into his mouth.

A few moments later, she lay snuggled in his arms, breathing in the earthy male scent of him. Her bleary eyes finding it hard to stay open, she had one thought—tomorrow, she would show him the books and prove to him that he needed her as much as she did him.

# Chapter Twenty-Three

Waking with Blair in his arms, Finlay realized just how much he had missed her. Somehow, she had become everything to him.

Blair was his salvation.

First, he'd never felt so close to a woman, and she seemed to be accepting of his quiet, reserved nature. But she'd also found a way to give him hope, making him feel worthy of her affections, despite his deficiency.

Looking over at her now, he couldn't believe he'd been the one lucky enough to marry her. He was almost waiting for God to send a messenger that said, no, there was a mistake, he did not deserve her. But if that happened, he'd make a deal with the devil to keep her.

After slipping quietly from the bed, he pulled on his clothes and sneaked out the door, careful to keep it from clicking as he tiptoed out into the hall. He wound down the hall and stairs to his office. Once there, he discovered his account books were missing. He'd hoped to glance over them with a clear head this morning before heading out to survey the damage to the stable in the daylight.

At first glance, he thought perhaps Blair had put them back in the drawer, but when he opened it, there was an empty space where the books should have been. Maybe Andrew had shelved them somewhere. He'd ask the servant after he met with the Cameron men about the events of last night.

Stopping in the kitchens for a bite, he was pleased to see a well-stocked pantry. The cook even smiled and didn't make a fuss when he took from the food prepared to put out on the side table in the breakfast room. With the fresh supplies, the man's cooking had improved.

Stepping out into the early morning air, he took in the eerie fog that had settled with the thick mist blanketing the path like smoke searching out someone to strangle. He shivered but moved on to his target.

The stables were a good hundred yards to the west of the property, and he could barely make it out with the haze hovering like a low cloud. As he got closer, voices carried to him through the stagnant air despite the lack of a breeze.

Tristan and Malcolm were waiting as he stepped through the door. The smell of charred wood clung to the insides. A brutal reminder of last night's events. There was no sign of the injured stable master, so he asked, "Is the man awake yet?"

"Aye, he'll be here any moment," Tristan said. "I'm going to take a look around outside." The Cameron man swiveled and strode out of the stable.

Finlay inspected the damage—luckily one of the housekeeper's boys had seen smoke and had run for help. But all the lad had been able to tell them was that the stable was on fire. He'd seen nothing else, and the man they'd found on the ground passed out the night before had a large bump on his head.

Fortunately, the rain from the previous week had kept everything moist, and there had been sufficient buckets filled with water to douse the flames. Had the boy not been here, the structure would have been destroyed, and the stable master would have perished in the flames.

Abe, the injured man, slogged in.

"How is yer head?" Finlay stepped forward to inspect the damage. Last night there had been too much blood to make out the extent of the wound.

"It will be all right, my lord. Just needs time to heal."

"Tell us what happened."

"I caught a man slinking around out here. Seemed to know his way around. I saw him pull out a spyglass to watch the house. Likely, he didn't know you had full-time help now."

Finlay tried to think what was on this side of the house—his study, the dining room, the parlor.

"I yelled out 'hey'. Calm as you please, he walked up to me and asked if I'd see the lady or lord of the house this evening. He looked familiar, but I couldn't place him. Tall man, stiff, too, like a wooden soldier. I told him it was not proper calling hours, that he should leave and come back tomorrow when it was… And the next thing I remember, I was on the ground, your man pulling me from the building." He pointed to Malcolm.

"What did he look like?"

"It was already dark. I couldn't see well."

He'd banished thoughts of the attempts on his life when he'd become convinced his wife was innocent—he had brushed them off as unlucky coincidences. But the disregard of Abe's well-being and that of the horses brought back the fears there was something sinister behind the rock in his saddle and the arrow in the marketplace. Hell, if someone had followed him from Scotland to prevent him from speaking to the king, the man surely knew he was too late. His message was already delivered, so that made no sense, and this didn't appear to be an attack on him like the others had.

Tristan rushed in, out of breath and holding his side. "I've found something in the woods ye must see."

· · ·

Finlay was gone when Blair woke. She dressed quickly but carefully in the new pale lavender gown the seamstress had fitted perfectly to her curves. Not waiting on her new lady's maid to arrive, she pulled her hair into what she hoped passed as fashionable and finished it off with two matching ribbons.

Rushing into the breakfast room, she found it empty, but food had been piled high on the side table and remained untouched as if she were the first one up. She stopped in the study, but Finlay wasn't in there, either. He must have been through here, because the account books appeared to have been put away. Surely her husband would eat something before starting his day, so she headed for the kitchens.

"Have ye seen Finlay?" she asked the cook.

"Yes, my lady. He left about a quarter of an hour ago." He pointed out the back door toward the gardens.

Tramping on the still wet ground, she hurried to the entrance of the garden. She'd not been out on the grounds without one of the Cameron men accompanying her until now, so she reveled in the peace of the birds singing and the beauty of the rising sun. Shrubbery blocked the view in several directions, and she smiled as she envisioned the plans Tristan and the new gardener had designed to make a maze. She could just see herself chasing their children down the paths or even better, Finlay looking for her to carry her off to what would be a private bench in the center.

There was no sign of her husband, but when she slogged into the heart of the overgrown mess, movement caught her eye. Maybe there were deer living in the tangled brush. As she got closer, an echo of a twig breaking reached her ears, and she hesitated. Something didn't feel right, like she was being stalked by some wild animal.

A scream from the direction of the house rent the thick morning air. *Jenny.*

While pivoting, her hair got stuck in a bush, and when she moved, it yanked at the tresses. She rubbed her head as she ran back toward the kitchens.

The housekeeper was standing just outside on the steps, barking orders at someone in the kitchen, while her youngest son sat crying and holding his hand. Blood was everywhere, and dizziness assailed her. Fighting the wave, she determined she would not faint this time.

"What happened?" Blair asked.

"He cut his finger."

Kneeling down, she inspected the gash, a spot in between the child's thumb and pointer finger.

The cook showed up with a clean cloth to wrap it. "We need to get him to the village healer."

"I'll go with ye," Blair said. "Ye may need some help."

Jenny nodded, and moments later, they were in the stables, mounting horses for the short journey to the village. On a nice day, you could walk the distance, but time was important.

One of the new men was alone in the stables. He had a gash on his temple.

"Abe. Did ye hit yer head last night?"

"Yes, my lady," the man answered as he wobbled on his feet. Maybe the damage from the fire was worse than she'd expected.

"Ye should go get some rest until it heals. I release ye from yer duties for the day."

Abe helped hand the boy up to his mother. "Yes, my lady. I am not at my best. The master was here, and he just told me the same."

She thought she'd caught a glimpse of a group of men walking into the woods, but there was no time to find Finlay now. Hopefully the cook would let him know she'd gone to help Jenny.

In no time, they were in the village stables and she was helping the boy into Jenny's arms. They hurried down the street to the house of the village physician. The healer was able to see to the lad straight away, and it wasn't long before both boy and mom had calmed.

"We'll be all right now, my lady, if you wish to go back." Jenny held her son's hand as he lay on a bed, his eyes slowly shutting. The housekeeper settled into the nearby seat as if she were suddenly exhausted.

"Aye, if yer certain. I'm sure yer other boys and Andrew will want to ken how he's doing. I'll go reassure them."

Stepping out into the day and shutting the door behind her, she glanced up to see a dirty, disheveled man with crazed, angry eyes descending on her. Bruce Graham. Her breath caught. Pure menace stared back at her. It was the same kind of anger she'd seen in Henry as he beat her. Her belly knotted, and fear invaded her chest.

Turning the knob, she tried to push back into the healer's house, but Bruce grabbed her wrist and twisted back. He held on with a grip so tight she wanted to cry out in pain. His other hand pushed at her opposite shoulder, backing her to the door frame and pinning her.

"Ye have made me very angry, Blair. It's been impossible to get to ye with all those Cameron men about. They didnae leave ye alone for a minute."

"Let go," she screamed. She tried to pull free, but he used the whole of his weight to restrain her.

"Ye will be coming back to Scotland with me."

"Ye have nae claim on me. I'm married."

"No' for long. And I dinnae care. I cannae go home

without ye."

"What do ye mean?"

"What I didnae tell ye before is that the Grahams have exiled me. The only way I can go back is with a way to help their cause. Ye are the key to me getting my life back."

Fear snaked its way into her heart, so deep she felt it crash into the pit of her stomach. Was he desperate enough to kill Finlay?

The door swung in, and she stumbled back. It was Jenny with a large, club-like object in her hand. As the housekeeper came down on Bruce's head with it, his grasp on her wavered, and she was able to escape his hold. He staggered then stretched for her, but she'd just made it out of his reach.

"Run, my lady. Get help," Jenny ordered as she jumped in between Bruce and her, holding the staff up, ready to strike. "Go," she yelled.

Dashing back to the stables, Blair didn't look behind her until she was guiding her horse out. Bruce was headed straight for her on foot. He probably had a horse around here as well, so she dug in her heels and urged the mare to move at a fast gallop from the village back to Catriona House.

Almost there, she looked over her shoulder to see the toad had found his horse and was giving chase. She picked up the pace to a sprint. When she arrived at the estate, she was so petrified, she didn't even go to the stables, just stopped the mare in front of the house, dismounted, and ran inside.

There was no one about.

She bolted through, checking the parlor, the breakfast room, the study. Even the kitchen was empty. Grabbing a knife, she ran up to her bedchamber to see if Finlay was inside and heard a door slam downstairs. She couldn't be sure it wasn't Bruce following her into the house, so she locked the door and sat at the back of the bed, knife ready, just in case.

# Chapter Twenty-Four

Finlay followed Malcolm and Tristan as they took him on a twisting path from the stables, into the woods, and then toward the back of the house where the lavender fields began.

"Someone's been living back here," Tristan said. "I cannae believe I didnae find it earlier with all the work I've done on the grounds, but 'tis hidden well."

"What's hidden?"

"A makeshift camp. Someone's been watching yer house. More specifically, yer wife." Tristan swallowed. "There is a journal of sorts."

Tingles erupted under his skin. Who would be watching his wife, and why? Hell, he'd left her alone with some blackguard camped right outside his house.

When they reached the spot, he was astounded by the bravado of the unknown person. A plaid was draped across sticks that had been cut and formed into a makeshift tent. When he pulled back the fabric, he saw scraps of food that had been carefully wrapped in bundles, along with a spyglass and some sort of sketchbook. It took a moment to make the letters come into focus. The name Bruce Graham was inscribed on the front.

His fingers clenched into a fist. The arse who had abandoned his kin in a time of need and tried to force Blair into marriage. Bruce had been the one to follow them, which would have been easy for the man to do with his tracking skills. And that day they'd walked the estate to check for threats, this camp hadn't been here. Finlay was certain of it.

After stooping down to retrieve the book, he thumbed to the first page and froze—a charcoal drawing of his wife in front of a tapestry he'd seen at the Macnab castle. Flipping the page, he gagged when he saw an image of Blair clad only in her shift. Chill bumps gave way to anger.

In the image, Blair had been standing on the balcony, her hair blowing in the wind as she appeared to stare out at the fields of lavender.

His hands fisted on the pad, and he flipped to the next page. Another image of Blair, this time as if she were standing right here in front of him, watching him with those soulful eyes. His hands started to shake.

One more flick of a page and fury clenched like a vise in his chest—Blair nude, lying on a bed, staring up at the artist in invitation as if it had really happened, like the other pictures were rooted in fact.

Tristan held a small bundle up for his view. The man unwound a string holding the corners together, and stones fell from the fabric. They were identical in size and shape to the one that had been placed under his saddle on the journey here. Tristan turned over the material and held it out for Finlay's inspection. It took him a moment to recognize the scrap of cloth through the red haze in his vision.

It was a kerchief depicting the coronation of King Charles—he'd never seen it, but the name embroidered into the bottom right corner stilled his breath...Blair Macnab.

Until recently, a lady would have given it to her knight as a favor during a jousting tournament. Why did Bruce Graham possess something so personal that clearly belonged to his wife? Had Blair given it to him? He'd seen her with it in Edinburgh.

His heart closed in on itself. Bile rose in his throat. Tossing the book aside, he glanced at his men. "I've seen enough. I need to find my wife."

Stepping back out into the air, he turned to Tristan and said, "Put a guard on this place. We need to catch him."

A commotion toward the road drew their attention. A carriage veered into the long drive toward the house—his father's. He wasn't up for visitors right now. He needed to find his wife to squash the doubt the discovery on his grounds had sparked. Blair was innocent—he was certain—but damn if it didn't look like she had intimate knowledge of Bruce Graham.

He marched toward the front, and Malcolm followed. A *whizz* sounded just before pain exploded on his arm. Crimson liquid dripped from just below his shoulder, his white shirt soaking up what didn't ooze to the ground.

"I've been shot. Duck."

Malcolm did, but Brodie took off running in the direction of the threat. He'd only suffered a minor wound, so Finlay gave chase, following the Cameron man's lead. When they got to the front of the house where the shot had come from, the only animal there was Blair's horse. Shaking his head, Brodie glanced over at him. "Is that one yer wife's?"

Had she tried to kill him? He'd become complacent, spending all his energy on getting his message to the king and ignoring the threats to himself. Still, he had been convinced she wouldn't harm him.

His father's carriage pulled to a stop in front of them. After jumping out, his father ran toward him and yelled,

"What happened?"

Brodie called, "Finlay's been shot."

"Best we get inside. We dinnae ken where it came from."

Both of his brothers and Prudence alighted from the carriage, and he wanted to groan at how this day had gone from perfect to absolute hell.

Everyone filed into the house in front of him as he slammed the door.

• • •

After what felt like an hour of no movement or noise from the hall, Blair decided it was time to find her husband. She set her knife down on the bed as she switched into a gown without Jenny's young son's blood on the sleeve. It had only been a small amount, but the sight of it unnerved her.

Once finished, she inched toward the door and listened. As she cracked it open, silence met her, but the house's walls were thick and sounds rarely carried into the halls. Still, she had to find Finlay to let him know Bruce had come looking for her and that he might be in danger. She knew for certain this time—the toad's presence was real, and so was the threat he posed.

Sneaking down the back steps and avoiding the front of the house, she crept quietly through the back hall. She stuck to the shadows as she made her way to the chapel, because it was likely the last place Bruce would dare step foot, and perhaps the Cameron men or the king's guards were in.

Skirting in through the door, she realized she'd left her knife, her only protection, on the bed.

She found no one in the chapel and nothing she could use as a weapon. She glanced out the window to see Robbie talking and laughing with the nun who had come back from Oxford. Although flanked by guards, the pair strolled down a path on the secluded side of the house. It was odd to see them so at ease with each other, almost like they had known each other before. If they'd been nearer, she would have called out for help, but they were too far away.

She sneaked back out and went in search of Finlay.

• • •

Andrew had patched Finlay's shoulder, but no one had seen his wife or the housekeeper. The cook said something about the woman's son cutting his hand and the pair of them rushing to take the lad to the village healer. But if Blair was still in town, why was her horse here? His stomach was tied in knots, and he didn't know whether to be worried for her or if she was the cause of his current condition.

After setting up a round of guards to watch the house for her return, he tried their room. When he flung open the door, it crashed into the wall. Bits of plaster splintered and gave off a *clunk* as they hit the floor.

No sign of her. He hurried through the dressing area, the other room, then the nursery, but all were empty. Fear started to take root. According to Brodie, while Finlay was in Oxford, Blair barely left the house, preferring to stay in his study and analyze his books. Perhaps she wasn't in league with Bruce.

He rushed back into their chamber and caught sight of the bed. He'd believed there was hope for a bright future with a wife who wanted to be with him. He'd even dared to think she might care for him.

*Och*, he wanted to go back to that moment, forget everything he had learned today. He wished to cling to her and run away, relive the happiest moment of his life over and over again.

But could it have been a lie?

The sun darted from behind a cloud and flooded the room with light. Something on the bed, almost under Blair's pillow, caught his eye. Inching forward, he leaned down to inspect the object. *A knife.* His whole body went numb.

Had she planned to kill him in his sleep? If she was planning on killing him, he was lucky she'd not done it sooner. Had she conspired with Bruce Graham, the man who drew intimate pictures of her? Despite the evidence, he was having a hard time believing her capable of the betrayal.

As he stared at the dagger, he staggered into his study, anger and fear taking hold as his arm pulsed with pain. He pushed the door closed without waiting for the *click*.

# Chapter Twenty-Five

Blair heard raised voices coming from the study. She recognized Finlay's and was about to fling open the door and run into his arms, when she heard, "Bruce Graham," barked through the air. Her heart skittered, and she froze. Then came the words, "I have to ken if my wife is plotting against me."

*What?*

Pressing herself to the wall, she prayed she'd misunderstood. Why would he suspect such a thing? She'd told him everything.

She listened to Finlay's raised voice. "The kerchief had Blair's name on it. I saw her with it in Edinburgh."

The world around her dimmed as if she were under the placid waters of a loch frozen in time. Her ears hummed. Her heart ached, and her breath stopped. She tried to think back to the last time she'd seen her kerchief. It had been the morning Bruce had presented her with his ultimatum. He must have taken it. Tears, hot and wet, raced down her cheeks, but she was too shocked to wipe at them. Her shoulders trembled as fear took hold.

"Perhaps there is another explanation." A voice barely penetrated the haze. Was it Brodie?

"Could she have been in league with the arse the whole time?"

*Nae.* She shook her head. *Nae,* that wasn't true. But how could she prove her innocence, because she'd admitted to Bruce's attempted blackmail.

"She is a traitor. When I came to visit, I caught her rifling through your desk." *Och.* Was that Prudence?

Her world crashed around her. Instead of the jeers of her father's men, she heard the mumbled voices of Finlay's companions.

Everything she'd done to prove she could be more than just a wife had been for nothing. The deepest, darkest part of her swallowed her in a pain so deep her whole body went numb but also ached for what she had lost.

Her sister-in-law's voice cut through her drowning misery. "Why did you marry the heretic?"

Why would the lass say such a thing? They were friends, sisters.

Silence followed, and she was about to burst into the room to defend herself, but Finlay's voice cut through the air. "Because of ye two. The hell I went through as a child because ye couldnae see past that I was yer father's bastard."

No one responded. She felt herself tilting sideways, although her feet remained planted on the ground.

"I married her because a dead man's seed grows in her belly, and I didn't want that child to be treated the way ye treated me."

Her hand fell to her flat abdomen. She wasn't with child. Why would he think such a thing?

Now he thought her a traitor and believed she tricked him into marriage for the sake of a child. Henry's babe. Bile rose to her throat and burned. He could set her aside. Leave her. Break her heart. The rending of something in her chest had her swaying as the world around fell out of focus. Did he not love her in return?

She choked on nothing but air. If Finlay set her aside, her father would chain her to Bruce and send her away with instructions to never let her come back. Her husband would never again hold her in his comforting arms.

Her knees buckled, but before she hit the ground, strong hands caught her waist. She glanced up to see warm, sad, hazel eyes. The Earl of Middlesbrough looked at her with what could have been regret and sorrow. She shook her head and pulled free then picked up her skirts and fled down the hall. She had to find a safe place to think, so she could face this once Finlay had calmed down. There was no use trying to defend herself in a room full of men who all thought her a harlot and traitor.

She just needed to breathe. The lavender fields.

Once she broke out into the yard and sought out the peace of the fragrant flower, she could finally draw air into her lungs again.

Finlay had married her because he'd thought she carried Henry's bairn, which might have been the only thing that saved her from the fate he had planned. But she had no babe in her belly to prevent him from tossing her aside.

She was already branded a traitor. She wasn't. But how could she prove it to men who never believed women and thought of them only as bedmates? And how could she prove to Finlay that he had become the most important part of her life? She could no longer imagine a world without her husband, and it would destroy her if he sent her away.

She continued on toward the lavender until a dark figure stepped from the bushes and stopped her in her tracks.

• • •

Finlay's father cut into the room. He was all earl and commanded everyone's attention without saying a word. He pinned Finlay with a fury he'd not seen since his father confronted his brothers about trying to get him kicked out of Oxford. He'd never thought to see his father that angry again and definitely didn't expect it to be directed at him.

"Do you not have any feelings for your wife?"

Stunned, he didn't know what to say.

"I haven't seen a woman so upset since I told your mother I was pledged to another. She looked like her world had just ended."

His mouth went dry as his pulse quickened. "What are ye talking about?"

"Blair. She was standing outside and heard everything you said." His father pointed a finger at him. "That she was in league with a man named Bruce and that you had married her because she was with someone else's child. Did she know that? Because it didn't appear so."

Coming from his father's lips, it all sounded ridiculous. Blair had become his reason for being, and there was no mistaking the way she'd looked at him last night. She would never have done anything to harm him. The loss of blood and his brother's presence were the only reasons for this madness. She would have a good explanation.

"I have to find Blair." He couldn't let her go on believing she didn't matter to him. She was everything. He bolted for the door.

Rushing past his father, he dashed into the hall and looked both ways. She was gone. Turning back toward the earl, he yelled, "Which way did she go?"

"The kitchens."

Blair was nowhere in sight, so he darted for the door. He

held his hand above his eyes to shield it from the sun as he stumbled down the stairs. About thirty feet away, his wife stood facing Bruce Graham, who was ten feet from her. She was shaking her head and backing toward the house.

Bruce noticed Finlay and ran toward her. "Stop or I'll kill him in front of ye, Blair."

His wife froze. She swiveled to see him there, and he noticed sheer terror in her gaze. The arse made his way toward her as she hesitated.

"My lady, get away from him. I won't let him hurt you again." Jenny appeared from the direction of the stables. She rushed toward Bruce and Blair, a big stick in her hand.

"Stop," Finlay yelled at the housekeeper, holding up a hand.

"That man assaulted her in the village." The housekeeper pointed the club at Bruce.

"Bruce," he called. "She is married to me. If ye go back to Scotland now, I'll forgive yer trespass here." If he reasoned with the man, perhaps he could talk him down. He could sense his family standing behind him, and their presence was reassuring.

"Nae. She'll be coming back with me. I have no home to go back to without her."

Bruce's attention darted between everyone like a caged bird looking for escape. His clothes were dingy, and he'd lost weight and muscle since the last time Finlay had seen him. Desperation from his state of exile must be driving the man. He had to get Blair away.

"Is that why ye set the stables on fire last night? To get to Blair?"

"Nae. That wasnae me. 'Twas her and her friend."

Finlay looked in the direction Bruce pointed.

Prudence? Her gaze darted between everyone as her calm demeanor flipped to that of a rabbit cornered by a dog.

Impossible. She was the most pious woman he knew.

"She was with the tall man. The one who came to see ye on yer first day back."

"Mr. Gerrick?" Finlay assumed the man had left town.

"Aye. If that's his name. I saw him start the fire while the lass snuck into the house."

A scream rent the air when one of the new servants came out into the yard. His attention was pulled that way for only a second, but when he refocused on Bruce Graham, the man wore a wicked grin and had a pistol aimed at his heart.

# Chapter Twenty-Six

"Stay away from my wife. Harming me will only see ye to the dungeons," Finlay said calmly as the Cameron men joined Finlay's family in the yard. Brodie, Tristan, and Malcolm all pulled sheaths from their backs, readying their claymores in her husband's defense.

Bruce's jaw tightened as his hand on the trigger appeared to tense.

Although he didn't have his sword, Finlay looked like he was ready to charge. At least he was still calling her his wife.

"She will be going back to Scotland with me. She was supposed to marry me."

"What makes ye think that?"

"Because I need her. The Grahams willnae take me back if I cannae prove useful." Bruce reached for Blair, but she moved away, keeping just enough distance that his clammy hands couldn't wrap around her.

"Ye cannae have her."

All the men followed Finlay's advance, apparently undaunted by the pistol aimed at her husband.

"Halt." Bruce waved the gun to both sides, his hand steady as if unfazed by being outnumbered. When they continued to inch forward, he turned the gun toward her, and the men stopped. Sweat dripped down his brow. A breeze blew, and she caught a whiff of something like burnt paper, giving her the impression he'd fired the gun recently. If she'd only held onto that knife, she could drive it into Bruce's cold heart.

Bruce Graham was either going to kill her or her husband. It couldn't end any other way.

She was faced with a decision—either take the bullet and save her husband, the man who thought her a traitor, or let him kill Finlay.

There was no choice. Regretting that it would be the only time she'd ever be given the chance to do so, she mouthed the words etched on her heart and hoped Finlay could see she meant them with all of her being.

Rounding on Bruce, she threw her hands into his arm to force him to aim it toward the sky. She thought she heard Finlay scream something, but her head jerked back, and a loud noise rang in her ear, stunning her.

Bruce stopped struggling. He let go of her and gaped.

Red liquid streamed down her face, covering her eye and cheek, then she felt as if the world were tilting.

. . .

Fear gripped Finlay, holding him in a state of icy paralysis as Bruce aimed the weapon at Blair's head. Time stood still, and years ticked off his life. His wife stood taller, then stilled, looked at him, and mouthed, "I love ye."

His heart dropped into the depths of his belly.

"Nae." The word escaped his mouth, but he was already running. Covering the impossible distance in the blink of an eye, but also so slowly he thought the world would end before he could reach her.

He was halfway there when he heard a *bang* so deafening his ears rang. His wife fell to the ground just before he plowed into the arse and knocked him to the earth.

When he pivoted and rushed to kneel beside Blair, the Cameron men pinned Bruce to the ground and divested him of any weapons.

Finlay took her head in his lap as blood poured from her wound. Her eyes were closed, and her body lay limp. *Nae. Nae.* His gut twisted as he fought back the nausea. *Och,* God, nae, he couldn't lose her. And he had to tell her he was sorry, and that he'd not meant any of the things that he'd blurted out in his study.

She'd said she loved him. How had he ever doubted her? She couldn't be gone, but her body was lifeless. And he felt as if he were being ripped in two as his heart struggled to beat.

*"Nae, nae."* His eyes stung, the world around him spinning as his focus centered on the only part of his life that mattered, the woman who had made him finally feel worthy.

He placed his head to her chest. The sound of her breath eluded him, but that could be because his own frantic panting was so loud and painful that he couldn't think. When he lifted her back up, blood stained the front of his shirt.

He had to get help. Had to help her. His gaze shot skyward, praying for anything that would bring his Blair back.

Jenny knelt beside him, tearing the sleeve from her gown. "We have to stop the bleeding," she said. The lass pulled another strip of fabric as he nodded. "Hold her steady."

He cradled the base of her skull as the red liquid continued to pour from the wound near her forehead, soaking into his plaid. With all the blood, there was no way to judge the extent of the damage.

"The physician is in the village. I just came from there.

We need to take her now." The housekeeper tied off the strips.

Just as she did, Blair's eyes fluttered open. Hope flared to life as her eyes started to focus and moved toward him. He was vaguely aware of Jenny shouting at someone to bring him his horse.

His wife gave a small smile, as if to say, good, yer still here. Her eyes closed again. *Nae.* She had to keep them open. He had to know she was all right.

"Blair." She groaned but didn't open them. "Look at me." Her lids slowly rose again as if she were waking, groggy from an early morning dream. "Can ye talk?"

"Aye." But the word was weak and raspy.

"I'm going to stand up with ye now. We have to get ye help."

She dabbed near the injury.

He wanted to tell her to leave it be, but it was good to see her moving.

"Hold her head," he told the housekeeper as he slid his leg out from under her. Carefully cradling his wife, he lifted her in his arms.

Brodie rode up and held out his arms. Finlay gently placed her there as her eyes continued to open and close.

"Stay awake, Blair," he whispered to her as he turned to mount Hedwynn and noticed his father and brothers huddled around Prudence.

Brodie lifted Blair and drew her gently in.

"Thank ye." Finlay started out at a sedate pace, not wanting to rock her head and cause more damage.

But she looked up at him and said, "I'm fine. It's just the blood."

He picked up the pace. "Ye have to be all right. I cannae do this without ye."

A small smile lit her lips, and his heart started back up

again. Her eyes misted. "I amnae with child."

"What?"

"I'm sorry." A tear ran down her cheek. *Nae, nae, nae,* he didn't want to see her cry. "I dinnae have Henry's child in my belly. I never did. I dinnae ken why ye thought so. I never would ha—" She winced as a jolt from the ride shook her.

"Shh, 'tis all right," he said as he slowed the pace. But then his words churned in his head. In anger and confusion, he had said awful things, and she'd overheard all of them. And she'd never told him she was going to have a babe. He'd just assumed it. "I didnae mean those things I said."

"I never would have deceived ye about something like that." Another tear streamed down her cheek and disappeared into the blood. His chest constricted.

"I didnae mean what I said. I would have married ye anyway. Ye are smart and bonny and a Royalist. Ye're all I've ever wanted in a wife." His breath hitched. "I'm so sorry. I didnae mean it. Ye are all I've ever wanted."

And, when they had a child, it would be his babe that grew in her belly. He would have loved their bairn no matter what, but the thought of them sharing the whole experience together made his heart soar.

"That makes me very happy," she said, but she started crying in earnest now, convulsing with the sobs.

"Och, please dinnae cry."

She laughed then. Thank heaven she giggled. Closing her eyes, she snuggled the uninjured side of her head next to his chest.

"We'll talk about all this later. Ye are going to be all right, and we'll have plenty of time to straighten it out." He said it as much to reassure himself as her, but hell, he was worried, not knowing the extent of her injury.

In the village, he pulled to a stop in front of the physician's home to discover Brodie, Jenny, and Malcolm already there.

Once dismounted, with Brodie's help, Finlay entered the small space smelling of medicinals and whisky.

The healer said, "I cannot do my job with you in here. You will have to wait outside."

But Finlay couldn't leave her. What if...oh God, he couldn't even think it. He shook his head.

"I'll be all right." But, Blair didn't open her eyes. The words came out strained as if she was fighting the pain and didn't want him to know it. The healer crossed his arms and glared at him.

"Blair." He wanted to make sure she could hear him.

"Um hum."

"I'll be right outside. Yell for me if ye need me."

Jenny took his hand and pulled him toward the door. "Ye must let the man do his job. She will be fine."

Brodie placed a hand on his back and propelled him forward. Finlay went out reluctantly, and the breath once again disappeared from his chest. Pacing outside, he let everything roll around in his head. It was all he could do while he waited to find out if his wife would survive.

He turned to Brodie. "What happened to Bruce?"

"He has been detained. He willnae harm anyone ever again.

He kept pacing. Trying to think of anything except for what could be happening with his wife in that house.

His mind turned toward the other threat. "Bruce said Prudence was with Mr. Gerrick. My account ledgers were missing after the fire." It couldn't be Prudence. She'd always been so nice to him.

"She came to Catriona House while you were visiting the king. I saw her looking at your books when I brought refreshments in for her and my lady." Jenny closed her eyes and shook her head. "I knew there wasn't something right about that girl."

Brodie chimed in, "I think yer brothers are questioning her now."

Jenny went into the house to check on Blair. When Finlay tried to follow, Brodie stopped him. "I ken 'tis hard, but if ye distract the physician, he may no' be able to help her."

His eyes started to sting then.

"She will be all right. Head wounds bleed a lot, and she seemed coherent, so I dinnae think there is much damage."

He prayed the man was right, but all he could do was nod and keep moving, because if he stopped, his world might end.

# Chapter Twenty-Seven

"Och, it hurts." Gently tapping at the area on her temple, Blair sat up from what felt like hours of torture. The procedure had most likely only been half an hour of prodding and stitching, but it had reminded her of the cat attack in her youth. Thankfully, the physician's wife had been there to talk her through it. She'd even offered her a dram of whisky to alleviate the pain. She'd drunk it, but she wasn't sure it had helped.

"Yes, I imagine it does. You are lucky to be alive." The physician shook his head as he turned and ambled toward the exit after his wife disappeared into another room.

"Is she all right?" Finlay sounded anxious.

"Yes, she just needs a bit of time to heal."

"Can I see her?"

"Yes, you can take her home."

*Och*, but would he want her to go home with him? Her stomach turned, but she wasn't sure if it was from the drink, the injury, or the thought of being sent away.

Hands trembling, she swung her legs off the bed and

started to stand. The physician stepped back, and Finlay rushed to her side. "How are ye feeling?"

"It hurts." That wasn't exactly right, it felt like her head had been split open and throbbed as if someone were jumping on it repeatedly.

"I stitched her. The bullet skimmed her temple. I think it may have also cracked her skull slightly, although there is no way to know. But it looks like no permanent damage was done."

Finlay dabbed just under her wound, scrutinizing it. She imagined it was hard to see with the remnants of the blood that were yet to be washed away and had matted in her hair. *Och*, she must look awful.

She didn't know what to say but was saved by the physician's wife zipping back into the room. "This is a tincture that will help with the pain. Only a spoonful when you need it because it will put you to sleep. I suggest you go home, get cleaned up, use it, then take a nice long nap."

"Thank ye."

The woman held up a second bottle. "This one is a salve to protect the injury spot. Clean the area twice a day and then apply this." Finlay took the vials and inspected them.

Moments later, he scooped her into his arms and carried her through the door. "We need to talk about what happened, but I want ye to get some rest first."

All she could do was nod. Pain and fear mixed in a dizzying wave as they spiraled out of control.

Brodie and Jenny were waiting with the horses. Once Finlay was mounted, Brodie hoisted her up to join her husband.

Laying the uninjured side of her head to his chest, she was relieved that he didn't push her away. An arm coiled around her waist, drawing her closer to him. It was warm and reassuring. She wanted to savor the feel of him while she had the chance, so she remained quiet for the short return ride.

Once back at Catriona House, Finlay carried her to their room. They passed many concerned faces along the way, but he didn't stop. She heard him instruct Jenny to have a bath made for her. Why was he taking such care?

In the room, he sat on the bed without letting go of her. Being in his arms felt so right, but unbearable at the same time. She finally couldn't take it any longer. "Are ye sending me away?" Her eyes stung, but she wasn't going to cry again.

"Nae, ye are no' going anywhere, wife. I may no' let ye out of my sight for years." He placed his lips gently on the uninjured side of her head.

Servants poured in, carrying buckets of water while Finlay continued to hold her.

The door closed behind the servants, and Finlay's hands drifted down, starting to work at the laces on her ruined gown.

"I..." she started to protest.

"We just need to get ye cleaned up. I have to ken how bad it truly is."

Moments later, she was in the tub, and Finlay stepped out onto the balcony as she bathed. Once she was cleaned, she joined him. She sighed as she looked over the fields, the scent and sight of the lavender calming her.

"We have to leave tomorrow," he said, his fists clenched. "I wouldnae ask it of ye, but the king has demanded. Will ye be all right for the journey back to Scotland?"

"I think I will be all right."

He studied her from head to toe. "We will go slow if we need to." His fingers came up to caress just under her injury, the touch sending gentle waves of relaxation over her. "We have to talk about what ye said."

"What did I say?" She struggled to remember.

"Right before ye almost got yerself killed." *Och*, that.

She'd meant it, but now, in such an intimate setting where he could deny her, fear washed over her.

"Did ye mean it?"

"Aye. I wouldnae have said it otherwise. And I thought 'twould be the only time I'd ever get to tell ye."

"Tell me now."

Her heart skittered, and she gulped, ready to confess yet again that she had fallen for her husband. "I love ye." While whispering the words softly, a dam of emotions released. Happiness washed over her at the thought that he wanted to hear her say it.

"Say it again." His breath quickened.

"I love ye." With every part of her soul she meant it.

He drew her in, and his head dipped to her mouth, claiming it in a long, slow, soul-stirring kiss that left no doubt he felt the same. And she realized she had more than she'd ever wanted—a husband who trusted her as a partner, and one who had awoken feelings in her that spoke to her very soul.

Pulling back, his mesmerizing gaze held hers for just a moment, before saying, "And I love ye, wife."

• • •

As they sat down to a meal which had been brought up to their chamber, Finlay cleared his throat. "Is something troubling ye?"

"They are cheating ye."

"Who?"

"Yer brothers."

"What do ye mean?" He took her hand and held it on the table between them.

"Yer account book is written in code. I deciphered it, but when ye get to the numbers, they are all wrong. They kenned numbers and letters were hard for ye and purposely made it almost impossible to decipher. I'm so sorry that they were cruel to ye. Brothers should never do that."

He'd suspected the books had been altered, but now he knew the truth, because he'd had an opportunity to slip down and speak with his father while Blair napped. "'Twas Prudence and Mr. Gerrick." The Cameron men had detained Bruce and her, but he hadn't had an opportunity to question her yet about where the ledgers were.

They were out even now looking for the estate manager. His stomach flipped as he wondered what the pair had been up to and how it had led to assaulting one of his men and setting his stables on fire.

"Why would they do such a thing?"

"I dinnae ken. 'Twas more important that I see to ye. But I'm sure Father and the Camerons have pried answers from her."

"I'm so sorry, but 'tis good news yer brothers were no' behind it."

"Aye." Finlay's thumb caressed the top of Blair's hand.

Then, it dawned on him. She had discovered his secret shame and didn't care—she had not held it against him. A dam broke inside, and his eyes stung. Blair loved him despite his deficiency, and she had done all she could to help him. She wanted to help him.

"Ye paid four times more than ye should have for grain, and I cannae find evidence 'twas ever delivered. There is a charge for repairs to the stable that never happened. Jenny's boys can attest to that." She bit her lip as if she thought he'd be angry with her over the revelations. She kept going. "I sent for the estate manager to have him answer for his deceptions, but he cannae be found. My guess is he never will be, so I reached out to yer father's solicitor. All transactions will now go through me."

"Please forgive me for rushing into that before ye were able to return, but I didnae want the crook to be able to take advantage of ye and ruin Catriona House. I've destroyed his credibility with the villagers. Fortunately, I have found ye still had enough to pay for the repairs we've managed. The good news is not only can ye make this place magnificent again, but it can be profitable."

He wanted to speak, to say thank you, but he was choked with pride and relief.

Blair continued, "Ye have several fields no' in use, and I've contacted a perfume maker about what flowers are in demand. He would be willing to purchase more lavender. If ye are agreeable to the deal, the new gardener has experience in growing some of them, and along with the lavender, ye can turn a profit even higher than the allowance ye receive from Dwight."

How had he found this woman? Not only had she saved him from his solitude, but she had discovered a way to make him independent. Thomas would cut him off when he inherited their father's title, but Finlay had planned to live in Scotland, because he would no longer have ties to England. However, once the earl had given him this place, he'd seen only failure in his future.

Now there was a light, and she had blond hair and blue eyes and made his heart thump with an optimism that had once eluded him.

"Well, say something."

How could he say what he was feeling? How could he tell her she'd given him hope that he'd not had since he was a child? That she had made the world a brighter place for him and that there was more than only duty to a king and a laird. There was love for this woman.

He rose and drew her up to his side, then he kissed her slowly, savoring the feel of her lips. When he pulled back, he said, "Ye are amazing."

"Ye arenae mad at me."

"Nae, never. Ye can manage the books all ye like." Her sapphire eyes sparkled, and he continued, "Thank ye for giving me hope. Something I havenae had for a very long time."

"Thank ye for letting me be yer partner."

# Epilogue

Finlay and Blair sat together behind his large desk going through the account books that had been found among Prudence's belongings. They had been delivered to Catriona House by his brother. His father had sent a letter to Scotland to inform them Prudence and Mr. Gerrick, who had been located shortly after their departure, had been taken into custody by the king. They were to be charged with treason.

Apparently, Prudence had tricked Caldwell into marriage after sleeping with him, then telling him she was carrying his child. Shortly after she lost the baby, now resulting in suspicion as to whether she'd ever been with child. She had schemed to steal the earl's and his sons' fortunes. A Protestant with allegiance to Parliament, she'd seen Finlay's family, staunch Royalists, as an easy way to funnel money to her cause.

When they'd returned to Cameron lands, Finlay had taken Blair to meet his mother, and the two bonded straight away. It was a joy to see his wife happy in both of his worlds. Tristan, Seamus, and Robbie joined them again on this recent journey back to England, Brodie and Alan wishing to stay at home with their wives.

Robbie had returned in hopes of another visit with his family while in England, but upon their arrival, they received word the queen was being forced to flee Oxford. As soon as they had heard, he and the Cameron men had immediately set out for Exeter, the pregnant queen's destination.

Shortly after their arrival, Blair was inspecting the ledgers. She had already set out a plan with his allowance, and preparations for making the estate profitable were well under way.

Andrew knocked at the door and announced, "The Earl of Middlesbrough to see you, my lord."

Jumping up and running for the door, Blair hugged his father when he entered. "Och, I have a surprise for ye. Dinnae go anywhere while I go find it."

"Lovely to see you as well." His father chuckled as his excited wife bounded from the room.

"Father, glad ye were able to make it."

"Bruce Graham has been convicted of attempted murder. He also confessed to planting the rock on your horse. Thankfully, you and Blair will never have to see that man again."

"That is good news."

"I also have disturbing news. The bow you found from the attack in the marketplace did not belong to him. Bruce had spotted your wife, chased her, and then retreated when he saw she'd come back around to you. Are you sure you were the intended target in that attack?"

Thinking back, Finlay remembered who was next to him. "Robbie." He scratched his head. Had someone discovered the lad's identity and tried to murder him? "It must have been meant for Robbie. I'll have to let the Cameron laird ken there is a possible threat."

"I have other news as well."

"Aye?"

"Your brothers will be paying a call on you and Blair tomorrow to offer their apologies. I assure you, we have had some frank discussions lately, and they will be well behaved from now on."

"Thank ye." He'd had a talk with his brothers before returning to Scotland. And although their relationship was still strained, he'd discovered they only stopped talking to him after he'd shut them out. It had happened on that day long ago when his mother-in-law's tutor destroyed his self-esteem. They were most likely unaware of the humiliation that had plagued him for years. He'd only imagined at the time they were jeering at him. "How is Caldwell?"

"He is managing. Prudence passed from the plague that was infiltrating the king's camp at Oxford."

Silence extended a few moments as the earl pursed his lips, and Finlay glanced down at the desk, taking in the news. His heart ached that his brother had not been as lucky in marriage as he.

Taking a deep breath, he said, "I look forward to mending my relationship with my brothers. I think with Blair's help that will happen."

A knock sounded at the door, and Blair peeked her head in. "Are ye ready?"

The earl laughed and shook his head as she inched in from the hall. Before his father could answer, his wife pushed the door wide, stepped aside, and gave his father the first view the earl had had of his mother in years.

Later, after they'd made love and snuggled in for the night, Finlay placed his hand on his wife's expanding belly and gave her a soft kiss on the lips.

"I am the luckiest man in all of Scotland and England."

"I think yer father would disagree with ye right now."

He smiled. The pair had retreated to the drawing room after dinner and had been inseparable. Blair and he had given them their space to get to know each other again.

Smiling, he thought of all his wife had accomplished. Saving him, this house, his parents, and now preparing to bring their child into the world. His fingers traced the scar that ran along her temple, the reminder she had been willing to give her life for his. He would do the same.

The mark was also a reminder that he'd almost lost her. Every morning and night, he kissed it and thanked God she was still with him. He kissed the still pink line. She sighed, nuzzling against him. And he knew that no matter where they were, be it in England or Scotland, she would always be his salvation.

# Acknowledgments

Special thanks to:

Robin Haseltine, for her guidance and diligent attention to detail, her continued faith in me, and all the hard work and time she has dedicated to making the *Highland Pride* series the best it can be. She is a truly gifted editor.

Jessica Watterson, who will drop other things to have wine and cheese with me. She has been my advocate and sounding board. Fate found a way to bring us together, despite my poor choice in footwear, and I will be forever grateful she is my agent.

My best friend, my husband, for his love, support, and for understanding when the story calls and I forget what we're talking about, that I still love him and he will always be my real-life hero.

My kids and my parents, Jo Ann and David Bailey, for encouraging me and being proud of what I do.

Eliza Knight and Madeline Martin, for keeping me motivated and sane. I treasure our special bond and how we support each other every day.

My writing tribe for sharing their enthusiasm, love of the craft, and wisdom along with keeping me motivated and on track. I will always be eternally grateful to: Michele Sandiford, Harper Kincaid, Denny S. Bryce, Jennifer McKeone, Nadine Monaco, Keely Thrall, Gabriel Ross, Jessica Snyder, and everyone in WRWDC.

And as always, for you, the reader, who picked up this book and gave me a chance to share a piece of my heart.

# About the Author

Lori Ann Bailey is a lover of wine, country music, and chocolate. When she was around ten, she dreamed of becoming a country singer. She even penned her own song, but her brothers soon informed her that she didn't possess the vocal range to follow that dream. Eventually, she entered the business world where she worked as an assistant buyer before becoming a stay-at-home mom. In order to meet people when she moved to a new neighborhood, she joined two book clubs.

When she picked up that first book, something unexpected happened. She was hooked. Lori started reading for pleasure, only to discover she'd always had her own private reality dancing in her head. After convincing her husband to purchase a laptop, she began typing the bedtime tales she'd told herself since childhood. Now she writes novels to tell others her stories, just as she had in the song she'd written so many years earlier.

Winner of the National Readers' Choice Award and Holt Medallion for Best First Book and Best Historical, Lori writes hunky Highland heroes and strong-willed independent lasses finding their perfect matches in the Highlands of 17th century Scotland.

She has served two years as the Washington DC Romance Writers Program Director and is currently on her second stint of service to Romance Writers of America as a member of the National Workshop Committee. She's also a founding member of the blog RomanceontheRocks.com and a contributor to the podcast, *History, Books, and Wine.*

After growing up and attending college in Mississippi, she lived in Ohio, Manhattan, and London, but chose to settle in Vienna, VA with her husband and four children. When not writing or reading, Lori enjoys time with her real-life hero and four kids or spending time walking or drinking wine with her friends.

Visit Lori Ann Bailey in the following places:

http://loriannbailey.com/ - be sure to sign up for her newsletter for exclusive content and so you don't miss any news.

https://www.facebook.com/LoriAnnBaileyauthor/
https://www.bookbub.com/profile/lori-ann-bailey
https://www.goodreads.com/LoriAnnBailey
https://www.amazon.com/Lori-Ann-Bailey/e/B01JGPBQSO
https://www.instagram.com/loriannbailey/

*Don't miss the Highland Pride series...*

*Discover more historical romance...*

## THE MADNESS OF MISS GREY
### a novel by Julia Bennet

All of society believes former actress Helen Grey to be mad, but after a decade imprisoned in a crumbling Yorkshire asylum, she's managed to cling to sanity. When a new doctor arrives, Dr. William Carter, she finally sees an opportunity for freedom. Helen and Will need to work together if she's ever going to be free. It won't be easy, not when her mysterious benefactor is determined to keep her locked up and hidden from society forever. When Helen is entangled in her own trap and begins to fall for Will too, she must fight not only for her liberty but for her right to love.

## THE WOLF OF KISIMUL CASTLE
### a *Highland Isles* novel by Heather McCollum

Mairi Maclean is kidnapped on her wedding day. Taken north to Kisimul Castle, she is held captive. Alec MacNeil, The Wolf of Kisimul Castle, soon learns Mairi is not a docile pawn in this game of war between neighboring Scots. When he finds his enemy dead, he takes his wife to replace the one that was murdered. But Mairi refuses to bend to his will, and the passion that flares between them threatens to tear Alec's strategy apart.

## HOW TO LOSE A HIGHLANDER
### a *MacGregor Lairds* novel by Michelle McLean

In this Highlander *Taming of the Shrew* meets *How to Lose a Guy in 10 Days* tale, Sorcha Campbell and Laird Malcolm MacGregor are determined to break the bonds of their forced matrimony. To do so, they'll have to keep their hands, and hearts, to themselves, or risk being permanently wed. But there's a thin line between love and hate, and even their feuding clans might not be enough to keep their passion at bay.

Made in the USA
San Bernardino, CA
22 November 2019

60280193R00173